The Power
of a Magnificent Romance!

Beauty and the Beast

Other **BEAUTY AND THE BEAST** *Novels*
from Avon Books

BEAUTY AND THE BEAST
by Barbara Hambly

MASQUES
by Ru Emerson

Beauty and the Beast

SONG OF ORPHEUS

A Novel by
BARBARA HAMBLY

based on the series created by
RON KOSLOW

AVON BOOKS  NEW YORK

AVON BOOKS
A division of
The Hearst Corporation
105 Madison Avenue
New York, New York 10016

First Avon Books Printing: November 1990

AVON TRADEMARK REG. U.S. PAT. OFF. AND IN OTHER COUNTRIES, MARCA
REGISTRADA, HECHO EN U.S.A.

Printed in the U.S.A.

RA   10   9   8   7   6   5   4   3   2   1

For
Ron Perlman, Linda Hamilton, and Roy Dotrice,
whose extraordinary talents
brought it all to life

To the Reader

As you know, the written word and what appears on a screen are two completely different media, and things that work on one frequently do not work on the other. This is the perennial pitfall of the novelizer, and it would be ludicrous to pretend otherwise.

In adapting the three telescripts which I elected to novelize in this book, I have used my own judgment in how they would be done, and I know there will be people who will object to the choices I made. In some cases these changes were minor—scenes omitted or merged together, or a regular character interjected back into a scene that would have been hers if the actress who played her had been available for filming that week. In some cases I performed a major chronological shift, which, incidentally, I checked out with the production staff of the television show first. I did this in the hopes that the story would work better *as a book* than would a straight transcript of three episodes, and that I would be able to develop the common theme of all three stories more effectively if they were thus intertwined.

To those who would have preferred a straight transcript, I apologize, and can say only that I had reasons for making the choices that I did. I hope that those who object to this will not find that it detracts fatally from their enjoyment of the stories as a whole.

One

"CATHERINE, this is Elliot. . . ."

And Catherine Chandler sighed, shutting her eyes and her teeth—hard—at the sound of that crisp, virile voice on the answering machine's scratchy tape. At the end of the day this was *not* what she needed . . .

"Look, we need to get together and talk. Let me take you out to dinner some night next week. Call me, please. You know my number."

Yes, I know your number, thought Catherine with weary anger, turning away from the still-running machine to round the end of the counter separating the kitchenette from the soft shadows of the living room, wondering what was left in the refrigerator. *And no, I will not call you, not now or next week or ever . . .*

"Catherine," went on Elliot's voice after a long moment, "I love you. I want you. Please call me."

Her hands were shaking a little—with the chill of the March night she'd just come out of, or with tiredness, or with an emotion she'd rather not delve into at the moment—as she opened the refrigerator. Her cleaning lady had left untouched most of a quart of milk and polystyrene box containing half a club sandwich from lunch yesterday with Jenny Aron-

1

sen—everything that hadn't been so old it was about to achieve sentience.

Dinner with Elliot Burch frequently meant Lutece or the Algonquin, or some very exclusive Tuscan bistro in Little Italy, although her co-workers were still ragging her about the occasion when she'd told him she had no time to meet him for lunch and he showed up at her desk at the New York City District Attorney's office complete with a caterer, lobster, and champagne. After a week of cheeseburgers hastily snatched at Tummy Time or one of the other greasy spoons that sprouted like fungus around City Hall Park, it didn't sound bad.

I love you. I want you.

Was that so bad?

A year ago it would have been enough, and more than enough.

She came slowly out of the kitchen, and stood where she could see herself in the narrow mirror which backed the long-legged Italianate table in the hall.

She studied the slim, almost fragile-looking silhouette dispassionately, the delicate oval face with its full lips and decided chin, the wide-set green eyes which always made her look younger than twenty-seven, the medium-short, silky hair that was a mixture of fair and brown. It was hard to think of herself as attractive at the end of an eleven-hour day of interviewing witnesses and searching records at City Hall. She felt rumpled and infinitely weary, grubby despite the smooth tidiness of her bronze silk shirt and noil skirt, and in any case after last April—nearly a year ago, now—she had never quite been able to see her own face as it was. She kept remembering it as it had been . . .

She shook her head to clear it of that horrible vision, turned away. It had been her beauty, Elliot had said, which had drawn him first to her . . . "I'm an aesthete." He'd grinned. "So sue me." As indeed, she'd been attracted to his strong good looks and his air of blazing energy, even before she'd realized that he was a multi-millionaire with a sense of humor and great personal charm.

She could almost hear her friend Edie's incredulous voice saying, *And you threw that AWAY?!?* as if she'd deliberately dropped a diamond tennis bracelet in the trashcan. She smiled, thinking of all the matter-of-fact advice Edie had given her on the subject of men. And it was true, in fact, that she'd wrapped up the diamond tennis bracelet Elliot had given her, along with the assortment of Armani silk scarves, the Opium perfume and the solitaire alexandrite earrings, and mailed them back to his office.

She did miss him. That was the worst of it. That was what still stung her with shame.

Edie would understand part of it . . but never the whole.

No one would understand the whole.

Tiredly, she walked on into the bedroom, slipping off her brown linen blazer as she went. In spite of the fact that it was nearly eight-thirty at night she had just returned from work . . . *No wonder I feel like I've been run over by a car*, she thought, glancing in passing at the clock. It had been a more than usually trying day, a morning spent pounding pavements, tracking down witnesses on a playground-shooting case on the West Side—Catherine still had trouble comprehending that an argument over a can of spray paint could result in the death of a sixteen-year-old boy—and waiting in a sleazy coffee shop near a construction site on West 123rd Street for a man who was supposed to give her some information about a protection racketeer named Max Avery. The afternoon, and far into the evening, had been spent in writing up the fact that no witnesses remembered seeing anything, that the man in the coffee shop had thought better about showing up, and all the other dry, laborious, soul-breaking detail of a dozen other case-reports that had to be researched, documented, date-stamped, filed, and ready to go on District Attorney John Moreno's desk Monday morning. *Make that a bus*, she thought. *A BIG bus.*

Beyond the French windows that opened onto the terrace, the lights of Fifth Avenue could be seen, glittering sharply beyond the spiky black lace of Central Park's trees. Those trees were just coming into spring leaf, the grass beneath them still wet from this morning's rain . . . just like her shoes, Catherine reflected ruefully. She took them off, remembering how, back in the days when she still worked for her father, it had been one of her greatest pleasures to play hooky on rainy spring afternoons, buy a hot dog from a street vendor and go walking in the park, for the joy of smelling the new grass and hearing the mellow sweetness of itinerant jazz musicians and the scrunch of wet pebbles underfoot.

Corporate law might have been dull, she thought, gently massaging the crick out of her neck,[1] *but at least I got home at a decent hour . . .*

But it was something she knew she could never go back to, as she knew she could never go back to Elliot—as she could never go back to being the person who would have loved him, or the person who could look at her face in the mirror and see beauty there.

And as her fingers worked at the stiffness left by hours of sitting over a court report and a cup of stale coffee, they came in contact with the scar that ran down in front of her left ear, the scar that she usually covered by combing her hair forward . . . the scar that still hurt on days like this, when the weather was damp and cold. It was about three inches long, a deep downward slash, as though she had been cut with a knife.

Then beyond the dark windows something caught her eye—movement in the dense shadows of the terrace.

She stepped quickly to the French doors, brushing back the gauzy screen of white curtains that covered them, but such was the overcast dark outside that she could see nothing in the building's shadows. She hesitated, remembering the man who hadn't shown up that afternoon—remembering other witnesses in the Avery case who'd "changed their minds" after Avery's boys had come calling on them or their families . . . but after a moment she unlocked the door and stepped outside.

The night scents rose to her, misty and yearning; damp grass and wet pavement, the pungence of exhaust muted by the distance to the street, even as the noise of traffic on Central Park West was muted. Her breath steamed faintly in the diffuse glow from the room behind her. The asphalt that paved her terrace was puddled with water, and beads of rain clung, glinting like diamonds, to the hardier tub-plants which she'd already moved out there. The raw cold spoke of more rain to come.

There was a noise behind her.

An almost-soundless footfall—she turned her head. Someone—some thing—stood at the far end of the terrace, on the little dais among the shrubs and potted trees. The dense gloom all but hid that cloaked and silent bulk, six and a half feet tall and visibly massive through shoulder and chest. But the dim light from the windows showed her a hand, monstrous, powerful, furred with coarse red hair, and

5

caught the glint of claws; showed a beast's fanged muzzle within the shadows of the hood and reflected luminous amber in two glowing eyes. Feral, powerful, it was a shape to have materialized out of civilization's nightmares, an animal shape utterly at odds with the glitter of New York's lights, the bustling throb of traffic in the street below. It moved toward her . . .

. . . and Catherine stepped to meet him, holding out her hands, to be gathered into those massive arms and to feel the touch of the taloned fingers, light as a dancer's on her cheek and hair.

"Catherine . . ."

A voice like rough-cut blue amber, dark and gentle and warm. She looked up into the face of the beast, a lion's face framed by a long, rough mane the color of honey—not human at all, save for the love, the sorrow, the wisdom in those deep-set blue eyes. "Vincent," she said. And they embraced.

Vincent stayed until nearly midnight, knowing she had to be at work the next morning—upon occasion, talking far into the night or, as they sometimes did, reading to one another, anything from Dickens to Mary Renault, they had kept each other awake until almost dawn. Sometimes talking, sometimes playing Bach on her stereo—"I don't think there's anything in the world so final as the silence after Bach," he said, and she smiled.

" 'Music to build the Great Pyramid by,' my father calls it."

He chuckled, a deep rumble in his chest, like a lion's purr. "Like John Donne, an acquired taste. Thank you," he added, gesturing through the French door, for they were sitting on the terrace still, Vincent having an instinctive caution about entering her apartment or indeed any room from which he

6

couldn't escape immediately and at a second's notice. By that time the night was very cold, and it would definitely rain by morning. He had draped around her shoulders a portion of the mantle he wore, a great, sleeved garment, made like his other clothes of scrap leather and rags; it was permeated with the smell of woodsmoke and tallow and the faint, musty odor of the damp earth. "There is very little recorded music in my world. We must rely on what people know, and can play. That . . ." His clawed hand sketched a gesture, as if shaping again the themes of the "Passacaglia" and "Fuge in C Minor" from the shadowy air. "That is magical."

"I wish I could do more," she said quietly, looking up at him. A neighbor's cat, picking its delicate way along the terrace railing, paused, ears pricking at Vincent's unfamiliar smell, then pirouetted on the baluster and sprang away. "There are so many things I wish I could give you."

He considered the matter for a moment, and when he spoke, it was not the platitude that others would have made of the words. "You give of yourself," he said, quite simply. "Your generosity, your friendship . . . the way you have helped those of us who were in trouble. There *is* no more than that."

She shook her head. "You know what I mean."

His face—strange, unhuman . . . monstrous some would have called it, though she did not find it so— was ill-equipped to smile, but his eyes smiled, like sunlight on water, sunlight that he would never, could never, see. "With what our friends in the world Above bring to us, and what the world Above casts aside, we have everything we need."

And perhaps that was so. Maybe not, she thought later, her mind echoing the old Rolling Stones song, what they want . . . but everything they need. And

7

how many people had even that, in her world . . . or in his?

After he had gone she lay awake in her bed, looking at the ghostly squares of light cast upon her bedroom ceiling from the street far below, and thought about his world.

The world Below.

She had seen it once, and only briefly, though she had sojourned there for ten days. She had been mugged, assaulted, cut to pieces with a knife; Vincent had found her bleeding to death in Central Park, and had taken her Below, for she had to be taken somewhere quickly and his was a face and form he dared not show to any in the world Above.

And in the secret underworld which lay below the level of Manhattan's subway tunnels, they had saved her life, people who for the most part she had never seen because of the bandages that covered her eyes. She had heard their voices, heard the messages they tapped out to one another on the drain-pipes and cable conduits . . . people who had left the world Above, for whatever varied reasons, and who formed the small, tight-knit community of the Tunnels . . . people who had taken the infant Vincent in, all those years ago, when whomever had birthed him had cast him out in horror to die—whatever he was, human or monster or something in between. And so they had met, though now, nearly a year later, it seemed impossible that she had not known him all of her life.

A plastic surgeon—the best that her father's considerable money could buy—had eradicated the knifescars, except for the extremely deep one in front of her left ear that would have required several further surgeries to correct. Her father, her friends, and indeed everyone else she knew, had wanted to forget that it had happened, forget that she had been missing those ten days, and had seemed to take it for granted that she, too, wanted to forget.

But she could not, nor did she want to. She could not unknow the knowledge that such things could happen, and did happen regularly to the innocent everywhere in the city—she could not turn aside from the gratitude to the people who had saved her. She could not forget Vincent, and the love that had grown between them, a love which she could never hope to explain to anyone who knew her, a love rooted deep within her soul like a flowering tree.

After the assault she had left the law firm where she had worked for her father, had gone to work in the offices of the District Attorney, and in the months that had followed had from time to time encountered people from the secret world Below. A deaf girl named Laura, who had been the witness to a murder, a boy named Kipper who had led her to a child-selling racket operating in the city's foster-homes. The man whom Vincent called Father, patriarch of that sanctuary world whose medical skills had saved her life.

But Vincent's world itself remained closed to her, a secret, as it was a secret from nearly everyone Above. She knew that there were Helpers, a trusted few who had connections with that quiet world beneath the city streets, who gave them what assistance they could in terms of food and fuel and news. But the people of Father's community lived for the most part by salvage, existing on the copious wastage of a throw away culture, dwelling in the steam-tunnels, in the hidden mazes of disused subway lines and forgotten water-mains, and in the caverns and tunnels of the granite bedrock far beneath the surface of New York's streets. Not an easy existence, Catherine guessed, but one which they preferred to the luxurious cruelty of the glittering world Above.

We have all we need, Vincent had said.

She moved her head on the pillows, turning her eyes to the shadowy shapes of her room: the pale, modern furniture, the sandstone-colored desert scapes of the paintings on the walls, the gauzy white webs of window curtains with their stirring shadows, the lace and silk of pegnoir thrown over the foot of the bed . . . treasures of her world, evidences of what people liked to call The Good Life—or, to use the more modern parlance, An Eighties Lifestyle, conveniently forgetting the hundreds of thousands of people in the Eighties whose lifestyle wasn't nearly so chic.

And her mind went back to Elliot Burch, and all that he could give her—remembering that message-tape she'd erased unanswered, as she'd erased all his messages before. A year ago—maybe even six months ago—Elliot Burch and all that he represented, that graciousness of living, that material ease, was something she would have welcomed.

But in the Greek myths, those who had been guests in the Underworld, those who had eaten of its food, tasted of its streams, were never quite free of it afterwards, despite all the songs of daylight the minstrel Orpheus could sing. Like them, Catherine knew that she, though the world Below was closed to her, would never be the person she had been before she had gone there—before Vincent had come into her life.

She was thinking of that world and its secrets as she drifted into sleep.

Oil-lamps were still burning in Father's chamber when Vincent reached it. From the crooked tunnel which led back to the Long Gallery his quick hearing picked up the muted echo of voices: Father's, Winslow's, Cullen's. Behind him in the gallery people were still abroad, though it was late even in terms of the eternal night in the world Below. Mary, the tunnel midwife, called out to one of the orphan children in her charge to come to bed, the soft sweetness of her voice punctuated by the whispered clang of the steam-pipes as Pascal, from the central cavern of the Pipe Chamber, relayed the messages along. With absent-minded habit Vincent picked out the maze of Morse and "single-tap" that made up the little man's code—*Cesar says Pell Street grocery dumping produce tomorrow night, arrange pickup—Benjamin from Sara, rehearsal next week okay?*

Then, more clearly, from the lights ahead of him, he heard Father's deep, cultured voice say, "We've finally put our finger on the source of the erosion on the upper levels under SoHo . . . there's a leak in one of the city's storm drains."

"If we could divert the flow of the drain . . ." said Winslow, and Cullen the woodcarver spoke up diffidently.

"Mouse really should be here to hear this . . ."

"You can get gray hair waiting for him," retorted Winslow, and by his tone the tunnel blacksmith was not pleased. "He ain't exactly the most dependable . . ."

As Vincent stepped through the rough-hewn stone opening of the vestibule to Father's multi-level chamber he heard the clattering dash of Mouse's footsteps in the tunnel behind him. The three men grouped around the octagonal mahogany table in the chamber below looked up toward Vincent, and Mouse came bursting past him, out of breath, a stocky boy of sixteen or seventeen—even Mouse wasn't sure—with guileless blue eyes and a rude pudding-bowl shock of blond hair which was, Vincent saw, liberally streaked with the yellowish mud typical of the tunnels south of Wall Street.

Vincent and Mouse paused together at the top of the short flight of iron steps leading down into the main part of the circular chamber. For a moment Father's sharp, blue-gray eyes rested on Vincent, and his mouth under its short gray beard tightened grimly, as if he could smell upon his adopted son's mantle and hair the lingering remnants of Catherine's perfume. Then his eyes shifted away and with a chuckle that sounded only a little forced he said to Winslow, "Well, we all know Mouse and the concept of time."

"Time?" Mouse grinned jauntily, but Vincent could see that neither the glance Father had given him, nor that careful silence, had been lost on the boy. "Easy. Early—you come before Mouse. Late—you come after." And grasping the iron handrails of the stair he swung himself lightly down into the room.

Vincent followed, feeling again Father's unvoiced *No comment*.

And it grieved him, that between the two people he most cared for in his life this wall of silence should exist.

It was not that Father—and though Vincent knew intellectually that there was no biological tie to this sturdy, grizzle-haired old man he had and always would regard him as his true father, the man who had literally given him both physical and emotional life—disliked Catherine or disapproved of her as a person. In their few meetings, on the thresholds of the Tunnel World either in the great culvert in Central Park or in the dark steam-tunnels below Catherine's own apartment building, he had seen that the old patriarch respected that slim golden woman, respected her for her personal courage in overcoming the effects of the attack which had brought her in touch with them, respected her still more for her

12

dedication to helping other victims, other innocents, which had led her eventually to her work with the District Attorney's office. He recognized in her the heart of a crusader, an idealist whose intelligence forced her to recognize that the world is not an ideal place—recognized in her his own sense of justice, his commitment to law as the only protection for the weak.

Recognized in her, in fact, all those things which claimed Vincent's respect and love.

It was Vincent's love for her which Father feared.

Beside Father, Cullen the woodcarver looked up from the maps that strewed the study table and grinned at Mouse. "Where the *hell* you been, pal? Swamping out the bottom tunnels?"

And now that Vincent saw the boy in the better lighting of the oil-lamps on Father's table, he could see that Mouse's clothes were all streaked and smeared with the same yellow mud that daubed his hair. Mouse shrugged, evasive as usual, and said, "Working," with a returning grin that took any sullenness out of his words.

"On something useful, I hope." Father ducked his head a little, eyes glinting piercingly between the steel rims of his square-cut reading glasses and the jutting grizzle of his brows. Going by Mouse's track record, Vincent thought this wasn't too likely. Mouse's inventions, like Mouse's incessant explorations of the farther reaches of the Tunnel World, were seldom motivated by practicality. Father didn't pry further—partly because it was not his nature and mostly because he'd known Mouse long enough to know that the young man would eventually reveal any discoveries that came to anything—but turned back to Winslow, a tall and massively-built black man who for years had been the blacksmith, the iron worker, the heavy mechanic of the Tunnel World. "It's vital that we deal with this soon . . ."

"Before the city crews wake up, and come down here looking for the problem," the big man agreed. In the hazy amber glow of the kerosene lamps, and of the dozens of candles perched everywhere about the chamber on any horizontal surface not already covered by Father's books, his bald scalp gleamed like pickled walnut. Fully as tall as Vincent and even more heavily built, in his bulky mantle pieced together from leather scrap and an old red blanket he dwarfed Father's stockiness and Cullen's tall, gangly thinness.

"We could go out and survey the area tonight," put in Cullen, rubbing his unshaven chin with the long fingers of an artist which protruded from the cut-off gloves he wore—gloves which they all wore as protection against the Tunnels' damp chill. "Take some measurements . . ."

Father looked down at the maps spread out on the table before them, the map of the highest levels of the Tunnel World, with the routes of steam-pipes, water-mains, pedestrian underpasses which had been dug and forgotten, and the old private subway tunnels which had once served the basements of millionaires' mansions now long torn down, all superimposed upon the lines of the old stream beds and ponds which centuries ago had dotted Manhattan island. "We'll need to reroute the storm drain temporarily," he said, frowning through his reading glasses. "I don't know why they ever put a drain through there anyway, it cuts directly across the old line of Cedar Creek. Now we can use either the old service main beneath the Broadway line, or . . . now look, Mouse!" he protested in exasperation, "pay attention! This is important!"

Mouse, absorbed in examining a grubby wad of

14

rags which he'd taken from his pocket, replaced it hastily and nodded, but looking sidelong at him, Vincent could see that the ramifications of simple repair work were the farthest things from his mind. Father's interest in the Tunnels was practical, founded on a desire for the safety of all who lived Below. Mouse's, Vincent knew, was aesthetic; the young man truly loved the dark and twisting world in which he had grown up, in which Vincent had found him eight years ago, a silent, wary, feral child who to this day had no recollection of where he had come from or how he'd gotten down there. The matter never seemed to bother Mouse much. The ultimate pragmatist, he lived very much in the present. And he explored, digging and crawling and searching far beyond the area occupied by Father's small community, not to better understand the mazes beneath Manhattan, but because he loved them for their own sake, even as Cullen carved, not simply because he wanted a fork or a candleholder, but out of the sheer joy of the texture of wax or stone or wood. Mere questions of getting a job done bored Mouse.

The youth was still tagging behind, fingering again his muddy packet of cloth and whatever it contained, when he, Winslow, and Cullen departed to investigate the leaky storm drain, leaving Vincent standing in the glow of the pendant oil-lamps which hung from the book-lined gallery encircling Father's chamber. It was now very late. The rumble of the subway lines had dulled to an occasional shudder, deep in the granite bones of the island above. Now and then a pipe clanged, sleepy messages relayed from one corner of that hidden world to another, like night-thoughts on the verge of dreams. Father rolled his map slowly together, his heavy shoulders bowed. He did not speak for a time, but he scarcely needed to. Vincent knew the cause of his troubled silence—and indeed, they had been through this a dozen times in the last several months.

Quietly, he said, "I don't do this to displease you, Father. You know that."

"I know," said the old man wearily. He removed his glasses and looked up, and in his eyes Vincent read the anxiety that lay behind his disapproval. "And you understand that if I am—displeased—by your visiting this woman, by your seeking her out in her own world, it is because I fear for your safety, and for the safety of us all." He rubbed his eyes tiredly, and limped to the roll-top desk at one side of the room, a massive oak fortress whose top was a waxen forest of candles set in a mottled lava-flow of ancient drippings, and whose pigeonholes bulged with roll after roll of maps. Piles of faded blueprints, boxes of discarded WPA archives and old ConEd records, ancient real estate surveys and clipped articles from archaeological journals heaped the floor around it, all logged and docketed in Father's scribbling, nearly illegible hand—the raw materials from which, with painstaking care, he was slowly forging his record of the lightless world below the subways, the world in which they lived.

"It's bad enough to think of what would befall you if you were trapped Above," Father went on, his voice sharpening with urgency, "if for some reason you couldn't get back here by daybreak. You've had some perilously close calls as it is. Caged up, stared at, treated like a freak and a monster . . . if you weren't simply shot out of hand by some terrified gun-owner."

And he surveyed his son's face, the face of a lion, a monster, a beast within its long frame of tawny mane. Only the eyes were the eyes of a man, wise and gentle and accepting of what he was. Father sighed, and shook his head, having learned long ago that humanity is not enough. He went on, "But your capture would endanger the rest of us, would endanger the entire existence of our world. We depend upon secrecy, upon being left alone . . ."

"Father, I know that," said Vincent quietly.

The older man drew in his breath, almost angrily, to retort, then let it out, knowing that he had no right to dictate, no right to speak the words. He and Vincent had been over this time and again, since Vincent had first gone Above to seek out Catherine, eight months after their first meeting—since Vincent had first admitted to himself that he loved her, that he could not let his life pass without seeing her again. Then, speaking of what lay at the heart of his anger, he said, "And I'm afraid you'll be hurt. Badly."

"I know that, too." And they both knew that now the subject was not some freaked-out gang member or unnerved cop.

"All my life I've feared this," said Father softly. "That someday this would happen—that you would want a world that you cannot have."

And that, too, Vincent knew. "If I cannot have it," he replied, "then at least I can enjoy of it what I can. I roam the streets and alleys of the city in the dark hours; I walk the woods of its park, as I have always done. Is this so different?"

"You know it is."

And Vincent nodded, lowering his eyes.

"Her world is a world of peril—to all of us, but especially to you. Please—be careful."

Father was right, of course. As he climbed the short flight of iron steps which led up to the vestibule of that great, book-filled chamber, and so out into the hazy torchlight of the Long Gallery and the darkness of the Tunnels again, Vincent reflected that he had always known this, even back in the days when his excursions to the world Above had comprised merely long midnight prowls of the city's silent back streets or quiet perambulations of the park.

This he had always done, since his childhood. Aware that he would be shunned at best—and possibly hunted and killed—because of what he was, Vincent had always kept a wary distance from the world Above. Yet that world and its people had always drawn him. In Father's books he had studied it, read about its wisdom and its follies and the lives of its people; all his life he had roamed, not only the mazes of subway tunnels and water-mains deep below the streets, but the streets themselves, and from the shadows had observed the dwellers of the city of light. In its squares and alleyways he had seen the worst of its scum and riffraff, drunks and addicts and whores, but through those glowing windows, in those odd side-turnings, he had seen other things as well: old Jewish couples doddering quietly hand-in-hand, helping one another up porch steps under the glare of the cold street lamps; a child patiently fishing an abandoned litter of kittens from behind a broken wall. Father had never liked these rambles, had always been apprehensive, but, aware of his hunger for air and freedom and experience, had never forbidden him to go. And he himself had always been extremely careful about keeping from sight, about never putting himself into any position where he could be seen and the inevitable questions asked.

Then he had met Catherine. And for him, all the world had changed.

Browning's words returned to him:

18

A tap at the pane, the quick sharp scratch
  And blue spurt of a lighted match,
And a voice less loud, through its joys and fears
  Than the two hearts beating each to each . . .

"Vincent . . ."

His footsteps had turned toward the outer tunnels, as he shrugged his great mantle of scrapwork and rags closer around his shoulders. His booted feet made no sound on the damp cement of the floor. Frequently before he slept he would patrol as far north as the Harlem River, miles beyond the area where most of the Tunnel dwellers lived, checking the iron gates and bars that defended the periphery of the inhabited Tunnels, checking the state of floors and walls for water-leakage, for Manhattan's deadly subterranean quicksands, for signs of decay, checking the air for the anomalous smells of gas-pockets and broken water-mains that might spell danger to those who lived Below. All the young men of the community took their turns at patrol of the inner perimeter, but Vincent, with his sharper senses and night-sighted eyes, was the guardian of the farther Tunnels, the watchman of the many gates.

But at the sound of Mouse's hurrying tread he looked back. The little man emerged from a cross-tunnel, hands in the pockets of his shabby gray sacking vest, the mud on his boots and trouser-knees caking and dry.

"Father's angry with you?" Mouse fell into step with him, looking up at him with some concern. Being so often in Father's bad books himself he was familiar with the signs.

"He's afraid," said Vincent. "Afraid for me . . ."

"Afraid of Catherine? Your Catherine?"

Vincent nodded. He had spoken of her to Mouse, when the little tinkerer had accompanied him on his workshop to see what his friend's latest projects were. "Afraid of her world," he said, his deep, slightly grainy voice echoing despite its softness in the low curve of the roof overhead, "of my journeys Above."

Mouse shrugged expansively. "Above—no problem. You run—you hide . . ." He gestured, spreading square, sturdy hands in the fingerless ruin of shabby knitted gloves. Then, looking up at Vincent a little more timidly, "She nice? Nice to you?"

He nodded, smiling inwardly at that simple analysis. *Nice*, he thought. The joy of being able to share whatever he thought, whatever he felt, with someone whose heart he trusted down to the marrow of his soul. The ease of her company, her quick and caring intelligence, her awareness of the hardship and evil of the world and her strong courageous joy in life. The fact that she saw him as Father, and Mouse, and his own friends Below saw him, as what he was . . . the unshakable trust between them. *Nice*. Yes. Entirely apart from the love which drew him to her, the love that ran so deep in him that at times it frightened him . . . Yes. It was nice.

"She your friend?"

"Yes," said Vincent softly, though what was between them was deeper than friendship, deeper than love—an understanding without questions, as if they had known one another through lifetimes past.

Mouse hesitated, reading the longing in Vincent's face, wanting to help but not knowing how. Then he fished from his pocket the mud-caked cloth he'd been fiddling with earlier in the evening, and he pressed it shyly into Vincent's hand. "Give her a present, maybe? Because she's your friend?"

"You don't have to . . ." began Vincent, deeply

touched that Mouse would have that concern for his troubles.

"Your friend, my friend," insisted Mouse more firmly, pushing the packet back when Vincent moved to return it to him. "Good to you. Father . . ." He shook his head. "Father doesn't understand."

No, thought Vincent with a sigh, *he understands too well.* Vincent had never asked the old man what had made him so wary of the world of day, had never asked him why he had sought the sanctuary of the Tunnels so many years ago, but he knew that Father, unlike many of the Tunnel Dwellers, never even made brief forays Above, distrusting and fearing the world over their heads.

And perhaps, he thought, Father was right. His love for Catherine was hopeless, in that he could never be a part of her world . . . he would always, as Father said, want something which he could not have. But what he did have with her, their stolen evenings together, went far beyond any other joy he had known. And in a strange way that was enough, and more than enough. It was his instinct to trust his heart, and his heart told him that no matter what might come, their love was a thing to be treasured.

He was glad at least that Mouse, if he did not understand, nevertheless supported him in this.

"Thank you, Mouse," he said, looking down at his friend. "What is it?" His clawed hands, surprisingly deft, started to unwrap the packet, and Mouse said quickly,

"Not here!" He threw a swift glance over his shoulder, as if fearing they'd be observed. Then he grinned apologetically, and said, "Better she unwrap it."

"All right." Vincent, used to Mouse's quirky

secretiveness, carefully bestowed the crusted little bundle in a pocket of his mantle.

Mouse smiled. "Have to go help Father now," he said, and added, conspiratorially, "He's lost without Mouse." And, satisfied that he had in some measure alleviated his friend's griefs, he darted away after Winslow and Cullen into the darkness.

Two

"VINCENT," said Catherine worriedly, turning the grubby packet over in her hands, "you don't think he . . ."

"Stole it?" The coarse topaz brows slanted down as he turned the thought over in his mind. Mouse's attitude about tools and equipment left unattended on construction sites Above was notoriously cavalier, though he would never have taken even something he wanted very badly from the chambers of any of his friends. "Mouse hasn't 'taken' anything in—oh, weeks."

Catherine chuckled ruefully. Though she had never met Mouse she felt, from Vincent's stories about him, that she knew him. She'd heard before about his forays Above and hated to think he'd get into trouble over a present for her.

More seriously, Vincent said, "Rest assured, wherever he found it, it came from his heart."

"Because I'm your . . . friend?" She slipped the packet into the pocket of her white silk kimono, and looked up into Vincent's face. It was late Saturday night and she had come home trashed, exhausted by a day of unpaid overtime spent chasing out to Jersey in quest of the elusive informant in the Max Avery case in the hopes of running him to ground at home on his day off. To her questions about kick-

23

backs, about men beaten up, about payoffs and graft
he had replied simply that he had never heard of
Max Avery or any of the victims of his strongarm
tactics. And all the while he had been talking to her,
a big, tired-looking man with a beer gut and a face
like a pallet-load of wallboard, his eyes had kept
sliding to the windows, where his two children
could be seen romping with the family mutt in the
weedy front yard. That kind of fear, that terrible
implied threat, was something Catherine had never
had to deal with in her days of advising marketing
firms about tax-free disinvestment options, and she
had no idea how to deal with it, no idea what to
say. The smell of fear had been thick in the air of
that little house and the memory of it clung to her
clothes and hair like cigarette-smoke after a party,
as she'd driven back furious and pitying and frustrated to the city, wishing there was something she
could do to change the situation and knowing there
was not. Two and a half hours of patient sitting in
a traffic jam outside the Holland Tunnel had not
improved her mood.

She had reached home with a throbbing headache, to find another imperious message from Elliot
on her machine. She had been shaky with anger
and, once that rage had calmed out of her, close to
tears of sheer weariness. Vincent's appearance at the
terrace window, as she'd sat at her dressing-table
leaning her head wearily on her hand, might have
been a coincidence, but she doubted it. In the
months past, when she had been in physical danger
from some of the tougher thugs her work brought
her in contact with, Vincent had known, and had
come to her rescue with the terrifying ferocity of an
animal. Now, even as he'd sensed her danger, he
sensed her pain, knowing that the one thing in the
world she craved was the gentleness of his com-

pany, and the strength of his shoulder beneath her cheek.

Foolish as she had felt about her weakness, she was infinitely glad for the bond between them, the psychic awareness of her feelings which had brought him to her side. The fact that one of the folk of his forbidden world—Mouse, whom she had never met—would send her a present simply because she was Vincent's friend brought her embarrassingly close again to tears.

She turned her face away, not wanting to worry him with what was, at bottom, simply exhaustion and the struggle to cure a myriad of ills which in the end could never be cured.

But he seemed to understand. His voice—the voice she had known him by before ever she had seen his face—vibrated gently in his chest where her face pressed to it, reassuring as the strength of his arm upon her waist. "What is more precious than a friend?" he asked. "We who live Below have few possessions, so we value more deeply the things we have. Food. Shelter. Quiet. Friends. Without each other, we would be lost indeed."

"Yes," said Catherine softly, closing her eyes. "Yes, without you I would be lost indeed."

And so she did not think again about Mouse's gift until the following afternoon.

She came home at five, later than she'd planned, after a morning spent doing laundry and replenishing her diminished larder and an afternoon spent getting the stuffing knocked out of her at Isaac Stubbs' Academy of Self-Defense—a rather dignified name for that echoing gray loft on Pell Street, but if you could defend yourself against Isaac when he really came after you, she had learned, you could defend yourself against almost anyone. She was sore and bruised and starting to stiffen up as she let herself into the apartment, glanced at the clock and groaned, and went to the bedroom to dial Jenny Aronsen's home number, praying her friend would still be there. *Dammit, if Jenny and I could put together all the minutes we've been late meeting each other we could spend a week on the Riviera . . .*

"Hello, Jenny? Cathy . . ." She perched on a corner of the bed, winced a little as she pulled her Reeboks off, and mentally reviewed the contents of the 'fancy' end of the wall of built-in closet for something appropriate to a champagne literary reception. "Look, I'm running a little late . . ."

"Cathy, if you desert me I'll slit my wrists." Jenny sounded uncharacteristically frazzled—hardly a surprise, reflected Catherine, recalling the effort involved in putting together even a simple cocktail party for her father's clients in that big old apartment which he still occupied in Gramercy Square. This was Jenny's first solo attempt at organizing a high-end book signing, and Alain Viso, Catherine knew, was one of Harwick Publications' biggest guns.

"I'll be there," promised Catherine. "Just give me time to shower and change and I'll meet you at the bookstore. Save a copy for me."

"I kiss your hands and feet," Jenny replied solemnly, and Catherine laughed and hung up. Five thirty-five—allowing forty-five minutes for makeup, that meant dinner on the run . . .

She grabbed her white silk kimono from the padded bench at the foot of her bed to head for the bathroom, and stopped as it swung heavily under the weight of Mouse's package in its pocket. The memory made her pause and smile, touched all over again that Vincent's friend would have sent her a gift, simply because he was glad that she was good to his friend. And though she was in a hurry, she stopped to unwrap it, wondering what one of the

Tunnel dwellers would consider an appropriate gift. It could be almost anything . . . Vincent's chamber, she remembered, was full of strange bric-a-brac, souvenir World's Fair pillows, old chandelier lustres and gilt-glass Christmas tree ornaments, anything beautiful and bright . . .

She gasped.

In the muddy wad of cloth, unfolded in her hand, lay a necklace. Dirt clogged its delicate filigree, fragments of mold still clung to its smooth-polished green stones, but enough of the grime had been rubbed away to show the gleam of gold underneath.

Twenties costume jewelry? she thought, turning it wonderingly in her hands. *Victorian?* Something about the delicacy of the workmanship, those tiny flowers and clusters of minute granules along the close-curled leaves, said *age* to her. They didn't do that kind of workmanship anymore, certainly not on anything valueless enough for someone to toss away for Mouse to find. It was one of the most extraordinarily beautiful things she'd ever seen, and though it would, she knew, make her even later to Jenny's reception, she carried the thing into the kitchen to clean it up.

"I still don't understand what it is you think we need." Winslow ducked his bald head under the arch of one of the several doors that led into Mouse's chamber. The Mousehole, as it was known to most of those who dwelt Below, was one of the deepest inhabited chambers of the Underworld, far below the usual levels of human abode and reached by an odd assortment of trap-doors, hatchways, and twisting passages which were booby-trapped, not out of malice or paranoia, but more out of Mouse's odd reclusiveness and regrettable sense of humor. Once reached, the chamber was large, irregularly shaped, and low-ceilinged, half laboratory and half junk shop, filled with an incredible jumble of unfinished projects, old vacuum tubes, tangles of hose and wire, dismantled clocks and pachinko games, dangling mobiles wrought of model cars, makeshift tools and Rube Goldberg-esque perpetual-motion machines whose mazes seemed to start and end nowhere. The glow of dozens of candles, set everywhere at random amid the junk, unevenly augmented the weird reflections of bunsen burners, plasma globes, Christmas-tree lights and a lava-lamp hooked to a creaking homemade generator the size of a couch.

Mouse dived across the cluttered chamber to a huge old steamer trunk in one corner, Winslow and Cullen picking their way cautiously at his heels. Their survey of the leaking storm-drain had revealed that it could, indeed, be repaired before another rainstorm, provided a temporary channel for the water could be found; and Mouse, as usual, had claimed to possess "just the thing."

"Gizmo," he explained unhelpfully, rooting among half a dozen dismembered telephones, part of a defunct typewriter, and enough copper wire to string a fence around Manhatten Island. "Know it's here someplace."

Winslow rolled his eyes. "Great," he muttered, half exasperated and half amused. Over on the workbench, Arthur, Mouse's pet raccoon, made a noise like a mechanical footfall-rattle and dipped his pointed black nose into an ornate goblet of water on the table beside him. "Well, find it. We got work to do . . ."

"Okay good, okay fine," agreed Mouse, throwing a skate-key and a handful of coaxial cables over his shoulder and rummaging deeper.

Cullen drifted over to the workbench, chirped a

greeting to Arthur and reached out to scratch the little animal's ears. But the raccoon chittered and ducked away behind the remains of a massive vacuum-tube radio set, bright eyes peering from behind the dusty glass. Cullen grinned, studying the impossible chaos strewed across the table with an artist's interest. He was sculpting a chess set as a gift for Father at the next Winterfeast, and Mouse was going to be one of the white rooks, the round, snub-nosed face peering, like Arthur's was now, from among a tangle of machinery. It would be tricky shaping cable and tubes out of the pine he'd picked for that piece—maybe he could fit Arthur into the composition somehow . . .

Then he paused, startled at the sight of something on the table, and glanced doubtfully across at Mouse.

"Mouse, where did you get this?"

Mouse and Winslow looked up. Cullen held up the thing he had found—a plate, made of metal and very dirty, save where Cullen had rubbed it on his coarse knitted arm-warmer. In that one small place, it showed the sheen of gold.

"Found it," replied Mouse casually, and returned to his search.

"It looks like gold," said Cullen worriedly.

"Is gold," said Mouse, looking up again. "Makes good wire, once you melt it down."

"Gold?" Winslow surged to his feet, crossed the room in a stride. "What are you talking about?"

Cullen held up the plate for him to see, their eyes meeting doubtfully as Winslow took it. They both knew Mouse well enough to fear that he might have gotten himself into real trouble this time.

"Check this out!" Cullen picked up the goblet from which Arthur had been drinking, turned it over, the water splashing out onto the floor, to look for an antique maker's mark on the bottom. "Silver . . ."

"Mouse, where did this come from?" asked Winslow uneasily, visions of probing squads of detectives rising horribly to mind. *Damn Mouse and his 'taking' . . .*

"Hey!" Mouse sprang to his feet and snatched the goblet from Cullen's hand. "That's Arthur's! You spilled his water . . ." He looked from Winslow's dark, bearded face to Cullen's thin unshaven one in the swimming candlelight, seeing their thoughts in their eyes, and added defensively, "Found it. Didn't take it, didn't steal it. *Found* it."

"Where?" demanded Cullen suspiciously, knowing how flexible Mouse's definitions of words could be. "Up top or down here?"

Mouse's voice was smug. "Below. Secret place." He reached up to pat Arthur's head as the raccoon swarmed nimbly up his arm and clung to the rough sacking of his vest with little black hands.

"Is there any more of this stuff?" asked Winslow.

Mouse shrugged, elaborately casual with his secret. "Don't remember."

"You *sure* you didn't steal it?"

"Winslow, he couldn't have," pointed out Cullen quietly, holding the golden plate up to the pulse of the candle-glow. "Look at the condition it's in. A man owns a solid gold plate, he washes it once in a while." Their eyes met.

He had a point, but Winslow had to be sure. *Father'll kill him . . .* "Mouse, show us where you found this stuff."

Mouse frowned, puzzled at the sudden eagerness in his voice, and the way Cullen reached out to touch his arm. "It's only gold," he said.

"Mouse, just show us!"

"Okay good—okay fine," agreed Mouse, shrugging again. Then his eyes sparkled with conspiratorial delight, and his voice dropped to a dramatic whisper. "But you have to keep it *secret*."

The tunnel was not deep—fifteen or twenty feet—but lay well beyond the Tunnel dwellers' usual haunts. It was situated below Manhattan's financial district, where the geology changed and pockets of quicksand and seepage made exploration alternately perilous and disgusting; a disused sewer, Winslow surmised, still redolent with the reminiscence of times past. There was a place where the brick of the wall had cracked, showing an older tunnel in the yellowish soil beyond. Scattered bricks and an old two-by-four or two gave ample evidence that Mouse had dug through, exploring, probably sheerly out of curiosity. Winslow had grown up Below and like most boys of the community had done his share of exploring, but his was basically a pragmatic mind. It was enough for him to know how to get from one place to another—he avoided the lower levels and the far-flung corners, not from fear, but simply from lack of interest, and lack of time.

By the dim light of the makeshift miner's hat which Mouse had constructed from a football helmet and two flashlights, Winslow glimpsed something that looked like rotting wood, and a fragment of what might once have been iron.

"This way," whispered Mouse, boosting himself up and wriggling down the muddy length of tunnel. Wrinkling his nose, Winslow followed, Cullen bringing up the rear with another lamp. By the echoes there was a chamber of some kind ahead. The dual beam of Mouse's lamp flashed on more wood, a bluish haze of dust and cobwebs, and there was the overpowering stink of salt, rust, and damp rot.

Then they emerged, slithering through a freshly-

hacked hole in what seemed to be an old wooden
wall to drop three or four feet down to the canted
floor of a room . . .

"Mouse, what *is* this?"

Mouse grinned, spreading out his arms with the
delight of discovery. "Found it," he said proudly,
and his voice echoed in blackened rafters almost
unseen in the stuffy gloom.

The floor tilted at an angle of perhaps fifteen
degrees, enough to have long ago precipitated such
furniture as the little room contained—what looked
like it had been a table, two crude chairs, a plank
chest—into a jumble of cantilevered shadows at the
side of the room, but not enough to have dislodged
the moldering remains of the rug from the floor,
nor the mildew-blackened bedding from the bunk
affixed to one wall. On a rusted iron chain a crude
lamp hung, its shadow like a weirdly dangling skele-
ton that groped and twitched with the movement of
the men's lights. Everything was filmed with mold,
even the whitish curtains of cobweb that festooned
the rafters overhead, and at their footfalls, the plank
ceiling leaked water and dirt. As the light of Cullen's
torch passed over the wreckage of furniture it caught
the glint of metal deep within the blackness.

"Hey . . ." He reached in, wondering if it was
another silver goblet, another golden plate, but it
was something else. "A sword!" He made a
delighted pass through the air, his thin face suddenly boyish in the creepy shadows. "An old cutlass
. . . avast, me hearties!"

"It's a sunken ship!" Winslow held up his lantern,
illuminating more closely the decaying wooden walls,
the jammed wreck of a small door that would not
open, a porthole beyond which nothing could be
seen but the silt-fine earth of this part of New York,
and darkness. It was weirdly silent here—even the

rumble of the subways did not penetrate, or else it was muffled by the leaden soil. The familiar, soft clang of the pipes could not be heard. The mutter of the three mens' voices, even, sounded muffled, as if smothered under the webs and dust of three centuries.

Cullen lowered his sword, gazed around in fascination. "How'd a ship get down here?"

"Like Father says, Old New York," offered Mouse, picking his way carefully among the broken furniture at the bottom of the room. "Might have been water here, long time ago."

"We're damn near under the Battery now," pointed out Winslow. "Shoreline could have changed . . ."

But Cullen had turned away, still exploring, delighted with the strange storybook quality of their find. "Look at this!" Dust billowed up as he pulled the shredding remains of the carpet aside, dimming and fuzzing still further the smouldering spots of the lanterns in the thick blue gloom. Beneath the carpet was a hatchway.

"Open it up," Winslow urged, even as Cullen knelt on the slanting surface to pry at the swollen wood. Winslow helped, using first the antique cutlass—which promptly broke—and then his own big buck-knife to try to get purchase on the splintery wood.

Mouse stood back to watch, his head tilted a little to one side. At last he said, "Stuck shut. I can open it."

And with a wicked grin, before either man could stop him or ask how he intended to accomplish this, he yelled "AHOY!!!", took two running steps forward, and jumped on the hatchway with all the force and momentum of his body. The wood shattered with a splintery crash and Mouse plunged down into darkness.

"You crazy little . . . !" Winslow lunged forward, holding his lamp down, for a dizzy second wondering how the hell they were going to haul their friend back up the tunnels if he'd managed to break a leg, always supposing the hatch didn't open into a chasm a hundred feet deep, or filled with quicksand . . .

"Mouse! You all right?" Cullen crowded up beside him, holding down his lantern in an attempt to enlighten the impenetrable murk below.

"Dark down here . . ." came Mouse's voice, not more than ten feet beneath them.

Winslow's breath blew out in a gusty sigh of relief. "You're going to get yourself killed one day!" he yelled, and reached his lamp still further down towards the twin upturned white beams of Mouse's hat. *If I don't kill you myself*, he added mentally. "You can't just . . ."

The bobbing light twinkled on something below them in the darkness, something that flashed and gleamed. Winslow broke off as he realized what it was—what it had to be. "Oh, my God," he whispered. Beside him, he heard the hissing intake of Cullen's breath.

Mouse had fallen into what had probably been one of the lowest holds of the ship, never intended for anything but storage. It had contained mostly food, now long since perished. But there had also been an old leather chest there, half rotted and crumbling, which had split open with the impact of Mouse's body, spilling forth its contents . . .

And its contents was gold. Here a jewelled cup, there a massive crucifix, elsewhere the frame of a gleaming mirror, caught with that secret flame the flashlights' prosaic beams; gold and silver coins lay in drifts between them, draped with seaweed-like tangles of thick-linked ornamental chains, ropes of soft-shining pearls, pendants the size of a man's palm; plates, goblets, jewelled tiaras, rings, reliquaries . . . a pirate's hoard of treasure glittering softly in its den of eternal dark.

Winslow and Cullen were stunned speechless, but Mouse merely picked up a heavy pectoral chain and waved it aloft, grinning proudly, "Found it. Told you!"

The leather chest itself could not have been lifted by one man, or two, even in its heyday—under the weight of the treasure it split and crumbled, dumping coins, necklaces, tablewear of baroque pearl and enamel in clattering rain about Mouse's feet when he tried to pick up one end. At length he shoved as much as he could about his person and had Winslow pull him up through the old hatch, and emerged into the shadowy lantern-light above like a King of Fools, with a jewelled tiara on his rumpled blonde hair and a prince's ransom of pearled chains around his neck, rubbing and clashing softly on the tattered sacking of his vest.

"Look at this," whispered Cullen, gazing raptly at the gleaming ornaments. "Just *look* at it!"

"I see it," said Winslow softly. "I don't believe it, but I sure see it."

"More down there," pointed out Mouse, setting down the heavy candelabra he'd brought up under his arm and systematically emptying doubloons from his pocket as if they'd been fistfuls of subway tokens.

Cullen's green eyes gleamed in the dim glow of the flashlights' beams. "How much more?"

"Lots." Mouse untangled the necklaces from around his shoulders, dropped them on the broken table—which Winslow had righted—with the lanterns and the coins. He didn't think any of the necklaces were as pretty as the one he'd given Vincent to pass along to his Catherine, the one he'd found, with the golden plate and the silver goblet, amid the dusty ruin of the table and chairs. He was glad it was the one he'd given her. A person who was good to Vincent, a person who was a friend to him Above, deserved the prettiest, and in Mouse's slim experience girls liked delicate things.

"We should bring it up," said Cullen eagerly. "We should bring all of it up."

"I'll bring my chest," offered Mouse, not certain he liked this new tone in Cullen's voice but wanting to help his friend. He looked at the treasure heaped upon the old table, gleaming against the blackened wood like a bed of embers under its centuries-deep incrustation of dirt. "We found good stuff, right?"

"Better than good, Mouse," breathed Winslow, his white grin huge with delight in the lamplight at this Tom Sawyer dream-come-true. "Better than good."

Mouse grinned back, pleased they appreciated his cleverness in finding such a thing as this, then turned and sprang up to the entry-hole in the wall. Cullen, unbelievingly running the jewelled chains through his fingers, whispered, "Not bad . . . not bad . . ." But as Mouse's fur boots vanished through the hole in the wall he seemed to remember something forgotten, and called out after him "Mouse!"

But Mouse's footsteps were already clattering away down the tunnel outside.

"Mouse, don't tell anyone!" yelled Cullen after him. "You hear? This is our secret!"

There was no reply. Uneasily, Cullen turned back to Winslow. "I don't think he heard me."

"Don't worry about it," he advised. "He ain't gonna tell nobody but his damned raccoon."

"He doesn't understand what we found, does he?" whispered Cullen, pacing back to the table, running his hands lightly, reverently over the gleaming things piled there around the lanterns. "It's just so much shiny metal to him."

Winslow looked curiously over at his friend's thin, dark-stubbled face, then back at the treasure, objects beautiful and incredibly precious which had, he realized for the first time, probably been stolen by violence at the cost of their original owners' lives. "Yeah," he said softly. "And maybe he's the smart one at that."

But Cullen, holding to the lantern-glow a sapphire the size of a walnut and staring intoxicated into its depths, scarcely heard.

Three

"So—how do you think it's going?"

Catherine looked around her at the dark panelling and discreet opulence of Adderly's Books. Its floor-to-ceiling wood shelves, carved Oxford-style stepladders and comfy red-upholstered chairs constituted an elegant and learned rebuke of every brightly-lit chain emporium of the latest in paperback bestsellers in New York. *We* can be successful *and* literate, Adderly's seemed to say—and indeed, seemed to prove. Archaeological works were their specialty, and they had the best collection in the city of both new works and vintage editions—whether you were after Jones' classic *Hovitos Treasure* or a rare 1939 printing of Horatio Smith's *Lost Antiquities of Bavaria*, you could find them there. Thus Adderly's was the ideal locale for a champagne reception and book-signing in honor of one of the best-known adventurer-archaeologists of the latter half of the twentieth century.

"Seems to be going great," she said.

Jenny Aronson relaxed a little, as much as any hostess ever relaxes. "I was so nervous . . ."

And well she should be, Catherine thought. She'd heard Jenny's horror stories of signings where no patrons had showed up at all and the authors involved had spent three hellish hours playing

"Hangman" behind the virgin stacks of their latest works and trying to look unconcerned.

No such danger here. The big room was flatteringly crowded, men in suits or sports jackets and women in stylish dresses nibbling hors d'oeuvres and sipping the medium-priced California champagne Jenny had convinced Harwick to spring for, chatting softly, mostly about Alain Viso's newest work, *Re-Discovering the Lost City of Petra*. Chamber music—Mozart or Rossini—murmured discreetly in the background. Jenny, in shimmering blue jacquard that set off her angular dark beauty, had kept things circulating adeptly, introducing the right people to one another and recognizing the various minor celebrities who had been invited.

Watching the throng, Catherine mentally played "Dress Derby," a game which had helped her through many of the more boring social events of her debutante days—the winner so far was a strapless silver lamé number with stiffened cylinders of fabric sewed vertically all around the skirt, giving the general effect of a rocket-ship in a 1930s Flash Gordon serial. Particularly in contrast with this view of appropriate wear, Catherine felt pleased with her own choice of dress, simple black velvet which set off the opulent delicacy of Mouse's necklace to perfection.

Viso himself, in fact, was probably the only one in the room dressed casually, probably because he knew everyone would expect an archaeologist to be wearing a safari jacket, albeit one which had originated at I. Magnin. A charming, white-bearded Frenchman in his sixties, he had been signing steadily since eight o'clock, now and then pausing—just long enough—to chat with the people in line or to exchange archaeological anecdotes with his friends.

Catherine smiled reassuringly at Jenny. "Alain

Viso's a fascinating character—you're going to sell a lot of books and everyone at Harwick will be very impressed. And besides," she added teasingly, "even if the party *and* the book were disasters, I'd still be your best friend."

Jenny's worried look melted into a grin—that was something, though she'd known it, she'd needed to hear just now. *Vincent is right*, thought Catherine, her mind straying briefly back to last night's quiet encounter on the terrace, when all she could do, tired and trashed and teary, had been to sit in the sheltering circle of his arm until she felt better. *Without one another, we would be lost indeed.*

"Thanks, pal. Here, he looks like he's finishing up, would you like to meet him?" The pleased brightening of Catherine's face was all the answer she needed; Jenny hustled over to winkle Viso, who had risen now to his feet, out of the cluster of fans around him.

Catherine remained near the book-lined wall, cradling the copy of *Re-Discovering Petra* which Jenny had given her—which, unlike many of the Harwick publications Jenny had passed along, she actually intended to read—in her arms. She was glad she had come. For months following the assault she had avoided parties, even after plastic surgery had removed the scars left on her face—and she still occasionally woke, shuddering, from nightmares of stumbling into some upscale social event with her face slashed and ugly, as she had seen it that first hellish moment in the mirror, when she'd taken the bandages off her eyes. But with Jenny's gentle, persistent help—inviting her to small gatherings rather than the big society parties that her father would have thrown—she had gradually gotten over this dread of showing herself in public, this sensation that they would all know what she *really* looked like, or had looked like, and she was glad of it, for she enjoyed parties, enjoyed watching people, observing from the background. *Vincent*, she found herself thinking, *would enjoy this, too, inveterate people-watcher that he is* . . .

Part of her felt a pang of regret that this was an experience he would never get to enjoy, and part of her smiled at the mental image of him in evening dress—which would suit his broad-shouldered height—his long saffron mane caught back in a black velvet ribbon as they did in the eighteenth century . . .

And peripherally she was aware of a man standing beside her. She took no especial notice of him beyond the awareness of his distance from her that becomes second nature to all practitioners of a martial art—something which is not quite readiness—until he spoke.

"Excuse me," he inquired politely, "are you with the publishing house?" And he made no attempt to disguise the appreciation of his glance as it travelled over her.

She smiled, and shook her head. "No . . ."

"A collector?" He was, she saw, superficially a very good-looking man on the sunny side of forty, his light brown hair streaked with sun-bleaching as well as incipient gray, his rugged face tanned, lined, and rakish. His smile was charming, but there was something hard and a little cynical about his cool gray eyes which said, *trouble*.

Nevertheless, he was handsome and the atmosphere was one of pleasant small talk and light flirtation. She smiled again and said, "Not really."

"Jonathan Thorpe." He extended a hand, well-manicured but very strong—the hand of a man at home with tools, Catherine guessed by the firm, light, dry touch. "I'm he 'without whom this book

41

could never have been written'." And he nodded towards the copy of *Re-Discovering Petra* in Catherine's hands.

"Catherine Chandler." Instead of shaking her hand he raised it gallantly to his lips, only the slightest of mistimings giving away that it was a gesture used deliberately to impress. He kept his eyes on her face, but the way he did so was a little unnerving, for there was something almost predatory in his gaze, and he held it several beats too long.

"Is there something wrong?" she asked uneasily, and his gray eyes smiled and warmed, apologetic and complimentary at once.

"I was merely admiring your necklace," he said. "It's very unusual."

"Thank you." Her hand strayed to it, briefly, and she smiled again, thinking of Mouse and his scavenging. She had found in her jewel-box a pair of filigreed Victorian earrings which both complemented its ornateness and were large enough, in concert with a careful job of makeup, to conceal the knife-scar in front of her left ear. They gave her, with her wide green eyes and brown-blonde hair, the burnished look of antique gold.

She had the impression he was about to ask her something else when out of the tail of her eye she caught a glimpse of Jenny approaching, with Alain Viso close behind. Thorpe saw them, too, and with a hasty "Excuse me," left Catherine and moved swiftly to intercept. "Alain," Catherine heard him say, "have you seen Gerstner's new book on Egypt? It's really extraordinary . . ."

"Gerstner!" sputtered the Frenchman indignantly, reacting to the name of the man Jenny had said was his most vociferous academic rival, and Thorpe took his arm and steered him deftly away from Jenny and Catherine. "Gerstner's a tomb-robber, a vandal . . ."

Gesticulating furiously, the archaeologist seemed not to have noticed that he'd been deliberately deflected from an introduction, and seemed to have forgotten all about the fact that he was going to meet someone. Jenny's eyes met Catherine's and she gave her an apologetic shrug. "Later," she promised.

But Catherine was somehow sure that this man Thorpe would unobtrusively manage to keep Viso away from her for the remainder of the night.

Whatever hopes for secrecy Cullen might have entertained evaporated when he pulled himself up out of the storage-hold into the old ship's cabin again. With Mouse's departure he and Winslow had lowered themselves down into the black, dusty pit, to explore more fully by lantern-light the low-beamed chamber they had only glimpsed, searching its farther corners to see if yet more treasure were there. They'd found a number of candlesticks and reliquaries and another small sack of gold coins—a sack which crumbled under the weight of the metal when they tried to lift it—and, in a far corner, a ladder, which they'd propped under the hatchway so they could climb out, though Cullen had his doubts about the state of the decaying wood. At the creak of footsteps in the cabin above he called out "Mouse?" and clambered up . . .

. . . only to find not only Mouse, but Mouse's friend Jamie—a thin, fair, tomboyish seventeen-year-old girl in a makeshift miner's helmet—and three of the Tunnel children, Kipper, Dustin, and Eric, excitedly whispering and staring around them in the slate-dark gloom.

"Is this where the treasure is?" demanded Kipper, darting towards the open hatch.

Cullen caught the boy around the waist, holding him back, a sudden, irrational fury at Mouse sweeping over him. "Stay outta there!" he ordered, as Kipper struggled indignantly, dark eyes sparkling under unruly black curls. "It's dangerous down there! The walls are rotting, floor's busted out . . . and you sure know how to keep a secret!" he added accusingly, rounding on Mouse.

"Only told Jamie," Mouse grinned sheepishly, putting an arm around her waist as if that excused everything. "Needed a hand with the trunk . . ." He gestured back at the hole in the wooden wall, through which the guttering flicker of a lantern could be seen. Quite clearly, Mouse's old steamer trunk, heavy in itself and now filled with picks, spades, unlit torches and a coil of rope, had proved too big to haul through the narrow passage into the ship. He shrugged, his casual wave implying that three or four others intimate with the secret—not to mention whomever else *they'd* told, thought Cullen dourly—was no great matter after all. "Kids saw us, followed."

Winslow's bald brown head appeared through the hatchway, and his dark brows shot up at the sight of the little crowd in the cabin.

"I wanna see," clamored Dustin, barely able to keep still with excitement—Eric crowded forward, the lenses of his glasses flashing in the reflected beam of Jamie's helmet.

" 'Don't worry,' " quoted Cullen sarcastically, " 'he won't tell nobody but his damn raccoon'."

Winslow hooked an elbow over the edge of the hatch, drew his massive shoulders further out and cast a curious look at Cullen's brooding face. "What's it matter, Cullen?" he asked. "The gold belongs to all of us." He turned back to the others. "Jamie, you light the torches. You kids, I want you to stay back where it's safe, you hear? Mouse, you bring some picks? We gotta enlarge that hole some to get the trunk in and out . . .''

For a moment it seemed to Winslow that Cullen would speak, but in the end he didn't. He only fetched a spade from the tools in Mouse's chest, and went to work widening the hole and, later, loading the treasure in Mouse's old steamer trunk to carry it out. But his glance, when it fell on the others—and later on those who, hearing rumor of the treasure, showed up to watch, or help, or get in the way—was one of increasing sourness, and as they worked on through the night, he had less and less to say.

In view of the uneasiness she had felt about Jonathan Thorpe, Catherine was not altogether surprised to get a phone call from him Monday morning at the D A's office, asking her out to lunch. "I know the decor's not much," Thorpe said apologetically, as he ushered her into the rather grubby confines of the Cafe Olympia on Murray Street, "but you have my word, these are the best cheeseburgers east of St. Louis."

"They'd have to be," agreed Catherine, looking around her at the miniature wasteland of faded formica and tattered vinyl, with its population of gaudily-dressed street hustlers, gray-coveralled mechanics, and Puerto Rican women chattering in Spanish over that day's *Spécialité du Jour*. Over at the next table a long-haired gnome of a man who looked like he'd been installed with the counters sat with his nose buried in a copy of *Fevre Dream*, oblivious to all around him.

Thorpe gestured expansively as a skinny waitress brought them cheeseburgers, Pepsi, and chips. "Put me in a jacket and tie and I can eat coq au vin at Lutèce with the best of them, but you can't imagine how good a cheeseburger can taste until you spend six months in Greenland living on Eskimo—er—delicacies.''

Catherine laughed. She didn't trust the man as far as she could throw him—which thanks to Isaac Stubbs' lessons was probably ten feet on a good day—but he had an undeniable roguish charm.

"Fortunately," she said, "I can only imagine. Have you worked with Viso a long time?''

"Officially?'' He cocked a sun-bleached eyebrow at her. In a brown leather jacket and well-faded jeans he seemed as much at home as he had last night in his tailored tweed sports jacket; though the sun had bleached his hair and lined his face, his hands, she noticed, were smooth, not roughened with the work of digging as she had seen that Alain Viso's were. "Officially, I've never worked with him at all. But the truth is, a man like Viso needs a man like me.''

"I see," said Catherine. "And what kind of man is that?''

"A man who has an ulterior motive when he asks a beautiful woman out to lunch.''

"Is that a compliment,'' Catherine asked, "or should I be getting nervous?'' The twinkle in his eye was definitely Clark Gable—a good-hearted rogue bearded by somebody like Bette Davis—but some instinct warned her that this man was only being as honest with her as he was because he'd guessed that a snow job wouldn't wash. Still, he was right about the cheeseburgers.

"The necklace you were wearing last night,'' said Thorpe, leaning forward across the battered formica and coming right to the point.

"Well, that's blunt enough,'' she said, amused in spite of herself.

"Would you consider selling it to me?''

The request startled her—she set down her cheese-burger, momentarily at a loss for how to respond. No one had ever asked her to sell them her personal jewelry before—it was as if he'd suddenly offered to buy her shoes. "No," she said at last. "It was a gift."

"Well, there are gifts . . . and there are gifts." Thorpe cocked an eyebrow at her wisely. "That necklace is quite old—and quite valuable."

A man who worked with Alain Viso—who had, according to the *Petra* book she'd skimmed last night, been in on Viso's discovery of the Assyrian tombs in Chagar Bazar—would not regard even the most well-made of Victorian costume jewelry as either old or valuable, and Catherine frowned, considerably disconcerted. "I—I didn't know . . ."

"Maybe there's something else you didn't know," he said gently, folding his hands before him and studying her face. "Whoever gave it to you probably obtained it by . . . shall we say, less than legal means?"

Not stealing, TAKING. She could hear Vincent's amused, exasperated imitation of his friend Mouse's eternal semantic argument with Father. And yet . . . something didn't fit. She knew the world of the Tunnel-dwellers only through Vincent, but in her heart, she knew Vincent too well to know that he would live with, or associate with, thieves. Uneasily, she said, "I don't think so . . ."

Thorpe regarded her gravely, like an older brother or a rather good-looking uncle faced with an innocent girl's dangerous naïveté. "If there's one thing I'm expert on," he said. "it's the law regarding private ownership of antiquities. If you won't sell me the necklace, at least tell me where you got it."

She shook her head, and gathered her red-and-blue silk scarf from the bench beside her. "From a

47

secret admirer," she said, with a small inner smile at how true that statement actually was. She slid from the booth and rose, glad that this was the sort of place where one paid for one's food first. "Well, Jonathan, I really should be going."

He didn't push it—either from consideration or, she suspected, because he sensed that to do so would rouse her suspicions and do him more harm than good. "Fine." He smiled. Then he gave her another of his wise looks and said, "If you change your mind and decide to sell . . . well, discretion is my middle name."

I'll bet it is, she thought. "I'll keep it in mind." But as she picked her way out among the crowded tables to the door she felt his eyes on her back, and was glad she had given him neither her home telephone number, nor her home address.

In the soft radiance of his candlelit chamber, Father pored over the maps strewn across the octagonal oak table before him. The WPA survey of 1937 showed where new sewer-lines had been laid along Prince Street when the new blocks of apartments had gone in, but no mention was made on the map of the steam-tunnels which had warmed the old Barrington, the small but ornate luxury apartment house which had been there up through the Twenties. If they hadn't been torn out or incorporated into the sewage system of the newer apartments, there should be a connecting system through to the old brick Civil War water-main that ran under Broome Street. He'd have to ask Vincent about that area . . .

He sighed, and pushed up his reading glasses to rub his eyes. There was no proper map of what lay beneath New York's streets, not even in the City Planning Department—every time new construction went in, or a water-line had to be repaired, or cables laid for electricity or this new cable television system, Father knew perfectly well that men from City Planning made a guesstimate from three or four different maps and then dug a test-bore to see what was really down there. And as for what lay on the deeper levels, it was anyone's guess, even after all these years. They really couldn't continue like this, on oral tradition and rote memory—even old-timers like Mary still got lost upon occasion, if they went deep, for instance to visit old Narcissa in her cave down near the Chamber of Winds. It was all very well for Kipper to teach Eric and Ellie, the newest children to arrive in the tunnels, the more-traveled ways, but it was a long and painstaking process, and there were always cases of people thinking they knew the way when they didn't. It was Father's great fear that someone—a child, or a newcomer—would one day get lost in the labyrinths of Below and die before they could be found. There were over two hundred miles of subway tunnels alone—when you counted in the steam-tunnels, the forgotten and sealed pedestrian underpasses, ancient basements and disused water-mains . . .

He shook his head. They had been lucky so far, by means of patrols and warnings, to avoid contact with the city work crews, but all it would take was one careless incident, one inopportune encounter, for the peace of their secret world to be shattered by incursions from Above. And they had been lucky so far that those people who did get lost, they had been able to find, usually thanks to Vincent's knowledge of the tunnels and ability as a tracker. Still, a map was needed, a good map . . .

He glanced up as movement caught his eye, and he saw his tall adopted son standing in the rock archway of the vestibule. "Ah, Vincent," he said, taking off his glasses and looking up. "How is the work progressing?"

Vincent stepped down the short flight of iron stairs, his strange face troubled. "It isn't," he said shortly, puzzlement in his blue eyes. "I've just visited the site. No one is there."

"No one?" said Father, startled and concerned. "Not even *Winslow?*" Given the big blacksmith's usual hardworking conscientiousness, that was hard to believe. "Perhaps they've taken a break . . ."

"Then their tools are taking a break as well," replied Vincent, pacing uneasily, soundlessly in his soft boots, his heavy mantle billowing around him.

Father frowned, really disquieted now. Though they lived underground the community had need to be far more concerned with the weather than most of those who lived above, and another storm was predicted coming in off the Atlantic. Heavy leakage from the corroded drain could mean, at the very least, wading through the upper tunnels in that area, perhaps water-damage in the chambers of those who lived in that area—at the worst, evacuation of that portion of the tunnels to stay out of the way of the city work crews who would appear if the flooding got bad enough to spill over into the nearby subway lines. "They're all aware of the urgency of this . . ."

"Mouse has vanished, too," Vincent went on, half to himself, thinking aloud. "And . . ." He paused, frowning, as something else occurred to him. "None of the children seem to be around . . ."

Father opened his mouth to speak again, but Vincent raised his head suddenly, listening to the soft clanging of the pipes. Father heard the clumsily-rapped code-tap of Vincent's name, and then, with awkward hesitations, the code for summons used by the Helpers.

"It's Catherine," said Vincent, his slanted eyebrows pulling together over the flattened, tapering bridge of his nose. Not an emergency, thought Father, analyzing the uncertain signal, but definitely a request for him to come. It was something she did seldom enough that Father recognized it as important, much as he deplored the fact that she could do it at all. He signed his dismissal with a gesture of his glasses, held in one hand; Vincent inclined his head and turned to go.

"If you should see anyone along the way," added Father dourly, "remind them that there's work to be done."

And yet, he thought, drawing up his rust-colored robes over his shoulders for warmth as Vincent's tall form melted away into the shadows of the passage, *it was unlike Cullen and the others—and certainly unlike Winslow—to disappear that way . . .*

The interview with Jonathan Thorpe troubled Catherine sufficiently that, as soon as the paperwork on the playground shooting case had been turned in to Moreno, she took what she considered to be a well-earned few hours off to consult Hillman's, the jewelers with whom her family had dealt since her Great-Grandfather Heathcott's day. What they told her troubled her still more.

It was true, she thought, as she stole softly down the stairs to the cement-walled laundry room in the basement of her apartment building, that she only knew the folk of the Tunnels from what Vincent had told her, and from scattered, momentary encounters with them, though she had been instrumental in helping the two orphan children Eric and Ellie to become members of that community. Upon that occasion, Father had mentioned that the community as a whole must vote upon the inclusion of new

members, and that those newcomers must be trust-
worthy in all senses of the word.

It was true they lived by forage, she thought, that
they existed upon what the world Above had cast
aside—true, too, that Mouse had a semantic problem
with the difference between *stealing* and *taking* . . .

Even so . . .

The gawky young man from apartment 18c was
just pawing a load of jeans, rumpled shirts, and
threadbare boxer shorts out of the dryer and back
into the pillowcase in which he'd obviously brought
them down as Catherine entered the laundry
room—*They really ought to make the poor things take
Home Survival courses in High School*, she thought,
shaking her head as he shambled out, leaving a trail
of socks, lint, and hard little balls of shredded Klee-
nex in his wake. Swiftly, she crossed the room to
the service closet, opened it and, taking from under
her coat the pipe-wrench from her household tool
kit, slipped inside. Overhead a 60-watt bulb burned
blearily; by its light she crouched and lifted out the
heavy iron grate of the drain in the cement floor.

A ladder of rusty metal staples led down into
darkness. A thick cluster of pipes traveled down the
service-closet wall to vanish through the floor—by
the light overhead Catherine could just make out
their smooth columns in the sub-basement below.
She climbed nimbly down, pulling the grate back
over the hole after her.

The sub-basement smelled of mildew and damp
cement—it was cold down here after the warmth of
the laundry room above. Her heels clicked on the
hard floor, for she was still dressed in the linen
slacks and rose silk shirt she'd worn to work. Barely
visible in the shadows, the pipes ran down into the
floor of this lower chamber as well, down, she
knew, through the black deeps of Underground,

down to the vast and echoing Pipe Chamber, where she'd once seen a little bald man named Pascal sitting like a spider in an impossible web, surrounded by a hazy halo of candlelight, a wrench in either hand like drumsticks and a stethoscope on his ears, listening to the messages and relaying them on.

The pipe nearest the wall, Vincent had told her, when he'd shown her the code that spelled out his name.

She tapped a series of longs and shorts a little like the Morse she'd learned in Girl Scouts . . .

"The pipes go deep, deeper sometimes than even Pascal can say," Vincent had told her once, when she'd asked him about the secrets of that lightless world. "There are chambers six, eight hundred feet below the level of the streets, chambers only Mouse and I and maybe Narcissa, the old voodoo-witch, have visited—some chambers, I suspect, that no one knows."

And Catherine had been silent, thinking about that vast and labyrinthine world where Vincent had grown up, reading Father's books by lamplight, absorbing all the wisdom, all the culture, of a world he could never enter.

And standing there in the chilly dark, she wondered, for the hundredth time, about Father himself. Obviously a man of great culture, obviously with medical training, both of which he had passed along to his adopted son. A man of high moral standards, with a passionate sense of justice . . . what was it that had turned him against her world, Catherine wondered, remembering the wariness that lay behind the respect for her in those sharp, blue-gray eyes. What had made him choose to forsake all that the world could give to an educated and talented man?

Then, turning her head, she saw in the dark at

the far end of the sub-basement the gold-green reflection of eyes, the glint of light on a steel belt-clasp and on the small buckles of his boots. A moment later Vincent stood framed in the broken arch of bricks that led down into the maze of steam-pipes and old water-mains that comprised the high-est level of the tunnels, the first steps on the road Below.

Stepping forward, she clasped his hands in greet-ing, her own fingers warmed by the returning pres-sure of his. But looking up into his face, she saw worry in his eyes.

"What is it?" she asked, and he shook his head.

"Nothing. Just . . ." He paused, troubled about something, then shook his head again.

"Vincent," said Catherine quietly, "the gift Mouse gave me . . ."

"What was it?"

"A necklace," she said. "I thought at first it was just an old piece of costume jewelry, but . . . I've just been to a jeweler. It's solid gold." Vincent stepped back, his blue-green eyes widening with astonish-ment. "He wouldn't even begin to appraise it. He says it dates back to the seventeenth century . . ."

He was silent, digesting this information—his mind running, as hers had been all the way back from Hillman's, on the possible implications of that undeniable fact. At length he said, "Mouse some-times takes things from the world above, yes. But only the things he needs—tools, machine parts . . ." He shook his head. "But . . . a *golden necklace?*"

When he left Catherine, Vincent turned his steps southward, toward the yellow-gray mud and silty landfill of Manhattan's tip. That yellow mud had been all over Mouse's clothes and hair the other day, the day he had been fingering the packet he'd given to Catherine—the coarse burlap, as Vincent recalled, had been impregnated with it. Vincent's wide-ranging patrols took him far beyond the usual walks of the Tunnel Dwellers, and he could pinpoint to within a few dozen feet where the mud had come from, by its composition and smell.

The more he thought about the defection of the work crew, the more it troubled him, for it was totally out of character for any of them to simply down tools and go. The men of the community were an independent-minded lot, granted, but they would generally have the courtesy to tell Father they were abandoning a task, if that was what they chose to do for reasons of their own . . . and in any case they *hadn't* downed tools, but had taken them. And for them all to vanish *en masse* like that, and the children as well . . .

Vincent did not remember whether it was Sherlock Holmes or William of Occam who had observed that it was rare indeed for two separate bizarre and anomalous situations to exist simultaneously—that two sets of unusual circumstances were likelier to stem from the same cause than from different causes. His instincts told him that whatever was going on, the answer might very well lie in whatever place Mouse had found the golden necklace.

He took the Eighth Avenue Express as far as Fulton Street, clinging with powerful claws to the top of the car in the roaring darkness, wind clawing back his mantle and his hair. Then, abandoning the subway line he moved south, up a service shaft and along a narrow fissure in the rock, then through an old brick main when the rock of the island's tip gave way to ancient landfill . . .

Far ahead he saw the flicker of torches. His hearing, more acute than human, picked up the low murmur of voices, broken now and then by those he recognized clearly . . .

"Just think how old it is," he heard Mary's soft tones, reverent with admiration. "And so lovely . . ."

"Cullen says the frame is solid gold," came Jamie's voice, with a note of strange, yearning delight. "I'm going to hang it in my chamber."

"Oh . . ." said Mary, disappointed. "I know a woman who would love it. One of our Helpers, she's given us so much over the years . . ."

"But *I* want it!"

And then, more clearly still, Winslow's voice: "Coming out!"

"This is heavy," grunted Winslow, heaving the hand-sewn sack up out of the hatch ahead of him.

Cullen, still slouched on the ladder up from the hold below, muttered ironically, "Gold gets that way."

There was laughter at this remark as Winslow upended the sack into Mouse's steamer trunk, which had finally been squeezed through the enlarged hole in the ship's wooden side. Grimy as they were, the coins, pendants, candlesticks and shoe-buckles seemed to have a luminous quality in the yellow torchlight, a warm and seductive beauty, as if the things had life of their own. The crowd—and it was by now a considerable crowd—in the old cabin closed around the chest, eager hands reaching out to touch, to caress, to assure themselves that hidden treasures really did exist, and that good fortune occasionally deigned to smile upon humankind.

"It's amazing," whispered Jamie, her gray eyes shining.

"I think those old coins were called doubloons," breathed Mary.

People were grabbing now, picking up coins,

neckpieces, bracelets, running the chains through their fingers, hanging pendants around their necks to see how the jewels gleamed against their patched clothes. "Lookit this ring . . ." Dustin held up the immense solitaire sapphire which had earlier fascinated Cullen, and Kipper reached out and pulled it away from him.

"Hey, cut that out!" ordered Winslow, as Dustin's hand came back to slap the older boy. "Now!"

"What're you doing?! Here, put those back . . ." Cullen pulled the scuffling boys apart, snatched the ring and tossed it back into the chest.

"We're just looking," protested Jamie, though she kept a possessive hand on the gold-framed mirror she'd chosen to keep in her room.

"Cullen," said Mary, her soft voice troubled at the two boys' crestfallen faces, "this belongs to all of us, to the whole community."

"Sure," retorted Cullen. "We do all the work and now you're going to tell us who the stuff belongs to."

"Come on, Cullen," cut in Winslow. "We share down here. You know that."

"Fine. You can share *your* third."

"That ain't how it goes. . . ." Winslow's temper, always short, began to flare, and Cullen's eyes blazed.

"Don't tell me. . . ."

Other voices chimed in, angry, protesting, rising higher and higher; while the adults squabbled Kipper reached over quickly and seized the ring again, as another child dug greedily into the chest for an enamelled snuffbox and Jamie hugged her precious mirror to her breast. The low rafters flung back the sound of conflict, the passageway picking up the echoes. Mouse covered his ears, appalled at the chaos, shaken and confused at the unprecedented spectacle of those dark forms struggling in the shadowy lantern-glare.

"STOP THIS!"

There was shocked silence. Vincent's voice, seldom raised, bellowed in the tiny cabin like a lion's roar. In the hush as he leaned in through the hole in the wall, massive shoulders filling it, eyes glowing in the saffron frame of his mane, men and women looked at one another, and at the gold clutched so passionately in their fists.

"So this is where you've all been." Vincent's gaze travelled from face to face, then to the treasure scattered about the dirty floor. "Where did this come from?"

"Me." Mouse pushed his way hesitantly through the crowd. Alone of everyone in the room, he didn't have some piece of pirate gold, some bit of looted jewels, in his hands. "Found it down there." He gestured to the black hole of the hatchway behind him, the dirty tangle of broken furniture shoved into a corner, the shattered cutlass and the digging tools. "Dug it up."

"*We* dug it up," Cullen corrected swiftly. "Mouse and Winslow and *me*."

"Cullen . . . !" protested Mary.

"Now, come on . . ." stormed Winslow.

"Wait a minute," added Jamie, "I helped . . ."

"You didn't do anything . . . !"

"Enough!" cried Vincent, and at once the clamor ceased. He looked around at them, disbelieving, as if they saw themselves mirrored in his clear, puzzled eyes, they looked suddenly sheepish, hearing their own angry voices for the first time.

"This is completely unlike us," went on Vincent quietly. "We will have a council meeting and discuss it there . . . calmly, quietly . . . like friends."

For a long moment there was abashed silence.

Then Winslow and Mouse moved shamefacedly forward to pick up the chest, staggering under the weight of the gold. Mary, who had filled her pinafore apron with golden coins, dumped them quickly back into the box and reached to take a handle and help with the glittering burden. Others took up the tools, gathered lanterns and removed the torches from the walls, ducking their heads under the low lintel as they climbed up after Vincent into the tunnel again.

Only Cullen hung back, out of the retreating glow. In his hands were the things he had taken from those who would have taken them from him— a necklace of pendant pearls, a golden shoe buckle, a handful of doubloons, a golden fork. As the shadows closed around him again he shoved the things deep in the pockets of his long, billowy coat. Only then did he follow the firefly trail of the lights.

Four

"ASTONISHING," said Father softly. His hands passed with reverent wonder across the things scattered upon the octagonal study table before him: cups, coins, an opulent rope of enormous pearls; a massive armband hammered into the shapes of feathered serpents; handfuls of doubloons; Kipper's huge sapphire ring. Among them and all around them candles burned, and in the improved light the treasures seemed truly magical, warm and living things and absolutely to be desired. All around the table the whole community was gathered in Father's room, pressing to look over one another's shoulders, or clustered along the rail of the book-lined gallery above, and the marveling whisper was like the murmurs of the earth-winds that stirred through the deeps. For once the soft, intermittent clanging of the pipes was silent—Pascal sat perched on the iron stair which led up to the gallery, mitted hands folded, dark eyes wide with wonder at the gold.

"These are centuries old," went on Father quietly. "Dutch, Spanish, and I think . . ." He touched the armband with awed disbelief. "Yes, I believe this is Mayan. And you say there's more?"

"A trunk full." Winslow stood beside him, fists on hips, his dark eyes somber. Standing quietly near the steps up to the vestibule Vincent could feel the

60

interplay of tension in the room, the emotional charge that reminded him of the nights Above when lightning brewed behind sullen clouds.

His eyes sought out Mouse, standing, helmet off now, beside Jamie—moved on to Cullen, slouched against the iron rail of the spiral gallery steps, arms crossed over his chest and a brooding look in his green eyes. Curious, he thought, that simple metal could act as such a magnet for people's hearts. The things were very beautiful . . but he sensed that the tension in the room would have been the same had the gold been in shapeless lumps.

"Gold, silver, jewels, you name it," Winslow went on. "We left it down in Mouse's chamber. Damn thing was heavy."

"It seems impossible," remarked Vincent. "A ship buried beneath the city . . ."

Father shook his head. "The island's shoreline has changed dramatically over the centuries—at one time Water Street really *was* on the water. A ship could easily have been lost in the harbor or the river, covered over by landfill. Until now."

And there was a stirring in the crowd as they adjusted their minds to the miracle of these new-found riches. To the fact that, from being the poorest of the poor, they were—each one was, or could be—wealthy beyond their wildest imaginings.

Father went on, with perhaps, Vincent thought, a shade too much briskness, "Now we, as a community, must decide what to do with this extraordinary treasure. Our decision will be a great test of our good sense and loyalty to each other."

From the corner of his eye Vincent saw Cullen's head come up. Everyone else was looking at the gold.

"Think of the good this can accomplish," put in

Mary, coming up quietly behind him. "For all of us, the whole community."

"We can buy food, medicine," agreed Winslow. "New toys for the kids instead of castoffs . . ." And standing on the sidelines, Eric and Ellie, Kipper and Dustin and Alex looked pleased.

"Machines!" enthused Mouse, his blue eyes glowing. "Parts and stuff . . ."

"Our Helpers deserve part of this wealth," added Mary. "Some of them have so little, but they've always been there when we needed them."

There was a clamor of assent, people agreeing, disagreeing, suggesting other things needed, asking how much and calculating what each—if not necessarily all unanimously—thought fair. Vincent raised his arm, troubled somehow at this eagerness, and as they quieted he said, "There's a danger here you all seem to be ignoring." He looked from face to face—Mary's lined and careworn visage under the neat coil of her graying fair hair, Jamie's bright, eager gaze, Winslow and Pascal and Sarah and all the rest . . . gazing at the treasure with the eyes of those who saw all their troubles fixed. Doubtfully, he said, "A man buying goods with antique gold will not go unnoticed. The world above will want to know where he came upon such a treasure. To use any of this will pose a threat to our security." Bad enough, he thought, that he himself should run the risks attendant upon visiting Catherine, or that Mouse should flirt with the laws of the world Above. Catherine—not to mention every police procedural Vincent had ever read, and he was a reader of copious mysteries—had stressed over and over that no sudden influx of unaccounted-for wealth *ever* went unnoticed. This would surely shatter the secret which protected them, and he saw that worry, too, spring into Father's eyes.

Winslow shrugged. "No problem. We can melt it all down into bars . . ."

Father was aghast. "Wait a minute!" he cried over the mutter of assent. "This is not just gold! This is history, art . . . the archaeological significance of this find could be staggering! These things need to be catalogued, studied . . ."

"Tell me about archaeology the next time we run out of penicillin!" retorted Winslow. "We can't just . . ."

"Hold it." With a slight movement of his bony shoulders Cullen pushed himself clear of the shadows, and his voice, though soft, had in it a note which silenced them all. He stepped forward, lean and wry as an old coon-hound, and there was a look in his green eyes that was at once hard and angry. "Now, Winslow and Mouse can do what they want with their shares," he said, with a deadly softness, "but a third of this is *mine*."

Father stared at him, not quite believing what he had heard, as if without warning Cullen had slapped him. "Are you saying the community has no stake in this?"

Cullen's gesture brushed aside that shock, that unspoken accusation, unanswered. "What's mine is mine, that's what I'm saying."

"Everyone helped . . ." began Mary indignantly.

"Everyone came around to watch, you mean."

"I did more than watch!" protested Jamie, and Winslow cut in with, "I don't care who did what . . ."

"Cullen," said Vincent, deeply troubled by what he was hearing, by what he saw coming, "you've always had a generous soul . . ."

"Just because I carve things and give them away is no call for stealing what's mine." His voice was low and reasonable, but facing him, Vincent could feel the slow smouldering of a rage so deep Cullen himself was probably unaware of its true nature. "Don't look at me that way," he added softly. "All I'm saying is that fair is fair. This is a dream come true . . ."

"Dreams can turn to nightmares, Cullen."

"I know the difference between dreams and nightmares," Cullen replied, still in that even, logical voice, and the room around them was now profoundly silent, the deep rumble of the subways overhead sounding loud in the hush. "You want to hear about dreams? When I was selling door-to-door, I'd see all these houses, beautiful houses—swimming pools, trees all around . . . the furniture would always be so nice. My whole life, I had one piece of nice furniture, *one*, and Betty was so scared of getting it dirty she wouldn't take the plastic off it."

He paused, staring down at the gold on the table as it shone in the candlelight, his eyes seeing nothing of the people around him. Father moved as if he would speak, but after all said nothing. Vincent doubted that Cullen would even have heard.

After a moment Cullen went on, his hand straying again and again to the gold on the table, lifting it, turning the heavy chains, the massive armbands, holding them to the candleflame and gazing at the glow reflected in the precious stuff as if it somehow had the power to remake the past as it should have been. "I used to tell her, *Betty*, I'd say, *someday our ship will come in . . . we'll have nice things, too. I'll be able to spend time on my carvings. Maybe sculpt in marble.* Thirty years I told her that."

The heavy armband he held turned in his fingers, gleaming gently in the candles' waxy glow—his eyes, still fixed upon it as if unable to bear meeting anyone else's gaze, turned bleak. "The day she died, I looked around, and you know what I had to show?

A ten-year-old car with a bad transmission. I couldn't even pay the hospital bills."

"That was Above," said Father, all the hurt of his own winter of loss, his own nightmare despair, naked in his voice. "You have never wanted for anything since you have been with us."

"Cullen, we know the hardships you've suffered . . ."

"Vincent, you don't know anything." Cullen looked up, the patient exasperation of a man speaking to a naive and sheltered child in his voice. And then, suddenly angry, "All I want is what I found!"

Winslow's voice was hard. "*Mouse* found it."

Cullen stopped, blinking, and at the sound of his name Mouse came forward, troubled and ashamed. "Found it, yes," he said hesitantly, knowing that somehow what he had found had done this terrible thing, had turned the home he loved into a battleground and all his friends into shouting strangers, but not comprehending quite how. Trying to sort it out he faltered, "Winslow and Cullen said dig . . ."

"I want my fair share!" shouted Cullen, rage and resentment flaring. "We wouldn't have had any of this if it wasn't for me . . ."

"Listen to all of you!" cried Father, as the voices rose again. "Now just . . . listen to what's happening! If we're unable to deal with this matter rationally, humanely—then perhaps the best alternative, the *only* alternative, is to bury this treasure again in a place safe from all of us!"

Winslow swung around, furious. "And who elected you king?"

And as if gasoline had been tossed on a fire chaos broke out, an angry chaos of shouts and gesticulations, of people trying to make themselves heard, of people knowing their solution, and theirs alone, was right and fair and just . . . "Father's right!" "You're just as bad as he is!" "The treasure belongs to the whole community!" "You'd divide it up ten, twenty different ways . . " "Our Helpers deserve . . ." "Would you shut up about the fucking Helpers?!" Father cried over and over, "Order! Please!" and Winslow shot back at him, "Who says? You? I say we take a vote . . ."

Finally, maddened, Cullen turned and hurled the bracelet he had been holding back at the pile on the table, the gold ringing and bouncing among the flickering lights. "You're thieves, all of you!" he cried passionately. "Thieves!" And turning, he stormed towards the doorway.

After one swift look at Father's ashen face Vincent strode to intercept the sculptor, slipping through the crowd to block his way. "Cullen, we're your friends," he said quietly, wondering what he could say to bring this man back to his senses, to call him back from the terrible place where his mind seemed to be lodged. "Listen to Father . . "

But the eyes he met were the eyes of a stranger, eyes such as he had seen in those who prowled the alleyways Above. Cullen's voice was bitterly soft. "What are you going to do if I don't? Kill me?"

And he thrust past Vincent and out into the tunnels' dark.

In spite of the fact that Catherine knew that her friend Edie in Data had undoubtedly closed out the discos the previous evening, she'd found the programmer there early in the morning when she had come in. As usual, Edie had been noodling purposefully with the BIF System terminal, fine-tuning some program of her own, checking out the action on the bulletinboards, or thumbing through the mainframe out of sheer curiosity. She'd been more than willing to do a little extracurricular research on Jonathan Thorpe.

Catherine looked up now from the account of an almost unbelievable domestic dispute—did this man *really* think that his wife was going to put up with his mistress and her fourteen-year-old daughter living with them?—as Edie came around the corner of her cubicle partition; saw the wry twist of those generous bronze lips.

"That bad?" she asked, and Edie nodded.

"I had a feeling about that," Catherine sighed, setting aside the soap-operatic police report. "Tell me."

"Well . . ." Edie shrugged. "Thorpe hasn't found a way to smuggle the Great Pyramid out of Egypt yet, but according to these Interpol reports I figure he's working on it." She dropped a sheaf of printouts on top of the latest bout of paperwork on the Avery case. "Try bribery, theft of national antiquities, smuggling . . . He's wanted in Egypt, India and half of South America. You sure do pick 'em, girl-fren'." And with a saucy grin she returned to her station, her green and purple dress a bright splash in the drabness of the bullpen outside.

Catherine thumbed thoughtfully through the hardcopy, what she saw making her increasingly worried. There were counts of assault and breach of promise, too, and three counts of fraud which had been dropped with an abruptness which, in Catherine's experience, told its own tale. Thorpe not only played dirty—he evidently played rough, too. Not a man to give up lightly when he started to sniff out that something promising had surfaced.

And thinking about the steely cynicism of his eyes, she felt a shiver down her back.

Wherever Mouse had gotten that necklace, there might have been more. If Thorpe traced it back . . .

Father should know about this, she thought.

She left work early—nobody in the DA's office ever kept to regular hours, and for the last week she'd worked past seven o'clock every night—and in the dark of the sub-basement rapped out the coded syllables of Vincent's name. Though she had never since her return from the Tunnels after her assault been down to the world Below, she felt a part of it; its secrets were the trust Vincent had placed in her hands. These people had given her back her life— they *were* Vincent's life, his only shelter and sanctuary . . . but more than that they were . . . how could she call them friends? She'd never seen most of them.

They were Vincent's friends. And Mouse had never seen her, when he'd given her that necklace that had set this whole thing in motion. The fact that she was good to Vincent had been enough for him, as it was for her . . .

Whatever Father said . . .

When Vincent appeared she was shocked at how exhausted he looked, how weary, and how sad. She had meant to warn him about Thorpe, to ask him where Mouse had found the necklace he'd given her, but instead she only held out her arms and he stepped mutely to her, clasping her close with a kind of desperate strength, a gratitude that there was someone stable and sane to come to.

For a long time, neither spoke. Then quietly, with dispassionate calm that did not attempt to hide his grief and disbelief at what had passed, Vincent told her the story of the treasure, of his friend Cullen, of what was taking place.

"And now . . ." He shook his head. "Some of them are meeting in Winslow's chamber, arguing. Others have gone back to the ship. All they see now

is the specter of wealth. Even the pipes are silent—
Pascal has left the pipe-chamber. And Cullen . . .
no one's seen him since he walked out."

She reached out to touch the wide sleeve of his
mantle, hurting for him at this betrayal, this frightful
shifting of the foundations of his life. But looking
up into his face she saw that his own inner core was
unshaken—that it was not primarily for himself that
he hurt.

"How is Father?" she asked. Somehow it seemed
worse to her that Father should be hurt, for she
knew that his objection to Vincent's friendship with
her stemmed from his protectiveness of his world
and its secrets, his love for the people who looked
to him as their guide.

"He is . . . devastated," said Vincent, soft voice
echoing in the low brick vault above them. In the
dim light that leaked down through the ceiling-grate
from above, his blue eyes were sad. "Everything
we've worked for, everything we've tried to build
. . . He sees his dream crumbling."

And there was nothing, Catherine realized, that
Vincent could do to help him. That was perhaps the
worst of all. His great strength, his inhuman ferocity, had defended the Tunnels half a dozen times
against threats from the outside, but against the
dark side of the human heart, against the betrayal
of friends, of ideals, of dreams, he could do no more
than anyone. Cullen's parting words had been all
the more cruel because there was truth in them. All
Vincent could do for Father, Catherine knew, was
be there—as she could only be there for him.

"And how are you?" she asked, and he sighed, a
sound torn out, it seemed, from the roots of his
bones.

"Catherine, our world has never seen such tur-
moil and dissension. It's being torn apart . . ."

Her hands tightened over his, and in the returning pressure she felt again his gratitude simply to be able to come here, to be with her for a time, to know she would understand. So often she had drawn strength from him, had felt his protection, both physical and emotional—yet somehow she had no real consciousness of reciprocating for all of those times. It was simply that they were one, that the strength of one was the other's strength.

For a time they stood together in silence upon the shadowy borderline between their two worlds, bathed in the dim light that leaked through the grate from the room above. Then Catherine sighed, and said, "There's another threat, Vincent, maybe just as dangerous." His head tilted to one side, Vincent looked gravely down at her, not surprised. But then, Catherine thought, very little on the subject of human evil surprised Vincent.

"A man was interested in the necklace Mouse gave me. His name is Thorpe. He was quite persistent. I ran a check on him and found out he smuggles antiquities. If he comes across any more of this treasure he'll do his best to find out where it came from."

"I see," said Vincent softly, his head bowed so that his mane half-hid his face. "And Jamie told me she saw Cullen take some of the gold, back at the ship. The treasure is in Mouse's chamber. I had best speak to him."

But Vincent was not the only one to be seeking out Mouse.

Cullen had gone Above that afternoon, immediately upon leaving the abortive conference in Father's room. It was raining on and off, and cold—the storm Father had feared trickling its waters down the unrepaired drain to further exacerbate their problems. As

Cullen prowled the streets of Manhattan, checking out one dealer after another from a cautious distance, looking for something that looked rich enough to give him what he wanted but not big enough to be scrupulously respectable, he had huddled in his long, baggy, homemade coat and felt like a derelict. *God damn it,* he mouthed silently at the well-dressed women on the sidewalks, *how dare you stare at me that way . . .*

And, because he was furious with them—those false friends, those thieves below, those who would take from him the means of breaking his lifelong hell of poverty and loss—he blamed them for that, too—for the patchwork of salvage, of old scraps of wool and leather they pieced together, that made him stand out in the crowd. *I'm not a bum, dammit. My ship has come in . . .* And he smiled a little, ironically. *It came in 300 years ago, but it DID come in.*

He had a little bit of money, small change, barely enough for bus and subway tokens if he was careful. He blamed them for that, too. Damn people were too stupid to use money . . . It limited him to midtown, but that was fine—you couldn't get the kind of money he was looking for elsewhere anyway. He had gone back to his chamber for it, and, thrusting it in his pockets, planning what he would do, his eyes had fallen on his workbench. The chess-set he'd been carving for Father when all this had started lay there neglected among the shavings: delicate pieces, the white side portraits of those he knew Below—Father, with that shrewd little smile of his faithfully caught, the White King; Mary's worn, kindly face beneath the loose bun of her hair; Vincent's strange, lion-like countenance and somber eyes . . .

He knew it was some of the best work he'd ever done and the reflection that he wouldn't—couldn't, now—finish it filled him for a moment with an artist's terrible regret, then with resentment, and anger.

How dared they do that to him, how *dared* they? Make him feel like this . . What the hell did Vincent know about life Above? About desperation? About watching the one person you loved in the world slowly die of cancer, about the humiliation of standing in one line after another for hours in every social welfare office from here to Queens, begging for money for chemotherapy, for operations, for rent and heating in that last awful winter? About pawning your carving tools—three hundred dollars' worth of them, painstakingly accumulated through half a lifetime's gifts and scrimping—and the look on that stinking pawnbroker's face when he'd said, "Twenty-five bucks—take it or leave it." Cullen had taken it. At that point he would have pawned one of his lungs if he could have found a taker.

From the inner pocket of his long brown coat of old leather and blanket-scraps—a coat Mary had made for him, but he tried not to think about that— he took the jewels he'd pocketed in the confusion of the quarrel at the ship. His rooms had always used far more candles than most, because of the fineness of what he did, and Sara the candlemaker had never grudged him, and by their myriad light the interlaced golden chains of the necklace shimmered, the pendant pearls glowed almost luminous through the film of dirt. The bracelets—one an armband, the other a thick tangle of chain and flowers— felt heavy and substantial in his hands, the rings caught points of light deep in their crystalline hearts.

If he'd had this . . . If he'd had this . . .

Well, he thought, *I've got it now. And they can't take it away from me . . .*

That thought brought others; a remembrance of the world Above, and that mother-robbing thief of a pawnbroker's face. He wasn't going to deal with any goddamn pawnbroker this time . . .

But it didn't pay to be like these emotional babies, those helpless do-gooders down here in the Tunnels. It didn't pay to be anything less than ready for whatever would happen.

From among the tools scattered on the table—tools the children had brought to him, knowing his hobby, whenever they'd found them in their foraging through the dumpsters and throwaways, tools Winslow and Mouse had repaired for him, resharpened, re-fitted with blades—he selected the biggest curved knife he could find. He tested the blade with one callused thumb. It wasn't much, but if anyone Above tried to take from him what was rightfully his, it would do.

And then he had gone Above.

The place he'd finally picked was small, prosperous—though not ostentatiously so—and in a neighborhood far enough north along Park Avenue as to be out of the absolute limelight of midtown, the limelight which so often requires spotless reputations and impeccable respectability. When the owner, a prim-faced, balding man named Damon Edmondton, tried to conceal his start of surprise as Cullen unwrapped his wares on the polished oak counter, Cullen knew he'd come to the right place, a place where few questions would be asked.

"Seventeenth century Dutch," murmured Edmondton, holding up the necklace with its droplet pearls. "Fascinating . . . mind if I ask where you got these?"

Cullen returned the discreet curiosity of his gaze with a harsh stare. "You want them or not?"

Edmondton turned the necklace over in his fingers, considering, weighing up the gold against Cullen's makeshift coat and shabby, hand-knitted scarf. "I'll give you two thousand . . ."

"Do I look that stupid?" Cullen turned away, pacing the dim, sterile-looking shop with its cases of coins and autograph letters, its bits of ancient jewelry and arms.

"You can't blame a man for trying to make a profit, can you?" asked Edmondton with a thin smile of complicity. "How does ten thousand strike you? I'll write you a check here and now."

"Cash " said Cullen. "I want cash." No bank in New York, he reflected bitterly, would cash a ten-thousand-dollar check from a man dressed as he was, in the tattered absurdity of Tunnel makeshifts, a man who had no bank account . . . Christ, you couldn't even *open* a bank-account these days with less than a couple hundred dollars! Wasn't worth the banks' time.

Without money, you weren't worth anyone's time.

"Cash," said Edmondton, with the understanding of long experience. "Of course."

Ten thousand . . . just like that. It was that simple. And now he was rich.

Cullen leaned across the oak desk which separated them, his green eyes eager. "I can get more of this. Lots more. You interested?"

He could almost hear the wheels spinning in the man's brain, adding and subtracting, calculating ways and means. His eyes, pale and fishy-cold, gave away nothing. But he dropped even the pretense of negotiating an honest transaction, and he didn't, Cullen noticed, bring up the subject of provenance. "I can't move too much of this," said Edmondton after a moment. "There are certain—ah—bureaucratic difficulties, not to mention cash-flow problems. But I have an acquaintance who specializes in these kinds of transactions. I can arrange a meeting."

Cullen thought about it for a moment, debating the wisdom of involving a third party about whom he knew nothing against the difficulties of sounding out every antiquities dealer in town. He'd been lucky finding a taker on the first throw. Someone else might be moved to probe a little deeper into matters that weren't any of their business, might ask questions, at worst get the cops involved, at the very least hold things up.

And he wanted to finish this business. Finish it and get out quickly, get started on his new life. "Okay." He held out his hand. "The money."

"Of course," smiled Edmondton. "Excuse me." He had the good manners to leave the goods on the counter as he went into the office behind the store. Cullen paced restlessly, peering into the glass table-cases of ancient coins, the standing displays of small cannon and samurai armor, hearing through the closed office door Edmondton's muffled voice, the indistinct muttering and long pauses signifying a telephone conversation. Get some clothes, he was thinking—buy a car, find an apartment, maybe not even in New York—start a new life . . . When he returned the dapper little dealer was carrying an envelope, which he handed to Cullen without a word.

Cullen opened it, and riffled through what was inside.

They were hundreds, and it was a *fat* envelope.

He barely heard Edmondton saying, "I've arranged a meeting for you here tonight. At eight." He looked up to see Edmondton's dry little smile. "If that fits into your schedule."

Cullen shoved the envelope into the pocket where the jewels had been, and grinned, a dry movement of his lips. "That'll be just fine."

Five

SHAKEN and dismayed by the chaos in Father's room, Mouse had retreated to his Mousehole to seek the comfort of his work. It had been, in fact, the device he was now testing—a sonic echo transceiver—which had led him to the sunken ship in the first place, and for this reason Mouse toyed for a time with the thought of dismantling it and trying to make something else—a wireless communicator, or a device to confuse bats—out of the parts. It had all seemed like such fun, when he'd found the buried treasure, when he'd had a secret to share with his friends. Why had it all turned out so wrong?

In time, the familiarity of the quiet lab soothed him. Now and then he looked across at the chestful of treasure that Winslow and the others had left there, the gold seeming to shine in the light of the forest of candles which illuminated the room. Arthur was rooting cheerfully around in the great trunk, entranced as always by the bright metal and glittering gems . . . and it *was* beautiful, thought Mouse, with a stab of hurt. The most beautiful he'd ever seen. Yet everyone had acted so crazy, yelling and fighting—Cullen, his friend Cullen, had turned against them all . . .

He was glad when the jingling of tripwired bells told him someone was on his way down the main tunnel into the Mousehole, and delighted when he saw that it was Cullen.

"Cullen!" He put down his soldering-gun, hopped from the work stool where he was perched as the tall man slouched quickly into the room. "Everybody's looking for you . . ."

"Take a walk," snapped Cullen savagely, crossing to the chest and shoving the startled Arthur aside. He was dressed, Mouse saw, to go Above, in coat and cap and scarf, and his unshaven face was grim. Kneeling by the loaded steamer trunk he pulled two crudely-stitched leather sacks from the pocket of his long coat, and began to shovel treasure into them. "So everybody's looking for me, huh? I'll just bet they are . . ."

He worked fast, grabbing greedily whatever his hands touched—he stuffed a last handful of doubloons into one sack and tied it shut, holding it clutched under his arm as he began cramming candlesticks, cups, chains into the second.

"Not yours," Mouse protested. "Father said . . ."

"I don't care what Father said. You do what you want with your third. I'm taking mine."

Mouse got to his feet, upset and confused at this terrible change in his friend. Remembering the noise and chaos of the conference, he did not want to believe Cullen had really meant all that he had said to Father, to Vincent, to Mary. It made no sense to him. "Stealing . . ." he said, coming over to catch Cullen's sleeve.

"Not stealing . . . taking. Remember?" Cullen tossed the words back at him, and Mouse hesitated, knowing the argument was wrong but not at all sure why.

"Not worth it, Cullen . . ."

Cullen stopped grabbing and paused, turning to him with feverish, obsessed eyes. "I'll show you

77

what's worth it." From his pocket Cullen pulled an envelope, and, opening it, thrust it at him, showing him what was inside without ever letting it out of his hand.

But it was only a lot of hundred-dollar bills.

"Ten thousand dollars," Cullen said, and his voice shivered with the queer note that had disturbed Mouse so much. "For just half a dozen pieces . . ." And he jerked it away when Mouse reached out, curious, to touch.

Mouse shook his head, not understanding. "Only paper," he said. "Not as pretty as the stuff you took."

Exasperated and disgusted, Cullen turned away and went back to filling his sack. Though the first sack was heavy and awkward and the hard shapes of reliquaries and cups within kept jabbing him in the ribs, he would not put it on the floor beside him, but kept it tucked under his elbow against his body.

"Stop it, Cullen," insisted Mouse, angry now. "My stuff! Leave it alone!"

Cullen fumbled with the drawstring, knotting it awkwardly, and got to his feet. It was difficult to manage both sacks at once, for the weight of them dragged and shifted in his arms. In the hundredfold candle-shadows a film of sweat sparkled on his high forehead, and his eyes burned with feverish light.

Hurt and angry, Mouse stepped in front of him. He might be a little cloudy on what Father objected to in his forays to construction sites Above, but he knew absolutely that it was not "taking" to take something from a friend, especially when that friend had asked you not to. And worse than that was the way Cullen looked at him, the way Cullen treated him, as if they had never been friends—as if they had never known each other at all.

"Get out of my way, Mouse."

"No," said Mouse. "My stuff. Can't take. Won't let you."

Cullen shifted the unwieldy sacks over onto one arm, his body twisting under the weight of them, and from his pocket pulled his woodcarving knife. This was his ticket out of here, his ticket to a new life, and nothing was going to stop him. "I'm warning you, boy . . . I'm warning you . . ."

Mouse stared at it, almost too shocked to feel afraid. "A joke, right? Won't cut me. Not you."

"The hell I won't . . ." gritted Cullen through his teeth, and lunged around Mouse for the door.

"Cullen, leave it!" Mouse grabbed him by the arm, and the treasure-sack cradled in that arm dropped to the floor, the top pulling open to spill coins, rings, bracelets across the worn red gaudiness of the old Persian rug. Furious, Cullen tried to jerk free of Mouse's grasp, to re-gather the precious things, but Mouse hung onto him, dragging him away. With an inarticulate snarl of rage Cullen plunged the knife's short blade full-force into Mouse's body.

Mouse gasped, half doubled over, his hand fumbling at the wound. Blue eyes wide with disbelief, betrayal, and pain he stared at Cullen, as if he would ask him why. Then slowly his knees buckled, and with a little sob he crumpled face-down to the floor among the scattered treasure.

Cullen stood for a moment staring down at him, aghast. His hand, the blade, the handle, his fingers were all red with Mouse's blood, and for an instant he looked at them as if he truly could not imagine how they had gotten that way. Surely it hadn't been him. Surely he wouldn't have done such a thing . . .

But the weapon was in his hand. Convulsively he flung it from him, and clutching the remaining sack, he fled the chamber, leaving Mouse lying on the tattered red carpet in a welter of blood and gold.

And it was there that Vincent found him, nearly an hour later. Arthur the raccoon was nuzzling frantically at his face, desperately distressed at the smell of the blood, and he darted away to hide in the shadows behind the treasure-chest when Vincent entered the room. Vincent knelt swiftly beside Mouse, turned him over carefully and felt with sensitive fingers at his throat for pulse. Then he half-lifted him, cradling him in his powerful arms.

Mouse's eyes fluttered open. "Vincent . . ." he whispered.

"Be quiet," replied Vincent softly. "Save your strength . . ." No bleeding from the mouth, he thought, his mind ticking off the details of Father's medical training automatically; a lot of blood lost—it had soaked the rug in a huge, dark puddle—but no smell of intestinal perforation. Mouse's hands felt cold with shock, his lips clay-colored . . . Father would have to operate, and operate fast, provided Mouse could be moved at all . . .

"Cullen." Mouse's breath was the short, shallow sobbing of pain. "Took the stuff . . . for *paper*, Vincent. Just for paper."

"Did he say where he was going, Mouse?" asked Vincent quickly, thinking of what Catherine had told him, wondering if it were possible to somehow head him off and keep the gold from surfacing Above . . .

But Mouse's eyes closed again, his body racked with a desperate shudder of agony and grief. He only whispered, "My *friend* . . ."

Cullen's fingers fumbled at the trip-lever mechanism which controlled the sheet-steel gate to the outer tunnels—when it slipped back he had to wrestle aside a second gate of iron bars. Behind him in the old dry water-tunnel a torch burned in a crude wall-sconce, a reminder that this was the world Below, the world he was leaving—from here the way would be dark. The sack of gold he carried dragged like lead at his arm, his muscles burning already from carrying it up the crude stairways, the rusted iron ladders where the downshafts dipped to pass under forgotten streams and marshes . . . along all those miles of echoing dark.

The gate slid shut behind him. He remembered how he'd helped Mouse install the counterweights that balanced it . . .

In the glow of a streetlamp which filtered down through a storm-gate somewhere near he looked at his hand. The knitted glove he wore, and the fingers emerging from it, were stained . . .

He wiped his hand on his coat. *You have to do what you have to do*, he told himself, *to reach your new life. I warned him. I did warn him . . .*

The dream of the life Above, of the things the gold could buy, was calling him. Staggering under the weight of his gold he stumbled off up the tunnel, feet splashing in the puddles of seep-water, towards the nearest ladder which would take him to it.

Edmondton's place was dark, though the door from the alleyway behind it was unlocked. As he pushed it open, in the smudgy yellow streetlight coming through the windows from Park Avenue Cullen noted a rather elaborate alarm system, hooked up but not armed, on the door. He stepped cautiously into the front shop, looked around him at the darkly looming shapes of armor and cannons, like waiting monsters in the shaded glow of the single lamp on the broad oak desk.

"Hello?" he said softly, and set the heavy bag down beside the lamp.

Even as he noticed the line of light under Edmondton's office door he saw the shadows of feet across it, heard a voice inquire, "Mr. Cullen?"

Cullen wheeled sharply as the door opened, the light silhouetting a man of whom all he could see was the gleam of a brown leather jacket, and, where the light struck it, a mane of sun-bleached hair.

"Where's Edmondton?"

"Occupied." The man came closer. In his late thirties, with a rugged, handsome face and a rakishness to his steel-gray eyes Cullen guessed most women would have called romantic—Betty would have, anyway. But Betty would have followed up that observation with the remark that though she'd happily look at this man all day, she wouldn't touch him with a ten-foot pole . . . "We don't need him."

"He said he'd be here," said Cullen worriedly, as, with the casualness of one who owned it already, the man opened the sack, pulled out a bracelet and held it to the light. "I don't know you."

"Take it easy, Mr. Cullen." For all its relaxed pleasantness, there was something cold and terrible about that smile. "I'm the man with the money. What else do you need to know?"

And while he spoke he was taking out other objects and examining them, a ring, a tiara, a pendant of garnet and diamonds the size of Cullen's palm. And in the man's eyes, in the bright bar of light from the doorway behind him, Cullen could see, not merely greed, but an intelligence, a calculation, as if he knew precisely how much these would fetch in the open market. "Nice . . ."

Cullen swallowed hard, and wiped his hand uneasily on the skirt of his long coat, though all the blood was clean from it by this time—he'd checked a couple of times on the way here to make sure. "All I want is fifty thousand. It's worth a lot more than that . . ."

"Is this all of it?"

Thinking about the steamer trunk brimming with gold back in Mouse's chamber, Cullen hesitated, for one fleeting moment wishing he'd taken more of it . . . taken all of it. What would they do with it down in the Tunnels anyway?

Then he remembered Mouse, lying there among the spilled coins, and shame and horror and burning regret scalded him. How could he have hurt Mouse, of all people . . . ? His own words, 'All I want is my fair share,' came back like a steam-burn on his soul, and he stammered, "Yes."

But those steel-cold eyes had marked his uncertainty. "Then there's more." It was not a question.

"This is my share," said Cullen doggedly. "That's all I wanted—my fair share." He wiped his hand again.

"I only wanted what was fair," he went on, louder, trying to convince himself—perhaps trying to convince Mouse as well. His speech grew suddenly fast and hard. "They tried to rob me, tried to take what was mine . . . And it *was* mine . . ."

The man's voice was silken. "The world's reached a sorry state, hasn't it? You just can't trust anyone." And with a gesture as smooth and quick and natural as picking up a fork, a gun was in his hand.

It must have been in a shoulder-holster under that brown leather jacket—staring down the barrel of the high-tech silencer, the ruby laser of its sighting-beam printing a neat red spot between his eyes, Cullen literally could not imagine where it had come from.

He gulped, his mouth dry. "Please . . . we don't

have to do it this way. Just give me the money—
you'll never hear from me again."

"I never pay for anything." His smile was now
utterly cold. He replaced the tiara, the ring, the
bracelet in the sack, jerked the drawstring tight and
threw it across the desk at Cullen, the weight of it
jarring him back. "Here. Carry it. You're going to
take me to the rest of this stuff.

Horrified, Cullen tried to shake his head, but
could not. Shocked, scared, and sobered, he felt
exactly as men are said to feel when snapped from
drunken stupor by a dousing with icy water—a hideous sense of having waked to memories of something he could barely believe he had done.
Everything in him revolted at the thought of taking
this man Below, of unleashing this businesslike violence on his friends, on the people who had taken
care of him when he needed them, who had always
been there for him . . . Father, Vincent, Mouse,
Mary . . . But to the marrow of his bones, he knew
that this man would kill him without compunction
and without hesitation. The fear of death—the memory of that shocked horror in Mouse's eyes—turned
his blood cold.

Feeling the laser-sight like a crimson needle in the
back of his neck he led the way through the back
door into the alley, staggering a little under the treasure's golden weight.

"If Cullen ever shows his face down here again,"
said Winslow softly, "I'll kill him."

Raising his head from his hand, Vincent looked
across Father's conference table at the blacksmith in
the light of the handful of candles burning in their
worn bronze stands. Beyond Winslow's shoulder
the sheets which curtained off a section of the gallery seemed to shine, backlit by the strong glow of

electric lights, with Father's shadow and Mary's thrown upon them as they worked. Mouse had rigged that section of the gallery for power a few months ago to give Father better light for his map-making projects. Though the old man had refused to use it for fear of rousing ConEd's suspicions by a regular drain of power, it had served from time to time as an emergency surgery.

Vincent reflected that the thought that one day he might be saving his own life had undoubtedly never even crossed Mouse's mind. At sixteen, one does not think in terms of one's own death.

His eyes went back to Winslow, steady and sad. "And what will that accomplish?"

Winslow's voice was grim. "It'll make me feel good."

Vincent sighed. "No. There's been enough bloodshed."

And if Catherine was right about the man Thorpe, the man who sought to buy her necklace and was quite probably keeping an eye out for other pieces of the same treasure to surface, there very well might be more.

He had not yet told Father of what she had said. There had not been time. By the time he had carried Mouse up as far as Father's chamber, his friend had been in a bad way, despite Vincent's competent first aid—it was a long way up from the Mousehole. Even now, though part of him reflected that he should still try to go after Cullen, he knew that it was useless—by the amount that Mouse had bled, and by the stickiness of the blood itself, he knew Cullen had been long gone by the time he'd even reached Mouse's side. And that being the case, he was not about to leave Father's chamber without hearing if his friend would live or die.

"I don't understand." Jamie, sitting to Winslow's

right—one of a half-dozen of Mouse's friends who had come to Father's chamber to wait for news— looked up, the tears she had been unable to keep back trickling down her face and her voice strained and shaky. "They were friends. How could he do it?"

"He was sick," said Vincent gently. "He couldn't see us, or hear us. There was no one, nothing . . . except himself. It is . . . a disease that comes from Above. It's called greed."

Kipper, sitting on the winding iron stair, looked up sharply, and all heads turned as the curtain over the alcove moved aside. Father came out, pulling from his mouth the makeshift surgical mask he wore. In a surgical gown instead of his usual robes he seemed strangely out of place in soft candlelight, against the strange, archaic collection of old bronzes and mouldering books which surrounded him. Before Mary switched off the power Vincent saw in the bright lights how haggard his eyes were behind his reading glasses, how lined his face had become.

"He going to be all right?" asked Winslow.

Father nodded, and pulled the sterile cap he wore off his rough gray hair. "Fortunately there was no serious internal damage. The knife-blade wasn't more than a few inches long. We closed up the wound . . ." His gray eyebrows flinched down at the thought of the violence and strife, at the thought that anyone would do such a thing . . . then he sighed. "He's lost a great deal of blood, but he's young, strong . . . He's going to be all right."

Winslow swore, deeply and happily, and caught Jamie in his arms in a great hug of relief. The tension in the room seemed to snap like a steel band breaking, like rain coming, Vincent thought, after too long a drought . . . Benjamin and Sara, loitering by the steps to the vestibule, who had been two of the most acrimonious contenders over the disposal of the treasure, embraced, their delight in their friend's survival a mutually acceptable excuse to forget what they'd said to each other . . . to all their other friends . . .

And then, clear and far off, Vincent heard over the pipes the swift clatter of a message coming in.

Pascal was back in the pipe-chamber. Heads turned as all of them heard the urgency of the pipe-telegrapher's touch.

Intruder alert . . . Cullen seen by the Long Stair . . . man with him . . . gun.

And, a moment later: *Heading toward Abyss.*

Six

THE Abyss was one of those places where those who lived Below seldom went, seldom even thought of, for the thought was not a comfortable one. For the most part the world Below was one of old steam-tunnels and disused mains, of courses hewn in times past for subways or roads whose funding later ran out, of old chambers cut for various purposes long forgotten—but purposes, at least, human and understandable. The geology of Manhattan itself was a channelled scabland, a labyrinth of natural fissures, old stream-cuts, dry waterfalls, forming tunnels damper and muddier, perhaps, and with greater danger of quicksand pockets, but still prosaic once their dark ways were known.

But there were places that were different, shafts and rooms and tunnels incredibly deep, seemingly alien to the world from which Father and his people had come, and the Abyss was one of them.

It was Father's theory that the Abyss was a blow-hole of some kind in the basaltic rock common at that level—nearly seven hundred feet down—and that its cylindrical shape and perfect straightness was a fluke of nature. But others whispered that only human hands could have shaped that enor-mous pit, seventy feet across and falling straight as if measured with a plumb line to depths hidden in the utter darkness of underground, and filled—when a torch was dropped to illuminate it—with a slowly-swirling cloud of mist that masked whatever lay below. Certainly a human agency must have cut the shallow, broken steps that ran down from the cavern's entrance, hugging the curve of the wall, for perhaps thirty feet, before trailing out onto a ledge that narrowed to nothingness after another thirty feet or so of level rock—but for what purpose, and how long ago, nobody, not even Father, could imagine. It was a vision out of Poe or Hodgson . . . Over the years various Tunnel children had dared each other to visit the place, for the purpose of dropping things over the edge and counting out the seconds of fall, but no one had ever heard anything land.

In his constant quest for knowledge Father had once lowered a rope weighted with a fifteen-pound rock down into those misty depths. He'd twice spliced new hundred-foot lengths to the original line, all the cord he could find, but never had the pull of the weight slackened to indicate it had touched any kind of bottom. For the most part people simply stayed away, for the place was uncanny. The rocks of the cavern's ceiling gave off a greenish gleam, and the constant winds of that endless pit roared and groaned as no winds should, the echoes transforming the sounds into something disquietingly like inhuman words.

Cullen knew that they would meet no one on their way there, and that was as it should be. He'd walked enough patrols himself to know they'd been spotted, even before he heard Pascal's distant warning chiming over the pipes; he only hoped his friends would have the sense, once they knew he was heading for the Abyss, to stay clear. The man Thorpe with his high-tech weapon would slaughter

them, the laser-sight aiming even in total darkness—
a tiger among lambs.

And he, Cullen, was the one who had opened the
gate of the fold. He was the one who had brought
the attention of the outside world to them, the one
who had made it profitable for someone to find out
about this world that had sheltered him, these
friends who had taken him in . . . He was the one
who had tempted the invader in.

Self-reproach and horror burned him, as bad as
the sickened consciousness of what he had done to
Mouse. He had been stupid, selfish and stupid and
blind. Mouse could be dead—the Mousehole was
deep down, it could be hours before anyone came
. . . The leather sack of gold and gems weighed like
a dead thing in his arms. His muscles burned, for it
was a long walk down to the Abyss, down stair
after stair, tunnel after descending tunnel, and the
bitterness of shame was bile in his mouth, eradicat-
ing even his fear. He should have listened to Vincent, when he told him to accept Father's wisdom;
he still couldn't believe, looking back on it, that he'd
done the things he'd done, said the things he'd said.

He'd acted like a drunk—drunk on the dream of
the Good Life, drunk on the smell of money . . . On
his way down the alleys to the deserted tenement
basement that enclosed the nearest way Down Cullen had debated turning around and facing the gun's
deadly ruby eye, telling Thorpe to kill him and be
damned. Having lost everything in one world and
then been dumb enough to close the doors of
another world against himself he realized there
wasn't a hell of a lot of point to living anyway.

But glancing back over his shoulder he had seen
in Thorpe's cold gray eyes that even should he do
so, even should he die to keep the secret of the
world Below, Thorpe would not abandon his search

for yet more gold. Having suffered that fever himself, Cullen realized it now in the other man's eyes. He was a shark upon a blood-spoor now, and would search—probably starting with Vincent's friend Catherine—and would, eventually, find.

He couldn't let that happen. And that left only one way out: the darkness of the Abyss.

In a way it didn't matter if he died trying. The fact that Thorpe had mentioned his name to him on the way down here informed him clearly enough that the man didn't plan on him being around to pass that information on to anybody else.

They stepped through the crooked arch of stone that led into the cavern, stood on the top step in the smutted glow of the few torches Father insisted be kept burning there, the old stair being unrailed and dangerous. Looking back over his shoulder, shifting the leather bag in his aching arms, Cullen saw Thorpe gaping around him in awe, taken off-guard by the sheer immensity of the place.

"Where the hell are we?"

"You said it," said Cullen quietly. "Hell—where both of us belong." And with that he swung the sack of gold at Thorpe's gun.

The weapon went spinning, caromed off the wall somewhere behind them, clattered on the chipped stone steps. But Cullen had no time to think about it—Thorpe threw himself upon him like a tiger, hands reaching for his throat, and Cullen fell back a pace or two down the stairs, twisting and struggling to get free. The bag of gold landed on the stairs with a heavy, musical clang, nearly tripping them both—they staggered, stumbled, the rock of the steps slippery with damp, uneven beneath their feet. Cullen was tall and wiry, but Thorpe more massively built, younger and stronger and far more used to violence.

Cullen gasped, tearing the gripping hands from his throat; the next second Thorpe hooked his legs from beneath him, flinging him backwards, outwards . . . The edge of the stairs cut into his back and he felt blowing up around him the clammy breath of the Abyss. He flailed for balance, his head hanging out over the roaring blackness, but Thorpe's foot crushed into his chest, shoving him back and down.

Then louder, over the queer unhuman echoes of the chasm, he heard another roar, a savage bellow of animal rage. Twisting his head Cullen saw Vincent's massive shape silhouetted against the dim phosphorescent light of the tunnel entrance above.

Thorpe swung around, shocked and horrified at the terrible apparition. Fangs bared, eyes glaring gold in the semi-darkness, Vincent leaped, mantle swirling around him like the shadow of wings. There was a cry and the sudden smell of blood and Thorpe went pitching back down the stairs, rolling a few steps and then scrambling, going for the gun. Vincent started after him and Cullen felt his precarious balance go. He screamed, "Vincent!" and Vincent turned, catching his arm, dragging him back . . .

And in that second, Thorpe caught up his weapon and aimed.

In a confused blur of elongated time Cullen saw the red beam of the laser-sight burning between Vincent's eyes. There was too much distance between Vincent and Thorpe to be cleared by a single leap—the bullet would take him mid-air anyway . . . Though he knew that to stand would put him between the silent death of that beam and its intended victim, Cullen lurched to his feet, grabbing the only thing to hand—the leather sack of gold. It weighed a good fifteen pounds, and he flung it full-force down at Thorpe.

And the weird thing was, replaying it in his mind later, Cullen knew the bag didn't hit Thorpe hard enough to throw him off-balance. It cannoned off his shoulder, enough maybe to jerk his aim aside for half a second. He could still easily have killed Vincent—if killing Vincent had been the most important thing to him.

But it wasn't. Because as the bag went sailing off toward the Abyss's eldritch darkness, Thorpe grabbed for it.

And lost his balance.

And fell.

Cullen—on his knees now and shaking with shock, clutching Vincent's heavy mantle and feeling the strength of those clawed hands gripping his shoulders reassuringly, breathing again, just beginning to know that he would live—imagined he could still hear Thorpe shrieking, screaming as he plunged into darkness and mist, long after the sounds should have ceased.

It was to the Abyss, that they brought the treasure in the end.

Jamie returned to the box the gold-framed mirror, Kipper, the enormous sapphire ring. As Cullen bent to close the lid on the shining heap of gold Vincent added the golden necklace Catherine had handed to him earlier that evening, when he'd told her what they intended, the gift Mouse had given her because she, like he, was Vincent's friend. There are gifts, Thorpe had said, and there are gifts, and sometimes innocence is not enough.

Little had been said as they'd hauled the treasure along the tunnels from the Mousehole. But everyone who'd taken a turn at it—Winslow, Mary, Benjamin, Jamie, and all those others, even the children— seemed to realize that in their combined efforts as they struggled down the endless tunnels and stairs, they affirmed again that the bond between them was more to be treasured than any amount of stolen gold.

And so, on the brink of the Abyss, Father turned to them all, his haggard face calm now in the sulfurous flare of the torches and the phosphorescent corpse-glow of the Abyss's overhanging rocks. "Are we all certain that what we're about to do is the course we wish to take?"

There was a murmur of assent, hushed and weary: "It's the *only* course . . ." "It's caused enough grief . . ." "We don't need it. It shouldn't be here . . ." "We have to get rid of it . . ." "It almost cost us everything."

And so, Father thought, looking at the closed lid of the trunk, it had. The friendship that had sustained each of them in the hardships of life apart from the world Above; the community which upheld them, physically and emotionally; the security each felt in that bond. It had cost not a few, he reflected, a measure of self-respect, in the memory of things they had said and done. It had nearly cost Mouse his life. A confirmed rationalist, Father was not a believer in antique curses, nor in the ill luck that is said to cling to treasure bought with its owner's blood. Nor did he have any evidence that the treasure *had* originally been stolen, *had* been the gleanings of the pirates who had once coursed these New World coasts looting tidewater plantations and merchant houses alike. But in his heart he had always been sure that these things had been ill-got, and like so much of the world Above, could bring to any who touched them nothing but grief.

"It's time," said Cullen, and bent to push the chest to the edge.

There was a stir in the crowd, a murmur and a

start. Cullen looked up in time to see Mouse standing beside him. For a moment their eyes met, Cullen shaken with relief to see his young friend on his feet, and with guilt and grief, remembering that last, shocked look of surprise in Mouse's eyes.

Then Mouse held out his hand, and smiled, glad only to see his friend back safe and sound and cured of that strange Topside illness which had parted them. Reaching up, Cullen grasped the offered fingers, unable to believe that he had ever been sick and stupid enough to choose this treasure—"Just paper," as Mouse had said, after all—over the warmth of this man's friendship, let alone his life.

Mouse bent down, gritting his teeth as the stitches pulled in his wound, and helped shove the chest that they had found.

"Wait . . ."

It was Vincent's voice. They both turned, surprised; for Vincent, Cullen knew, had been among the most hurt, the most grieved, and—perhaps because of Father's upbringing, perhaps only because he was not entirely human—the least affected by the epidemic of greed. He had stood a little apart from the others, down on the ledge that overhung the Abyss's echoing chasm, his tawny head bowed. Now he stepped forward into the torchlight, his blue eyes troubled under the crease of his brows, the wind from the Abyss stirring the folds of his mantle, the long ends of his mane.

"We cannot do this," he said, deep voice low and urgent.

Gently, a little concerned by this unexpected cavil, Father replied, "We've agreed that it's the only way."

Vincent shook his head. "If we throw this treasure away, then it *has* defeated us," he said. "There may be no place for it in our world, but there are others, in the world above, who go hungry and homeless."

There was a stirring in the group as his words sank in. For the first time, without the poisonous distortion of resentment, Cullen thought of the black days after his wife's death, the days of having nowhere to turn; Mary's hand went unconsciously to her throat at the remembrance of the children she had lost; Jamie's fingers closed around Mouse's arm. Those who had been born Below, like Winslow and Pascal, were silent, too, either from their memories of living Above or from what they had learned by going there, by speaking to others, by sharing with those who had left that world behind. Living on what the world Above cast away, they were too familiar with what that world did to those without power and wealth.

Vincent went on, "Although we live separate and apart from them, we can never deny that we are all a part of each other. We cannot turn our backs."

Was that Catherine's influence speaking? Father wondered, looking down at Vincent, who stood, half in darkness, half in torchlight, like some strange demon guardian of these lightless realms. Or was it the people whom Vincent had watched for so long from the shadows of the city's alleys and the trees of the park, the people of the world Above for whom he had always felt such yearning compassion? Or was it just because Vincent was who he was, because he had not been touched by the greed for gold, because those strange, jeweled eyes saw so clearly? Wary as he was of the world Above, hurt by it as he had been, Father understood that this beautiful adopted son of his was right.

"So what did you do with it, in the end?" asked Catherine softly, looking out over the plumed lacework of Central Park's darkness, the flow of lights that even at this late hour crept down Central Park West like a shining river. Beside her, Vincent's strange, flattened profile was outlined against the ephemeral gemwork of the lights, the velvet overcast of the sky beyond.

"Left it on the doorstep of the St. Regina Shelter for the Homeless," he replied, turning his head to meet her eyes.

"I know them," said Catherine. "They're not a big outfit—in fact I think sometimes they have trouble making their rent—but they're dedicated."

"They are . . . people that I watch, have watched for a number of years, from alleys and shadows. I think one or two of the Sisters are aware of my existence, though not of who I am—they leave me food sometimes. They are good people, with their own needs met, and with a higher calling to shelter them from the self-deception that so often goes with this disease of greed."

He smiled a little, the soft muzzle quirking, and a note of deep joy came into his voice. "It took all of us to carry it, you know, dragging and straining together, up the steps, out of the Abyss, and then up all those stairways, all those passages; the whole community, even Father, whom I suspect still didn't think much of the idea, working together to give this gift. It was—a good thing to see. And," he added, mischief twinkling deep in his tourmaline eyes, "dragging it that distance gave any doubters once and for all a great distaste for so large a quantity of gold. Cullen knocked on the door, and ran back to shelter; I waited in the shadows to see that the Sisters did, in fact, take the treasure in. They will know how to dispose of it properly, with respect for its antiquity . . ."

"I wonder," said Catherine, putting her arm around his waist and leaning into the warming shelter of his cloak, "what they thought?"

Vincent said simply, "That it was a miracle."

Seven

FOR a long time Father sat staring silently at the clipping in the resinous candlelight. The pain he had long since deceived himself into thinking he had forgotten stirred to aching life around his heart.

The wreck of my memories . . .

. . . All I can say seems useless. Still I cling to the wreck of my memories, before they sink forever . . .

"Father?" It was Vincent's voice, worried at the sudden stillness which had come upon him.

Startled, Father looked up from the small square of newspaper he held, returning with a jolt to the present. From the other side of the chessboard Vincent was watching him uneasily, the ochre glow of the oil-lamps on the carved sideboard behind him making a shadowy halo of his mane. Father looked down at the small square of newsprint he still held in his hands, a cutting from the personals column—the *Times*, by the typography—which Dustin had brought him in an old hair-oil bottle only minutes ago.

The hair-oil bottle, with the message inside it, had been tipped into a storm-drain near Times Square . . . That had to be Lou. The jolly, white-haired barber was one of the oldest of the Helpers, who had been leaving food and books and information, newspapers and sometimes things like paints for Elizabeth

99

or drill-bits for Mouse or woodcarving-blades for Cullen, for nearly thirty years. As one of Father's oldest friends, Lou was one of the few who had heard him speak, in the early days, of the phrase, "the wreck of my memories"—who had seen the tears that came to his eyes at the words.

He got to his feet and turned away, shaken to his bones. *The wreck of my memories . . . I cling to the wreck of my memories . . .* Only moments ago the only thing in his mind had been the intricacies of gambits from the seventh Fischer-Spassky game, and how to use them against Vincent's neat, controlled strategies . . . along with a kind of wry amusement that in teaching his adopted son to play chess he had created a monster . . . no pun intended, of course . . .

And then this. Like the dropping of a bomb . . .

The dropping of a bomb.

Somewhere a subway rumbled past, leaving a deeper silence behind it that was broken, a moment later, by the mournful clanking of some message on the pipes.

"Father, what is it?"

"I always wondered when it would happen," he said slowly, almost to himself, wondering what, in fact, there was for him to say. "And now it has."

He turned back toward where Vincent still sat, his powerful, red-furred hands folded before him, at rest beside the tiny ivory army of captured pawns. Father's own hands, in the cut-off gloves and knitted arm-warmers he wore to protect him against the tunnels' chill, toyed with the clipping, turning it over and over, fingers shaking.

His words fumbled a little as he said, "I have never lied to you, Vincent. The things I've taught you about the world Above . . . the things I've asked of you . . ." And Catherine's name hovered unspoken between them for a moment. "So much of it was to protect you. But it was also to help me forget . . ." He faltered, uncertain, then went on.

". . . forget a world I once loved."

"I always sensed that," said Vincent softly, his head a little to one side, his blue eyes steady, questioning, calm.

Had it been that obvious? Father wondered. He had told Vincent about all those places that he would never see, that he himself would never see again: the way night looks, out across the rooftops of Paris if you happen to be sitting on one of those little iron balconies under the eaves; the pewter splendor of Pacific shore sand dunes on winter mornings where the only thing that moves is a single crying gull. The heartshaking delight of seeing Venice for the first time, the sense of seeing something wrought solely of light floating on water, the conviction that you can put your hand through any of its buildings; the leached dry silence of the Arizona deserts, waiting for something since the ruinous dawn of time. The unbelievable color of sunset sky. Was that why Vincent had never asked him, *Why did you leave all that? Why do you live Below?*

"Vincent," he said hesitantly, "there are certain things I have kept from you, about my life . . . before . . ."

That quality of stillness was perhaps the most remarkable thing about Vincent, the impression of being utterly grounded, utterly at peace—curious when you thought about it, reflected Father abstractedly, considering what he was like in action . . .

"Father—what are you trying to tell me?"

"That I have to return. I have to go Above."

Vincent was silent, assimilating this news. Even as he said the words Father felt queerly disoriented, as the realization came to him that he had not seen daylight for . . . surely it couldn't be . . . nearly thirty-five years . . . ? It would all be changed . . . It hurt, and in a strange way it frightened him. From the newspapers, from the people he had spoken to, he had known this intellectually of course, shaken his head over it, but somewhere in the back of his mind he had accepted the fact that it didn't really touch upon him, didn't really matter . . . would never really matter to him again.

"When will you go?"

"As soon as I prepare myself." He drew a deep breath. His voice, he was surprised to discover, sounded even and calm. "I'll be back by evening," he went on. "When I return, we'll talk."

But he had no idea what it was that he would say.

When Vincent left Father stood for a time, looking around him at the large, circular chamber, with its softly-glowing oil-lamps, its candles burning in a dozen wall-niches, its narrow gallery overhead, its books. They were his treasure, those books. There had been times, in the dark years when he'd first come Below, when they had been the only thing between him and the madness of despair. The room was filled with them, every horizontal surface heaped and cluttered—Book Club bestsellers of twenty years ago, leather-bound classics with faded inscriptions on the flyleaf, self-help tomes which he read with amused curiosity at the preoccupations of the upper world, and stripped paperback throwaways of book-stores on every conceivable subject . . . stacked the battered old furniture, filled the dark nooks under the turn of the iron steps. Above them and among them rose the odd things the world Above had cast away, as it had cast him: a delicate Victorian bust of a lady in an Elizabethan lace collar—a lamp formed of graceful bronze mermaids—a carved chair—an orrery with the constellations engraved around its central belt, and the dearth of outer planets a dead giveaway as to its age.

The world he had built for himself. Like the nacre of a pearl, he thought, to enclose himself away from pain. A world where he had been safe.

A subway rumbled by somewhere near, a reminder of the world he had left.

He could still be safe here, he thought. He didn't have to answer that advertisement.

But he knew already that it was, in modern parlance, not an option.

He took his stick from where it leaned on the carved sideboard, made his way to the alcove where he slept. It was tucked away under the gallery and behind the stairs. Above his bed, with its clean and mended sheets, the dull-hued quilts that Mary pieced together out of whatever scraps came her way, was a painting old Elizabeth had done from memory, of Hyde Park in the Thirties. He turned up the oil-lamp that depended from the low ceiling and moved to the great armoire that loomed in its darkest recess. Opening its doors, he peered into the shadows within.

Then reaching inside, he took out a double-breasted gray tweed suit, nearly new—pants, vest, shirt, even a tie, stylishly wide and striped maroon and blue. In the breast pocket of the suit jacket was a handkerchief, still folded; clipped to the lapel, a laminated staff badge which said simply, Chittenden Research Institute.

That, he put aside, interested to note that the anger he had once felt at the mention of that place was gone. He had given it up, as he had given up all those other angers . . . he only felt a curious sense of displacement, a wondering that it had ever taken place at all.

From the back corner, protected by a piece of sacking, he took a pair of sharkskin wing-tips—at least, he thought with a wry smile, the shoes would still fit. At a guess the suit would, too. They had enough, here Below, to eat, but there wasn't much opportunity for getting fat. From a shelf he took a gray fedora, and blew the dust from its brim; putting it on, he surveyed himself in the mirror on the inside of the cupboard door.

He had meant it only to be a perfunctory check, almost like combing his hair—maybe to check whether, after all these years, he would still "pass." But the face of the man in the glass arrested him, tugged at something inside, as if he had seen that face looking back at him the last time he'd gotten himself dressed like this . . . for the hearing . . .

A kind of shock. Surely his hair should be dark brown instead of gray? Surely his cheeks should have been a little plumper, not . . . not sagging that way under the grizzled beard. Those quiet years, each passing with the soft-footed rhythm of the world Below, swooped down upon him in a rush, as if all of them were happening at once. Surely there shouldn't be all those lines around the eyes, the spoor of hardship and grief. They hadn't been there before—at least, not until the end . . .

There was a cane in the armoire, too, a proper one, made by a cane-maker in London to his specifications and not like the stick he walked with these days, sturdy and comfortable as it was.

And this was the cane he leaned upon, later, all the long way across the Chasm Bridge and up the tunnels, up the turning iron steps of the Long Stair, up service-ducts and riser-vents, passing the torches set by Vincent and Nicholas and the others who patrolled the periphery. The music of the world below whispered behind him, the soft clanging of the pipes as Pascal relayed messages, channelled information . . .

He let himself out through the last of the gates. He hadn't walked this way in years, but he knew the route, having endlessly studied the old WPA and ConEd schematics, the subway routes and geological surveys, in his construction of maps of the world Below. At the end of a tunnel swathed in bluish dusk was a flight of concrete steps, and dimly he could see light at the top, the harsh glow of cheap electric bulbs, and even more dimly, hear the clamor of a subway station, a far-off murmur in the deep silence which still reigned here. The smell of humanity came down to him, too, above the dank underground scents of water and earth, a live smell, raw and unfamiliar—cigarettes, perfume and unwashed clothes, garbage and popcorn and car exhaust.

The noise and the smell and the light increased as he limped toward the stair. Uncertainty washed over him. Had Eurydice in the Greek myth, he wondered, felt this apprehensive tightening of the chest, as Orpheus' song drew her up out of the depths of the world Below? *Don't look back,* the myth had said, and he understood that. It would be so easy to turn around, to sink back into the comfort of the familiar darkness—to ignore the song of the upper world, terrifying and yet filled with the yearning of half-forgotten joys.

He climbed the stairs. The echo of his footsteps, so clear in the silent tunnels, was gradually subsumed in the sound of the world Above.

He ascended the newspaper-littered cement steps of the Union Square Station, and New York City smote him like a hammer of painted brass.

Jerky, restless music . . . the wail of sirens . . . voices raised in argument . . .

Eurydice, he thought wryly, *may have had the right idea after all* . . .

People—had there *been* this many people? The sidewalks were jammed with them; the sheer noise of their movement alone was like the steady roar of the sea. The streets were clogged with traffic, taxicabs the familiar color of cheap mustard pelting madly between buses, cars, trucks piled with produce and goods and daubed with a kaleidoscope of graffiti; the noise of brakes, horns, and bellowed vulgarity like the din of an oompah band. Father looked around him, squinting in the unfamiliar sunlight slanting through the buildings . . .

Unfamiliar? No . . . How could he have forgotten the chipped-crystal quality of spring evening sunlight after recent rain? How could he have lived so long without it? *It must be rush hour*, he thought; the shadows were already getting long. By the curb a man was selling hotdogs from a red-and-yellow pushcart, the smell of salty grease a song of mouthwatering delight; a girl pushed past him, the shortness of her leather skirt shocking and yet somehow joyously impudent . . . a little further on, where Lexington Avenue led out of the Square, amid a crowd of onlookers (*There really ARE more people, it was never as crowded as this, surely* . . .) he glimpsed an extremely lithe black teenager in jeans and a red sweatshirt performing what had to be "break-dancing," rolling and twisting on the square's cement pavement in a fashion regrettably reminiscent of what Father had seen of Kipper's and Dustin's attempts at the . . . er . . . *Is it sport or art?*

He jostled along Lexington Avenue, heading north. Some things were bizarrely alien, like the youth who passed him bearing on one shoulder a massive— *How had Jamie referred to them? Boom-box?* In a window a mannequin with a startlingly zebra-striped face modeled a suit of what looked like scarlet, jeweled sweat-clothes—Did women *really* wear their hair like that these days? Across the street people passed unconcernedly under a cafe-front which boasted the back end of a '63 Cadillac, polished and shining, overhanging the sidewalk, for all the world as if some careless motorist had rammed it into the second-floor wall . . .

Other things, like the closed faces of the homegoing men in business suits or the little knot of Hasidic rabbis furiously arguing Talmud as they walked along in their long black coats and side-curls, were comforting in their familiarity. Water puddled in the gutters and the sidewalks were littered with sodden newspapers, the blue shadows of the buildings had already swallowed up the street . . . buses surged past in a choking gray cloud of exhaust.

The flavor of New York hadn't changed. But so many of the buildings had. Walking up Lexington Avenue, Father scanned those monoliths of glass and stone, looking through plate-glass walls into lobbies where receptionists were putting on athletic shoes preparatory to leaving for the night. (*How very sensible* . . .) And 3122 Lexington . . . the address was unfamiliar, but at a guess, he thought, it would be where Alan Taft had his offices these days.

Alan Taft.

Dear God, it had been so long since he'd seen Alan Taft. His old friend's face rose before him now, pink and lantern-jawed and surmounted by a shock of dark hair. Father shook his head, the pain stirring again, like feeling returning to a limb long numbed.

He knew he must have seen Alan at least once or twice after the hearing, but had no recollection of it. It seemed to him, as he walked down the avenue in the gathering darkness, that the life he had known before all came to a stop, as if shut behind a wall, in the lobby of the Federal Building in Washington D.C., with reporters running toward him across the gray granite floor, flashbulbs popping, voices echoing from the ceiling vaults . . . "Can we have a question?" "What do you make of the committee's findings?" "Are you going to appeal?" "I said all I wanted to say at the hearing—I have nothing further to add . . ." Alan Taft had been beside him then, hovering just behind the two plainclothes marshals who had been his escort—surely it was Alan who had told the reporters, "No further comment."

He didn't even remember how he had gotten back to New York.

The fact that Alan would use the phrase, ". . . the wreck of my memories . . ." would mean . . .

Thirty-one twenty-two Lexington Avenue was a newer building, a monstrous skyscraper with a façade of black marble pillars rising toward the darkening spring sky. Lights in the lobby shone through two-story-high plate glass; a uniformed guard looked up from the desk as Father entered, but, evidently reassured by the suit and hat, made no comment. Times had changed, Father reflected—the guards evidently had television sets to keep them company these days. He wondered, for a brief second, whether even elevators had altered in the intervening years, but a few moments after his pressing the button to summon one, its door slid open. It was carpeted, even to its walls and ceiling, in the same flat iron-gray as the hallway . . . He shook his head. A directory which had taken up much of one lobby wall had listed the offices of Alan Taft, Attorney at Law, on the twenty-third floor. He pressed the button to ascend.

He was aware, in the long silence of the lift, of how hard his heart was beating, how fast. It was good—calming—to be off the street, out from under the immensity of sky, even that crevice of sky visible between the buildings, away from the jammed, homegoing mob. He hadn't realized how disorienting it would be to see that many faces he did not know. Crossing between blocks, he'd been aware of how completely he'd lost his ability to gauge the speed of oncoming traffic . . . And all those queer, tiny, snub-nosed cars . . .

What was he thinking about? he asked himself as the elevator sighed to a stop. He was about to meet Alan Taft again. His feet made little sound on the mauve carpet of the hall, the rubber end of his cane sinking a little into it as he walked . . . wondering what Alan would look like after all these years. Wondering how he had fared. Better than he himself, if he could still advertise as Attorney at Law in this obviously respectable building. But then, he'd been Anson Chase's lawyer . . .

The building was deserted at this time of the evening. Shut doors gave the corridor an air of cold, of unfeeling secrecy. His bad leg aching from the length of his walk that day, Father finally came to the door of Alan Taft's office, and turned the handle.

It was open. He stepped inside, conscious of the silence.

The place was lush in a light, modern way, graced with indoor plants and oak cabinetry—pieces of Alan's precious chinoiserie relieved the unremitting coolness of the pale walls. A partition wall of frosted glass separated the reception area from what had to be the main offices, probably admitting a good deal of light in the daytime. Though the receptionist had clearly gone, lights were visible through the partition in the inner office . . .

"Alan?"

Only silence greeted his words.

They would hardly have left the place unlocked, he thought, crossing the reception area and opening the inner door. *How on earth do the guards police a building this big, anyway?*

He stopped on the threshhold, shocked. His first thought, poking with his cane-tip at the whirlwind ruin of spilled file folders, scattered papers, books dumped from the shelves, as was that the place had been searched, hurriedly but very thoroughly indeed. The drawers of the filing cabinets hung open, briefs, notes, reports, dockets spewing from them and lying in a huge lake of paper all around; every drawer in the desk had been likewise ransacked. It was only when Father stepped around the desk itself that he saw Taft's body.

Taft was quite dead. Automatically noting the relative warmth of the hands and face as he felt for pulse, the absence of lividity, Father thought, *Not more than half an hour ago* . . . and then compressed his lips harshly. *Of course it couldn't have been earlier. Half an hour ago there would have been people around* . . .

And at the same time the part of him that was not a doctor, the part of him that was not the leader of a community, was crying Alan's name as if his old friend's spirit could still hear. His hand lay near the receiver of the overturned telephone amid the spilled papers—his neck had been broken, a brutal and efficient crime. His hair and mustache, Father saw with a queer stab of pain, had turned quite white since he'd seen him last . . .

And out in the hallway, he heard the sudden thunder of feet.

There must have been some kind of security device, a hidden camera or a trip-wire system like some of Mouse's—he'd been a fool not to think of it in a building this size. He was starting clumsily to his feet, hampered by his bad leg, as four policemen—not uniformed security officers, but NYPD—poured into the outer office, guns drawn and leveled as they slammed through the inner door.

"Move away from that desk," barked one of them, holding his gun in both hands, ready to fire.

Father stood frozen, his mind stalled on Alan's death, on the ransacked office, on those hideous replaying scenes of the past and on his fears for what notice of any kind would mean for his people . . .

"NOW!!"

Shakily, he moved into the open. Another officer grabbed his arm, all but threw him against the glass wall, kicked his legs apart and began to frisk him.

"Larry, we got a man down," called out the first cop. "Radio an ambulance . . ."

"Look, I'm a doctor," said Father over his shoulder. "He's already . . ."

"Shut up. Do it, Larry."

One of the cops detached a walkie-talkie from his belt, spoke tersely into it while the first man walked around the desk, then bent over Taft's body. A woman dispatcher's voice chattered over the walkie-talkie—ambulance on the way—1015 already filed . . . Father's hands were dragged roughly behind him, cuffed as he was pulled away from the wall and turned around to face the man as he came back.

And in his eyes, despairingly, Father read the officer's awareness of just how short a time Taft had been dead. Other voices were sounding in the hall now, a rising clamor—beyond the vast plate-glass window the sky was quite dark. "You're under arrest," said the cop, flipping a notebook from his pocket as others shoved Father towards the door. "You have the right to remain silent . . ."

111

Eight

CATHERINE had gone to bed at around ten, after an early dinner out with her father . . . early, because she had to be at the New York City Jail in the morning to take the deposition of an Italian restaurant-owner who'd tried to carve up his partner with a broken beer-bottle. But she hadn't seen her father in over a week, and missed him—as she still missed the regular routine of having dinner or drinks with him, which had been so comfortable before she'd started working for the D.A. A good-looking, pink-faced man with a carefully-tended crop of prematurely white hair and his daughter's green eyes, he'd shaken his head sympathetically over her adventures in New Jersey and Harlem trying to get information about Max Avery's extortion racket, and had regaled her with his own accounts of a corporate client who'd had him globe-trotting between the original Jersey—the Isle of Jersey—and the Cayman Islands, those two notorious havens of tax-avoidance, to help set up an intricate system of interconnecting directorates to keep at least a certain amount of the client's corporate profits out of IRS hands.

"There's a delicate line between tax-avoidance and tax-evasion," he said, spearing a fragile pillow of Il Forno's famous tagliatelli on the plate before him, "and I keep warning Linker to make sure he stays on the right side of it . . ."

"Oh, nonsense," grinned Catherine mischievously. "You just wanted a free trip to the Cayman Islands to get a little sun."

Her father laughed. "Believe me, if I wanted a little sun I wouldn't pick a tax-free zone, no matter how pretty it is . . . And speaking of tax-shelters," he added, as Catherine took a sip of her chardonnay, "you *are* coming to the fund-raiser for the Chamber Music Society I'm having at the house, aren't you?"

"Mmm, of course . . . the quartet'll be playing there, won't they?"

He nodded. "And they'll do the overture from *Marriage of Figaro* just for you." Then the smile had faded from his face and his eyes met hers worriedly. "I got a phone call from Elliot Burch, asking if he could be invited."

Catherine set down her wineglass, her hands feeling suddenly cold. For a moment she thought, *I can't very well dictate to Dad who he can invite to his own parties* . . . and then she thought, *But I can say what I want*. She wet her lips, phrasing it carefully in her mind, then said, "I'd really rather you didn't."

Charles Chandler nodded, accepting this. For a moment he looked at his daughter across the white tablecloth, the light of the candles in their crystal holders shining softly on her dust-blonde hair, the olive silk of her blouse, seeing her now as an adult, no longer the impulsive girl he'd known. In college, he thought, she'd have stammered, "No, that's fine . . ." then either gotten sick or been deathly quiet all through the party . . .

"Cathy," he asked gently, after a pause to phrase things himself, "what happened between you and Elliot Burch? I thought . . . well." He paused, not wanting it to sound like it did—that he'd been glad to see her with someone who treated her so well, a man he'd have been pleased and proud to have as a son-in-law.

You thought he was Prince Charming, smiled Catherine wanly to herself. *Well, so did I . . .*

And after the gifts he'd sent her, after the ballets and shows . . . after those walks arm-in-arm along the sidewalks *(and so what if he could afford a limo!)* watching the lights, joking, listening to the sweet melancholy of jazz sax on the streetcorners, marvelling together over the heartstirring bizarreness of New York . . . why not?

I love you. I want you . . .

Cathy, don't walk out on me . . .

"Elliot Burch—" she said slowly, turning her glass slowly around on the white tablecloth, her eyes never leaving the candle-reflection palely glimmering in the wine, "or rather, Elliot Burch's lawyer, but with corporate heads you know that amounts to the same thing—hired a firm of 'security consultants' to 'convince' a handful of old people to move out of a rent-controlled apartment building Burch wanted to buy and tear down to put up one of his own projects. They beat several of them up—firebombed the cellar—tried to cut electricity to the building . . . Dirty things. Vicious things."

"I see," said her father, and for a moment there was silence, as he tried to reconcile those tactics with the man who'd donated so lavishly to charities, who had treated him with such charm and respect. "Wouldn't it have been easier for them just to have moved?"

"If they could have found anyplace closer than Jamaica Heights where they could have rented an apartment for under four hundred dollars, maybe," returned Catherine, the bitterness of that old battle staining her voice. She looked up at him, her green eyes intent in the candlelight. "They were all on fixed incomes, Dad, six or seven hundred a month. And besides . . . it was their home. It had been their home for twenty, thirty years. Their friends were there, people they knew, people they could turn to . . ."

"I see," he said again, nodding, and she could tell he hadn't thought of that. Had not thought of the terrible fragility, the terrible dependence, of being old and poor. And indeed, never having wanted for so much as a dime in his life, why should he? There was no chance he'd ever find himself turned out of the spacious apartment Catherine had grown up in, that he'd have to depend upon the charity and kindness of others.

She could see he was troubled, and reached across the table, and touched his hand. "After that . . ." She paused, steadied her voice, and went on, "After that I couldn't look Elliot in the face."

And it was just like Elliot, she thought, returning to her cannelloni without much appetite, to imply a major donation to the Chamber Music Society in order to secure an invitation to a party where he was sure she'd be.

Thus, because she'd read a chapter or so of Alain Viso's book to put herself to sleep, she was dreaming of having dinner at an Italian restaurant installed in a rock-cut tomb in the lost, rose-red city of Petra when a faint tapping on the French doors of her room drew her from her sleep.

Turning on her pillows, she saw behind the floating white gauze of the curtains Vincent's dark shape on the terrace, outlined by the glow of the city behind him.

She rolled out of bed and in her white silk pajamas ran to unlock the French doors and step outside.

"I'm sorry to wake you, Catherine . . ."

"Something's wrong . . ." It wasn't late—not even midnight—but later than he usually made an appearance on weeknights. Unromantic, perhaps, but he was deeply considerate about the fact that she had a job. But even in the near-dark of the terrace, illuminated only the filtered reflections from the lights below, she could see the worry in his face.

"It's Father."

"What's happened?" *Ill*, she thought. He was the doctor for the world below . . . Vincent, she knew, had what medical training Father had passed along to him, but not enough to take care of him should there be a real emergency.

Vincent shook his head, and his voice was troubled. "He went above today, for the first time I can remember. He should have been back hours ago. He's somewhere in the city . . ." He turned to look out at the bonfire of lights below, their reflections glistening on the leather shoulders of his mantle, in the deeps of his eyes. "Catherine, I need your help."

"Of course I'll help."

He paused, made a small gesture of frustration and helplessness. "I should never have let him go alone . . ." But they both knew there was no way Vincent could have gone with him. And Catherine guessed, both from what Vincent had told her of the old man and from the few times she had met that sturdy patriarch in the shadowy no-man's-land beneath the subcellar of her apartment building, that Father was far too stubborn to ask for help.

"Where was he going?" she asked, wondering a little that anything would have drawn him back to the world Above. In their few brief meetings he had

116

kept to the shadows, not merely of the sub-basement, but of the dim archway that let into the tunnels below, as if, like Vincent, he was wary even of entering the places where humans dwelled. She knew he had always mistrusted Vincent's involvement with her.

Vincent shook his head. "I know that it had to do with his life before."

"When he lived Above?"

He nodded. The night was cool for March. The breeze that stirred his long hair, that fluttered the pale silk of her pajamas against her arms, smelled of the park's grass and water, an alien beauty in the thick hive of concrete and exhaust. On the avenue below a taxi honked, the sound transmuted to a kind of thin punctuation-mark in the dark.

"What has he told you about his life then?"

"Only that it was another life, lived by another person," he replied softly. "And that the memory of it was best forgotten. I know he was a doctor . . ."

Vincent had mentioned others besides himself moving back and forth between the two worlds—Mouse, like his little namesake, hoarding bright things away in some secret lair; Kipper . . . Laura . . . But Father? The part of her that was a lawyer, that dealt all day with the thugs and sleazeballs whose crimes paraded through the DA's office, thought with a horrible pang of compassion, *He's not streetwise* . . . Not even as streetwise as Vincent, who prowled the city's alleyways and the cold shadows of the park, listening, watching on the fringes of the world which could never be his.

It meant that Father might very easily be in serious trouble.

And he could be anywhere in the city. Conceivably—though he had told Vincent he would be back by night, which argued a destination within the Five Boroughs—he could be anywhere at all.

Gently, she asked, "Do you know his full name?"

Vincent shook his head. There was a strange kind of sadness in his voice as he said, "I have always called him Father."

While Catherine made the first round of telephone calls—to emergency rooms, to shelters, and, though both of them shied away from saying so, to the morgue—Vincent returned, at Catherine's behest, to the Tunnels, to search among Father's things for a starting point. Remembering her classes in legal research, though it had been years (*Thank God!* she thought) since she'd actually gone through the tedious process of a records search, Catherine had said, "Anything you can find will help us. A name, a place, a reference . . . some kind of starting point. Tomorrow . . . damn, I've got that deposition in the morning, but after that I can probably take off and make it to the library—they have microfilm newspaper files going back a century and a half . . ."

"Why wait until tomorrow?" Vincent had asked.

And Catherine had almost laughed. Of course—if there was an entryway from Below into the basement of her apartment building, it was only logical that there'd be one in the cellars of the New York Public Library. Knowing Vincent, knowing Father—and in a way she felt that she *did* know Father—they'd probably been regular, if unrecorded, borrowers for years.

She wondered if Father was scrupulous about returning books on time, like Jenny was, or whether, like Catherine, he kept forgetting to take them back . . . *At least he doesn't have to worry about those astronomical fines every month . . .*

"All right. Come back for me at one, with what ever you can find . . ."

Whatever you can find.

Vincent stood, hesitant and feeling oddly ashamed, in the doorway of Father's lamplit room, looking around him at the circular vault. Comfortingly familiar, the place he had always known . . . the room in which he had grown up. Without Father's presence, with the knowledge that he was somewhere, probably in trouble and unable to return, the room had a strange sense of emptiness that it did not have when Father was simply elsewhere, gone to fetch water from one of the fountains or gossiping with Elizabeth up in the Painted Tunnels. Remembering the occasions upon which he himself had been trapped Above, Vincent felt a profound uneasiness, and knew that Catherine was right in asking him to search the old man's rooms. Still, he felt loath to do it, to pry into another's possessions, to trespass upon the hidden details of another's life. Even if Father had been a stranger he wouldn't have liked it.

But he knew he had no choice.

He opened the center drawer in the rolltop desk, removed a thick packet of medical journal clippings—all since 1963, long after Father had come to the Tunnels—a folded sheet of notes on drain leakages, a Xeroxed article one of the Helpers had sent him about quicksand. He checked notebooks, thumbed open volumes for notes that might have been tucked into their pages . . . knowing all the while that if Father, like most of the others, had come Below with little or nothing, there would in all probability be nothing to find.

And so, for a long time, it seemed. Seated cross-legged on the worn Kirman that floored the chamber, surrounded with lamps and candles, by their burnished light Vincent sorted through Father's papers: the hundreds of maps that went into his endless self-appointed task of making a master-chart of the world Below; notes on the history of that world, taken from verbal accounts of those who had been born there, who had lived there longest—Pascal, Winslow, a woman named Grace who had been his friend Devin's mother, who had been the matriarch when Father had first arrived; medical notes on everyone who lived or had ever lived Below. There were medical journals, gleaned from the throwaways of the Columbia medical library or, more often, sent by Dr. Alcott, one of the oldest of the Helpers; bundles of clippings on every subject from industrial pollution to the slow demise of the railroads; boxes of old letters which Father had found tucked into the pages of he books which had, from a thousand different sources, come his way.

But nothing before a certain point in the 1950s— nothing that would relate to Father's former life. It was as if, in turning his back upon that world physically, he had done so also in his heart.

With a sigh, Vincent got to his feet, easing his cricked shoulders, his cramped neck. It was past twelve, and Above the ground the spring night was cold. He hoped Father was sleeping somewhere warm, somewhere dry—that he'd had food to eat. Night after night, in the alleys of the city, he saw men curled in the shadows of doorways, sleeping on the pavements like exhausted dogs.

Slowly, unwillingly, he crossed to the dark alcove beneath the gallery stairs, the room where Father slept. His sense of violating secrets grew, his unwillingness to pry warring with what Catherine had said. *Anything you can find will help us.* Only the thought that Father might be sleeping cold, sleeping wet, sleeping hungry made him approach the big armoire—only the recollection of his own trials upon those occasions when he had not been able to reach a way Down let him open the scarred walnut doors.

Within the armoire he found Father's clothes, the brown robe Mary had made for him, his leather vest and the assortment of sweaters and sweatshirts he wore beneath against the damp cold of the tunnels. Knitted arm-warmers, his boots, the thick knitted wrap Mary had made to give extra protection to his bad knee. His gloves, fingerless, battered, stained with ink . . . his stick.

Vincent frowned. If he had left his stick he must have had some other means of support, another stick or a cane . . . as he must have had some other clothes. The drawers below contained nothing but sheets and an extra quilt. The shelf above . . .

Vincent drew out the little square of plastic that rested on the front of the shelf, turned it to the light. Chittenden Research Institute—Staff. And a small red square.

As he moved the hanging robe aside something at the back of the cupboard caught his eye. He reached back, into its deepest shadows, and drew forth a framed picture, a black-and-white photograph carefully preserved behind glass. He held it up, to catch the light of the lamps.

It was a wedding picture. Father, his beard dark and his face younger and thinner and far less lined, stood in a tuxedo, his arm circling the waist of one of the loveliest girls Vincent had ever seen. She had something to her of Catherine's fair-skinned beauty— her light hair was coiled up under a sea of white veils and blushers, but her face, upturned to Father's, was radiant with joy.

Vincent felt his heart contract within him, with sorrow and pity for those two people, for whatever circumstances had shattered the bond he saw between them—for whatever it was that had separated Father and this girl.

Behind the photograph, between it and the cardboard that stiffened its back, was an envelope, without address or superscription, folded and creased. Vincent started to open it, but stopped, overwhelmed by a sense of betrayal. Looking at the photograph again, looking at the shining happiness on Father's face and on that of Father's bride, he understood the sadness, the depth of the wound that had made Father say, *forget a world I once loved.* He could not bring himself to pry into this last detail, force open this secret that Father had worked so strictly to keep closed.

He picked up his mantle from the brown leather chair where he had left it, slung it on and tucked the photograph and envelope away into one of its deep pockets. It was time to go. The rush of the subways had become less frequent, and the clanging of the pipes nearly ceased. From the Long Gallery outside Father's chamber came none of the talk and chatter of those who traversed it, coming and going to other places in the underground world. Catherine would be waiting, to help him pick apart the knotted skein of Father's past and find a thread which might lead them to his present whereabouts.

Earlier that evening, Police Lieutenant Kyle Parker and Detective Rinaldo Gutierrez had been attempting something of the same thing, though from the other end, working a present mystery and finding in it only a torn-off knot of the past.

"Still won't give his name, huh?" asked Gutierrez, glancing back through the soundproofed window into the interrogation room where the suspect in the Taft killing sat at the bare gray table, hands folded, strangely dignified in his silence. Stout, bearded, and graying, his cane leaning against the table at his side, even in the coarse blue jail denims he seemed very different from the general clientele of the City Hall Jail. The harsh overhead light made him look old and haggard—or maybe it was just that he'd come through the rolling-mill of Booking. Upper class, doctor or lawyer, Gutierrez guessed. He didn't have an ad-man's glibness, or an MBA's bustling aggression. But in Gutierrez' dozen years of experience on the Force, there were darn few upper-class professionals brought in who weren't screaming for their lawyers before they even saw Holding.

Lt. Parker, fair and beefy beside Gutierrez' dark, nervous thinness, shook his head. "*Nada*. And no ID—no driver's license, no credit cards, no business cards, no checks . . ."

Gutierez shrugged. "S.O.P. for a professional hit."

Parker made a noise of not-quite-assent in his throat. Gutierrez could see why—the man didn't look like your average Organization assassin. But then, who'd let a greasy-haired, stiletto-toting sleaze-ball in a shiny suit into their office in the first place? The most efficient hitman Gutierrez had ever seen had looked like a grocery clerk.

"Maybe,' said Parker. "But check out the stuff we *did* get from his pockets." He held out a bagged and tagged article from an evidence bin, marked simply, *John Doe GL2543*.

Detective Gutierrez flipped through the half-dozen dollar bills in the bag, then took a closer look and frowned. "Silver certificates? How long have they been out of circulation—twenty, thirty years?"

Parker held out another baggy, containing nothing more than two squares of pinkish tagboard. "Pair of ticket stubs from a Dodgers-Giants game."

"Brooklyn and New York . . . Ebbets Field . . . 1952." He shook his head, baffled.

"Twilight Zone, huh?" Parker glanced through the soundproofed window again, at the man at the table. He'd seen all kinds come through—raving angel-dusters, weeping husband-killers, kids so stoned their P.O. had to hold them upright in their chairs—but never a man like this, with his patriarch's face and haunted eyes. "So whatta you think?"

Gutierrez shrugged. "What I always think: why me?" And the the two of them entered the room to try their luck again.

Gutierrez studied the slender file on the table for a moment as Parker closed the door and took his stand beside it. John Doe GL2543 looked up, meeting his gaze without fear and without hope. The file didn't contain much—the arrest report from the officer in charge of the armed response at the office building on Lex, prints, a photostat of a newspaper clipping, a black-and-white mug shot. If Taft's office hadn't been ransacked, if Taft hadn't been trustee and attorney for the Chase estate and its multi-million-dollar offshoots, the whole case would have been held over until tomorrow, falling, as it had, on the borderline between shifts.

But here they were at seven-thirty at night, and, thought Gutierrez again, *why me?*

He lit up a cigarette and studied John Doe GL2543 for a moment through the blue-gray haze of its smoke. "Why'd you kill Alan Taft?"

Evenly, John Doe GL2543 replied, "I didn't kill Alan Taft. When I found him, he was already dead."

"I see. So you know him."

A brief pause—a look of consideration in those blue-gray eyes. Then, with a kind of weary grief, "I knew him, yes."

Cigarette smoke made a thin trail after his gesturing hand. "What were you doing in his offices?" And, when there was no reply, "You were looking for something, right? The place was torn apart."

Still no reply. Gutierrez tossed the photostat clip across the table at him—they'd traced it to today's *Times* and had found that it had been run all week. Someone had printed FTR in block letters across the top. "Maybe this'll help you remember. That's Taft's office address, we found it in your goddam *pocket!*"

The man said nothing, but under the grizzled beard the lips compressed a little, and his eyes, touching the clip briefly, looked away, as if the sight of the ad brought some obscure regret or pain.

" 'The wreck of my memories.' What's it mean?"

Still nothing. Gutierrez sighed, took another drag of smoke. *Why me?* It was his case, and he'd go on with it all night if he had to, but this silence was going to make it pretty tedious. "Maybe you wanna start by telling us your name, okay? Whattaya say?"

But what he said was nothing, like a spy under enemy interrogation, or, Gutierrez thought, like a pro who's been through this all before. Irritably, Parker leaned forward, jabbed a finger in the suspect's face, and snapped, "Hey, mister: *who the hell are you?*"

"Will you answer the question, please . . ." And the voice of that gray-suited bureaucrat in the center of the tribunal had prickled with irritation. "Are you now or have you ever been a member of the communist party?"

He had answered, "I am not."

And beside him, Alan Taft had sat quiet, hands on his notes, his eyes moving from man to man of the six or seven—how many had it been? He thought the scene would be branded on his recollection down to the tiniest detail forever but now he really wasn't sure how many had been there that day—members of the judicial board of the House Committee on Un-American Activities, while behind them the noise in the hearing room quieted to a dull throb, like bees in swarming-time.

'What is your occupation?"

"I'm a research physician. I was employed at the Chittenden Institute until . . ." He hesitated, wondering what to say about that, then simply settled for, ". . . until some months ago."

The outrage he had felt at being dismissed for telling them what they didn't want to hear had burned in him still, then; outrage, and shock. Looking back, he could only feel a kind of tired bemusement at his own naïveté . . .

"It is this Committee's understanding that your security clearance was denied for subversive activities . . ."

"I'm a doctor," he had said, his anger overriding the representative's bureaucratic monotone. "I was trying to save lives . . ."

"Please confine your answers to the questions asked."

And then his outrage, his disbelief that this injustice was actually being perpetrated, broke forth, and he leaned forward angrily in his hard oak chair. "Why is it that no one wants to hear that the Atomic Energy Commission has grossly miscalculated what constitutes a dangerous dose of radiation? Now, this is not Communist-inspired propaganda, this is a medical fact! My God, in Nevada they're exploding nuclear devices in front of your own troops!"

"I won't warn you again, doctor . . ."

And Alan Taft had laid a silencing hand on his arm. Alan was a lawyer—and as family attorney for a millionaire like Anson Chase, he would know more about the way politics worked than most. It was Taft who spoke. "Perhaps if my client knew the source of these allegations . . . ?"

'They were included in sworn testimony given before this committee."

Alan had been going carefully, not only because he was a lawyer, but, now seen in retrospect, because his knowledge of what was going on had made him afraid. But at twenty-eight years of age, when your career has been cut short, when you are facing the fact that no one will employ you, when you have been railroaded, not because you did something wrong, but because you did your job and were right, it is difficult to remain silent.

"Sworn lies is what they were!"

"We are not interested in extraneous matters. This committee is interested only in any subversive activities you may have been engaged in."

"Not interested?" The sheer Kafkaesque bizarrerie of the scene almost made him want to laugh, if the results of his tests had not been so terrifying, if the implications of what was taking place now were not so hideous, if so much were not at stake. "Medical research has linked radiation levels which we are being told are 'acceptable' to leukemia, bone-cancer, thyroid abnormalities . . ."

But the head of the committee had already hit the switch that shut off the microphone, cutting his reply from the people in the hearing room, cutting his protestations from the tapes of the proceedings. When he spoke, the representative's voice was cold as stone. "You will limit your testimony to the committee's agenda . . ."

The committee's agenda. Father regarded the two men before him in the harsh glare of the overhead light: the sharper, darker face of the man seated across the table behind the floating veil of cigarette smoke, the beefy red countenance of the younger man who had lost his temper. They, too, had their own agenda. *As inquisitors go, my friends, I have seen better.* They were tired, and angry because of it; frustrated by an uncooperative subject. They had his sympathy.

But he had the right to remain silent, and this time—for the sake of the world which had taken him in all those years ago, for its protection against prying questions—this time, he would exercise that right.

Nine

It was roughly two miles from Catherine's apartment building to the New York Public Library down on Fifth Avenue. Vincent led her through the steam-tunnels under her own building, where they edged along carefully next to the steam-pipes themselves, then along the echoing cement corridor of what had once been a pedestrian underpass, now long ago sealed up and forgotten, the dull thunder of the Eighth Avenue Local and the Sixth Avenue Express a distant vibration in the walls.

"Take this," whispered Vincent, pressing something into her hand, his eyes gleaming in the reflection of the flashlight she carried; she angled the beam to her palm, and saw that he'd handed her a stump of blue chalk. "The children all carry them in case they get lost."

"But I'm with you," she protested, and Vincent shook his head.

"Was it Seneca who said, 'Accept in your mind that anything which can happen, can happen to you'? In our world it never pays to take chances."

It was not the first time Catherine had traveled through the upper reaches of the world of the tunnels, the dark world Below. With Vincent guiding her she had no fear of getting lost, for he moved along the tunnels, up and down the twisting iron stairs and riser-vent ladders, with the sureness of a man walking the hallways of his own home. It was a damp world, the beam of her flashlight glancing sharply off water puddled underfoot or trickling in dark streaks down the curving walls, and a cold one, but one that held no especial dread. Along the walls of the tunnel, clusters of smaller pipes carried TV cables, electrical conduits, telephone lines—deeper down, Vincent had told her, the lines for old pneu- matic systems of communication between office buildings long-demolished still ran. Now and then she could hear the soft clanking of the pipes, and thought of Pascal, one of the few dwellers Below whom she had actually glimpsed, clattering happily away on the pipes in the vast central nexus of the Pipe Chamber like Ringo Starr on a good night.

They climbed a short flight of brick steps, her Reeboks making no more noise than Vincent's soft leather boots; slipped through a trapezoidal arch of broken brick behind a ceiling-high stack of damp cardboard boxes that smelled overwhelmingly of mildew. Catherine's flashlight showed her a big cement room filled with such boxes, redolent of decay and mice. They were in the basement of the library.

"You come here often?" she whispered, as he led the way up the basement stairs and unerringly toward the microfilm newspaper files.

He looked a little surprised at the question, and nodded. "At least I did until they started locking up their collection of musical recordings. We would take turns, my friend Devin and I—one of us stand- ing watch for the guard outside the soundproofed listening rooms, the other inside listening. We lis- tened to everything in those days . . . we were nearly caught, laughing at Bill Cosby's *Why Is There Air?*"

Catherine chuckled softly, then shivered a little, at the thought of coming here regularly, late at night. The long corridor outside the microfilm rooms seemed to contain a thicker darkness than the tunnels below, the cold dusty weight of the building and all it contained pressing down upon their heads. "Is it true the place is haunted?" she asked, and Vincent's blue eyes smiled in the flashlight-glow.

In the microfilm rooms, she searched the computer catalogue. Edie's instruction in the wiles of mainframe management paid off—in a very short time she figured out how to find the sections she needed. Any reference to the Chittenden Research Institute between the years—counting back from Vincent's recollections and Father's probable age—1945 and 1960.

It was a daunting stack even in microfilm which they carried up to the long row of readers on the library's main floor, and Catherine had the beginnings of a severe headache by the time she hit pay dirt.

"Here," she said, and Vincent, who had been sitting a little apart from her in the shadowy cavern of that giant room, listening for the footsteps of the guard, turned his head.

"This is from June of 1951. The Chittenden Research Institute was given a grant by the Defense Department to study the effects of nuclear fallout . . ." Catherine glanced at the legal pad she'd brought to take notes on, shifted the reader along toward the next reference, in November of that year. Vincent hesitated, feeling against his chest the square-cornered weight of the picture frame which he had been somehow unwilling to show Catherine, unwilling to bring into the light . . .

"Here it is . . . one of the research doctors claimed that the Chittenden Institute was misrepresenting his findings . . ." Her voice slowed, shocked and angry over what she read. "He was forced to retire when he called for the abolition of atomic weapons, the halt of testing . . ."

Vincent leaned toward her. Somehow in the vast darkness of the library which lay beyond the tiny pool of the microfilm reader's light the tale of that old injustice seemed very recent, as if it had taken place days ago instead of before either of them had been born. But then, thought Vincent, this place, these massive stacks crammed willy-nilly with wisdom and frivolity and facts which had been proven untrue, had been then as they were now, had seen all that and more come and go . . .

"His name was Dr. Jacob Wells," she said, and Vincent turned the name over on his tongue.

"Jacob . . ." Pascal and the other longtime dwellers in the Tunnels had told him that when Father had first come Below, all those years ago, they had called him Doc—some of the oldtimers still did. It was Vincent, and his friend Devin who had vanished into the world Above, and Mary who had called him Father, and in a few years the name had stuck.

"There's more . . . give me a second . . ." Her fingers hit the scan lever and the columns of type flashed by—weather predictions that had seemed so critical at the time; ads for *The Thing from Another World*, Edsels, and spike-heeled shoes . . . Then the fast-forward snowstorm jarred to a halt. There was no need for Catherine to search, for the headline was bannered across three columns of the *New York Examiner*:

ANTI-ATOMIC RESEARCHER NAMED COMMUNIST

Beneath it was a picture of Father, the younger,

dark, bearded Father, subscribed by the caption, "Dr. Jacob Wells." And beneath that, the subhead, *Stripped of Medical License.*

Catherine could only stare, mouth open, aghast. "Vincent," she whispered, but he was beside her already, his powerful hand on her shoulder. "He was *blacklisted*," she said softly, horror and loathing in her voice at what had been done. "Called before the House Committee on Un-American Activities . . ."

"I've read about that time," he murmured.

So had Catherine, in her high school government classes and later, at Radcliffe—Simon, the Columbia Law School radical she'd been dating in those days, had fulminated about them at some length, citing careers that had been ruined, men who had been unable to work under their own names . . . men who had accused their colleagues of being Communists because their politics were liberal or their attitudes disrespectful. But it had always seemed like some nightmarish fairy tale, on par with what Warner Brothers movie-Nazis had been to her before her work in the DA's office had introduced her to people who really had faded numbers tattooed on their arms. Father . . .

She shook her head, not able to take it in.

Vincent sighed, and removed the envelope from his coat. "I took this also," he said, "from his dresser."

The sorrow in his voice made her look up from the creased and grimy stationery to his face. She thought about what her own feelings would be, if she had to invade her father's desk, pry through his private papers . . . even to save his life. She would no more have done that, she realized, than she would have gone digging through Jenny's purse while Jenny's back was turned.

"You haven't opened it, have you?"

He shook his head, knowing she would understand. "I couldn't."

Gently, she said, "If we have any hope of finding him, we need to learn what we can about his life."

He nodded, with a kind of defeat. "I know."

It wasn't sealed. She had just raised the flap when Vincent added, "I found it behind a photograph . . . a wedding photograph."

Oh, no, she thought, seeing for the first time the enormity of what those old accusations had cost him. *No . . .*

Slowly, she drew forth the single sheet, thick, deckle-edged, and clearly very expensive.

Dear Jacob [she read],
   I am writing you from Paris, where my father has sent me. Spring has arrived early here, the time for lovers, and it's as if the season mocks my sadness . . .

And it seemed to Catherine as if the scents of that long-ago Parisian spring rose to her from the page—wet chestnut leaves underfoot in the Boulevard St. Michel and the steamy breath of *croque messieurs* and tar-black espresso on raw gray air . . . Tears quivered in her voice and she reached behind her, seeking Vincent's reassuring hand.

And in his cell at the New York City Jail, lying awake in the utter silence of the deepest part of night with the stink of the open toilet in his nostrils and only the distant, passing tread of a guard in his ears, Father, too, was hearing the words of that letter, as he'd heard them in his mind—heard them as if that beautiful young girl he'd taken to the altar were in the room with him, speaking to him—for all those years.

. . . But I am beginning to understand that loss is sometimes necessary. I know of no gentle way to tell you that my father has annulled our marriage. And I would be lying to you if I said that I fought him. I can't even blame him. Forgive me, Jacob, because I know you're innocent and still don't have the strength to stand by you. But you're strong. You will survive. Of that I'm positive.

All I can say seems useless. Still I cling to the wreck of my memories, before they sink forever. Goodbye, Jacob. I'll love you always.

Margaret

And in the dark of Underground, throughout the night the soft chime and rattle of the pipes continued, relaying information, asking questions, finding no answers.

"That's the word in from Chang," reported Pascal, straightening up from a particularly old piece of iron conduit, vintage 1940s, and removing the earpieces of his stethoscope from his ears. All around him, the enormous cavern of the pipe-chamber glowed with the molten light of hundreds of candles, stuck in the neck of wine bottles or propped in little mounds of their own drippings on the pipes themselves, a hazy galaxy of swollen amber stars. Even so, the vast room was cold. Its walls and ceiling vanished in the shadows of the limitless, angled jungle of pipes, and the strange runic shapes of curving metal and elbow-joints took on a queer kind of life in the fluttering light, as if this place were, in fact, some kind of organic heart.

Pascal rubbed a gloved hand over the bald dome of his head, and sighed. "He's heard nothing."

Winslow, slouched on a corner of Pascal's narrow bed, swore.

"Got to be up there somewhere," argued Mouse, fidgeting with the thinner metal rods Pascal sometimes used instead of wrenches for relaying messages which required a more complicated code. He dropped them back on the table, looked brightly from the blacksmith to the pipe-player to Mary, who was seated in Pascal's one comfortable chair, a rump-sprung Victorian which Winslow had re-covered years ago in the faded gold tapestry of an old curtain. "Knows the ways down. In trouble—hit by car—would phone a Helper."

"Yeah," agreed Winslow dourly. "Only all the evidence points to the fact that he *hasn't* phoned anybody."

"What did Lou say?" asked Mary, turning to Pascal and hugging the webby brown-and-gray folds of her shawl closer about her slender shoulders.

"Only that the ad was in this morning's *Times,*" replied Pascal, who'd had a long talk over the pipes with the barber as soon as it had become clear that Father was long overdue. "He said a long time ago Father had said something about the phrase, 'the wreck of my memories', and Lou remembered it—remembered that it had made him sad for some reason . . . I think he said they'd been talking about Lou's divorce or something. And Lou said he thought Father ought to see it. He says now he wishes he'd let well enough alone . . "

"I still say we ought to send out a search party." Winslow got to his feet and began to pace restlessly, his shadow lumbering after him a dozenfold, like a herd of ghostly monsters clambering and sliding along the pipes.

"Send one where?" asked Mary. "To prowl every back alley in the city, look behind every fence, in every vacant lot . . ."

"He could have been mugged. It's a jungle out

there, Mary, you can't *believe* how bad it is—and Father hasn't been Above in one hell of a long time."

"Vincent'll find him," declared Mouse confidently. "Bring him back safe."

"Jamie and the older kids have been Above, looking," pointed out Mary. "And we have the Helpers looking and listening for word . . ."

"Yeah?" grumbled Winslow. "And that seems to have done about as much good as if we'd gone down to old Narcissa and asked her to look for him in that crystal of hers."

"Might not be such a bad idea," teased Pascal, with a wan grin in spite of the growing fear that they all shared and which none would admit. "Now if we could get a lock of his hair, maybe some fingernail parings . . ."

"Don't need voodoo," said Mouse, shaking his head firmly so that his blond hair slapped back and forth on his forehead. "And don't need search party. Vincent'll find him."

Winslow sighed, slumped back on the bed again and folded his heavy arms. "Well, since there ain't a whole lot else we can do, I only hope you're right."

In a beautifully-appointed bedroom in an apartment on Fifth Avenue, a woman was lying awake. She could not see the clock from where she lay, and in any case the heavy, rough-woven gray curtains which shrouded the windows were lined and interlined to block out any shred of light, but she knew it was late, the cold deeps of the night. By the rosebud of light from the night-lamp her nurse had left she could make out the shapes of the familiar things in her room—the louvered doors of the dressing-room, the curves of her vanity and its circular mirror, the graceful shapes of the flower arrangements that decorated every horizontal surface . . .

The smell of the flowers was thick in the night air, sweet and pleasant, under other circumstances, she thought, but now stuffy, funereal . . .

Dammit, she thought, turning her head with an aching pang of discomfort, *I'm not dead yet*.

Beside the bed, the portable IV stand rose like a gallows, incongruous next to the small Kandinsky on the wall. The rest of the apartment still had much of the old-fashioned furniture and academy still lifes which had characterized it from her childhood, but in this room, with its pale pink walls and cool brightness, she had the paintings she had bought, she loved—modern, light, and quirky, like Kandinsky's strange floating stars and triangular people.

The queasiness, the giddiness, of her last chemotherapy was beginning to wear off. She moved one skeletal hand, to touch what was left of her hair, cut short now . . . Well, it scarcely mattered, she thought. It had been graying for years. Though the doctors hadn't liked it, though Alan—dear Alan!—hadn't liked it, she was glad Henry had brought her home.

Brought her home, she thought, exhausted in mind and spirit—home to die?

Beside her reading glasses on the low nightstand at her side she could see the *Times*. Her nurse must have brought it in. She couldn't remember . . . It had been in her things when Henry had picked her up at the hospital this afternoon—Alan had brought it to her only that morning, to complain about the ad.

"You can't expect after all this time . . ." he had begun, and she had turned away from him, tired— so tired. He'd paused, his irritation not quite concealing the anxiety he felt for her, the lined rosiness of his face puckering with worry. After a moment's pause he'd gone on, "The ad's run for seven days now. Do I have your permission to cancel this nonsense?"

"No!"

". . . Margaret . . ."

"Listen to me," she'd said, and Alan Taft—that oldest of friends, that most trusted of confidants— *My God*, she thought, *how long have we been together?* —had listened. She was, after all, his boss, as her father had been, and like her father, she knew how to make her will felt.

Quietly, she had said, "A day hasn't passed that I haven't thought of him . . . of seeing him again. Especially now." Now, she thought, that her CA– 125 was up to 190 and she'd seen the word *metastasized* in the doctor's eyes—when it was clear her time was running out.

"He dropped off the face of the earth thirty-five years ago," Alan had pleaded, putting down the newspaper with its ad on the white formica table beside her hospital bed. Morning sunlight filtering through the yellow curtains of her private room had fallen upon it there—had glinted on the hideous collection of medicine-droppers and syringes, on the IVs, the water-glasses, the whole sickening paraphernalia of the gravely ill. At over a thousand dollars a day, Margaret had hated the place. Taft went on, "We're not even sure . . ."

"I know he's alive." Her voice, with all its old firmness—the firmness acquired with such difficulty, such pain, over the course of a life of regret, had overridden his and cut him off.

And lying awake, safe in her own room, surrounded by her own things, listening to the far-off, desultory murmur of traffic on Fifth Avenue far below, she knew it now.

Ten

It was almost four in the morning when Catherine and Vincent left the library, slipping back down the basement stairs and behind the piled boxes of books, but Catherine felt a curious elation and relief. She had found the name of the woman—girl, really, because she'd been barely nineteen at the time— whom Father had married in June of 1950.

And to her shock, she'd realized that she'd met her.

The phrase, *Paris, where my father has sent me*, and an examination of the wedding-dress in the photograph Vincent had found, told Catherine worlds about the economic class of the woman who had signed herself Margaret. The dress was a Dior original, the lace alone must have cost seven or eight hundred dollars—1950 dollars. The background, Catherine recognized from doing bridesmaid duty for three of her fellow-debutantes, was the fashionable St. George's. It hadn't taken much search of the society pages to find the account of the much-trumpeted union of Dr. Jacob Wells and Miss Margaret Chase, only child—of all people—of Anson Travers Chase, one of the most powerful, most ruthless, and certainly most wealthy industrialists in New York's Upper Ten Thousand. He'd been dead by the time Catherine had made her debut—and by all she'd heard of him from her father, who belonged to the same club, was undoubtedly frying in the circle of Hell reserved for those who oppressed their fellow-man.

But Catherine remembered meeting the reclusive Margaret Chase at one of those enormous society parties it had been her misfortune to attend while her father still entertained hopes of getting her married off to someone suitable. A brief introduction, a shake of kid-gloved hands, an exchange of well-bred smiles and compliments on each others' dresses before each moved on to other social obligations, but Catherine had a recollection of a slim, fair, rather faded woman who probably would have been extremely beautiful if she'd had any animation at all in her fine-boned face.

An hour and a half, two cups of strong coffee and a shower later, Catherine put through a phone call to her father's friend Kim Baskerville, an elderly widow who had moved in the circles of old-money New York society for all of her life and, as she said, knew everything about everyone who was anyone. Kim, Catherine knew, rose early to feed her seven birds and three Pekingese—six-thirty would probably catch her just after her jog around Gramercy Park.

"Margaret Chase?" said Kim, and there was a deep twinge of sorrow in her voice. "Dear Heavens, yes, I know her address, poor thing, if she's there— she's been in and out of the hospital for months now with chemotherapy. Pancreatic cancer—they've operated on her twice, and now . . . Well, they say it's only a matter of time."

"Oh," said Catherine, as a piece of the puzzle dropped suddenly into place. "Oh, I'm sorry." That beautiful young girl—dying.

"Well," said Kim, her voice returning to its usual

briskness, "where there's life, there's hope, they say—only sometimes poor Margaret seemed so fragile. You'll probably have to deal with Mr. Dutton—Henry Dutton—he's been the closest to her since—oh, November, I think he met her. It's really wonderful how well he's looked after her. No reason why he shouldn't, of course—she's leaving his charity every cent of her money."

"Oh, really?" Catherine perched on one corner of a kitchen bar-stool, pulled the towel from her head and rumpled her hair with her fingers to encourage it to dry. Outside the window, gray rain had begun to come down again, a thin, steady drumming on the terrace, a reflection of the sorrow in that letter written in Paris all those springs ago.

"Oh, perfectly aboveboard," chirped Kim, hearing the thoughtful note in her voice. "People have to leave their money to someone, you know, and it stands to reason that a man who raises money for charities would make it his business to bring those charities to the attention of someone who is ill, and without family. I'm only glad she has a friend to look after her."

Maybe, thought Catherine, as she jotted down Margaret Chase's address and went to dry her hair. *And maybe I'm being unjust to a good-souled and hardworking man.* But in her experience in both the DA's office and among the upper crust of New York society in which she had been raised, she had never noticed the prospect of money bring out the best in anyone.

And Margaret Chase was dying. Catherine paused, looked away from her dressing-table mirror out at the gray morning outside, feeling again the stab of sadness at the desperate unfairness of it all. It had obviously been she who had put that ad in the paper, she who had sent for him, the man she had married all those years ago—the man she had said she would always love.

Catherine wondered whether Father had made it that far.

At seven-thirty, showered, made up, and dressed in chic red and black, Catherine was crossing the marble checkerboard floor of the lobby of one of the old luxury apartment buildings on Fifth Avenue,and tipping the uniformed attendant in the elevator to take her up to the Chase's penthouse mansion.

Henry Dutton met her at the door.

'I'm sorry to have come this early," she apologized, and he shook his head with a friendly smile.

"No, don't worry about it. You're clearly a busy woman, as I'm a busy man . . . Would you like some coffee, Miss Chandler?"

Since she'd been up since eleven-thirty the previous night she nodded, and he touched an intercom button to order it. It was brought by a young, dark, well-groomed man who handled the silver tray with its delicately scrolled Edwardian coffee-service without any trace of the reverent skill characteristic of the professional butlers Catherine had known. *Interesting*, she thought, her eyes returning to Dutton. Good-looking in a craggy way, light brown hair, light eyes . . . too light, she thought. Pale blue without warmth. In his gray slacks and neat blue sports jacket he had the air she'd met in other professional fund-raisers: busy, smooth, with excellent manners meticulously acquired.

The coffee was wonderful—Catherine had always been something of a connoisseur and months of drinking sludge at the District Attorney's office had sharpened her appreciation. It was thoroughly in keeping with the room itself, long, sunlit, its white walls recently painted and its lavish woodwork and wainscot still glowing with an original finish carefully maintained. The flower arrangement on the sideboard—yellow star-chrysanthemums, lupine, and asters—had clearly cost over a hundred dollars, though its blossoms were wilting now and needed to be dead-headed . . . The space of the room itself, nearly forty feet long across the front of the building, was a smug and quiet announcement of how much the place cost.

Over the marble fireplace a portrait of a grim-faced man in his forties stared down at them. The portraitist had obviously tried to make his subject appear magnificent, catching every detail of expensive haberdashery and furnishings as eloquently as a price-tag, but his skill had betrayed him; the man's mouth looked like a trap, and the shallowness of his soul showed through in the sly, ruthless eyes. As a compliment it was a dead loss, but as a likeness it was superb.

"Miss Chase's father?" she asked, and Dutton smiled.

"Classic robber-baron," he said, the note of fascination in his voice giving the lie to the disapproval in his words. "In his salad days he helped finance both sides of the Spanish-American war. Came through the Depression untouched . . ."

A movement down at the far end of the room made him turn his head. Catherine saw a middle-aged Hispanic woman in a nurse's uniform standing in a doorway. Dutton said, "Excuse me," and, rising, crossed the length of the room to speak to her. Catherine sipped her coffee, watching him—the nurse kept nodding, gesturing as if to say, No, it's nothing—Dutton was shaking his head. In time he laid a hand on the nurse's slim back and guided her back through the door, into whatever fastnesses of the apartment lay beyond.

Then he came back, his features expressing regret. "I'm sorry, Miss Chandler—Margaret just isn't up to visitors. Perhaps tomorrow."

"Tomorrow's fine," said Catherine, looking across at him as he took his seat once more in the chair opposite the couch where she sat. "Just tell me when."

"I wish I could." He sighed ruefully. "But her condition doesn't allow me to be that specific." He stirred cream into his coffee—looking across at those light eyes, that mouth that for all its mobility had a quality of hardness much akin to that of the portrait looking down over his shoulder, Catherine had the feeling that this man was putting her off. "Maybe I can help you with whatever it is?"

Catherine sipped her coffee. "I'm sorry. It's private."

The pale eyes narrowed with curiosity. "I thought you said you were with the District Attorney's office?"

"I am," said Catherine, with a polite smile. "It's still private." She set down her cup and reached into her handbag for a card, which she placed beside the silver-rimmed saucer. "My service number's on the card," she said, rising. "So you can reach me tomorrow, whenever Ms. Chase feels up to it."

"Of course," smiled Dutton, and showed her to the door himself. "Miss Chandler," he added, as he opened the door out into the private elevator lobby.

She turned back, raincoat over one arm, to face him.

He cocked an eyebrow at her. "Are you always this mysterious?"

She gave him her best rueful smile, apologizing without backing off or giving anything away. "Occupational hazard," she excused herself. There was something about this man which struck her wrong,

145

something that was too smooth, too calculating, though for the life of her she couldn't identify what. Maybe it was just Kim's mention of a fortune that size going begging, and this man Johnny-on-the-spot. "Thanks for the coffee."

And as she rode down the elevator, Catherine found herself wondering whether Father had managed to see Margaret yesterday evening, and whether Henry Dutton knew anything of the circumstances which had caused Margaret to place that ad.

Henry Dutton stood in the vestibule of Margaret Chase's apartment for a few moments after the door to the elevator lobby closed. Then, thoughtfully, he turned back to the living room, where the beefy young man who'd brought in the coffee-service was just picking it up. "Connor," Dutton said, and the young man put down the tray and came over to him. The neat jacket Connor wore did nothing to hide the width of his shoulders, the way he held his arms that was the telltale mark of pumping a lot of iron; his smooth, good-looking face was blank and rather cold.

"Alora says Miss Chase has been asking for you again," reported Connor, and Dutton nodded.

"I'll go see her in a minute." He motioned with his head back towards the outer door. "That woman who was just here . . ."

"Sir?"

"Satisfy my curiosity, would you?" said Dutton. "Find out what she wants."

Connor thought about it a moment, then moved his head in agreement.

"Good man." Dutton passed down the length of the room, then through a door and down a short corridor to the room where Margaret lay.

The curtains were partially open, and the thin

streak of April sunlight gleaming through made the light of the bedside lamp, which still burned, seem sluttish and dirty. Outside the rain had ceased, and, barely to be seen through the narrow opening, the glittering towers of Rockefeller Center, the fantasy shape of the Chrysler Building and the sharp spike of the Empire State seemed to float against the new-washed sky, clean and bright as a matte-painting in some unthinkable Twenties science fiction film. Margaret was sitting up in bed, hugging herself. Her face looked ravaged.

"Margaret . . ." Dutton strode towards her, concerned.

Her eyes turned towards him; she sighed. "I feel as though I've been asleep for half a century." She ran a hand, thin and splotched with the discolorations of chemotherapy, through her short-cropped gray hair, and made a noise that could have been a bitter laugh. "God, I must look awful."

She did, but Dutton smiled warmly, "You look as beautiful as ever."

"I look like hell." And for a moment there was something in the firmness of the mouth that was like the strength of the man in the portrait in the room outside. Then she sighed, relaxing a little, and went on, "But I think a walk in the park would do me good. See a little real green and smell some fresh air."

Maybe buy a newspaper, thought Dutton—there was a stand in the building's lobby—and he said soothingly, "I don't think that's a good idea. You should be resting." And he crossed to close the blinds again, cutting out the sparkling day.

Margaret rubbed her hands across her face, looked around her for her reading glasses, for the clock that usually sat on the nightstand beside them. But the nightstand contained only an assortment of pill-bottles, a tumbler of water—even the *Times* with its ad had been taken away. "What time is it?" she muttered.

Dutton sat in the chair beside the bed and took several pills from the little cup the nurse had prepared. "Time for your medication." It wasn't, in fact—it was an hour or two early—but, Dutton thought, it was probably better this way.

"Damn those things."

He held them out to her, smiling coaxingly. "You should be grateful for 'those things'."

Her voice was bitter, but with the granite strength that long suffering can sometimes give. "I hate pain killers. A little pain is good for the soul."

"Now, come on," urged Dutton, his voice picking up just the thinnest of edges. "I have a meeting with the Planning Commission about the shelter we'll be building, and it started five minutes ago." And he held out the pills again, half rising; she flinched back a little as his shadow fell over her, as if his physical size and power held the implication of a threat.

"Please, Henry," she moaned. "I'd rather not."

His voice was coaxing but inexorable, "Come on, come on, Margaret, take your medicine now . . . doctor's orders."

Their eyes met, hers filled with a hopeless weariness, the knowledge that it didn't really matter. And why not? she thought. Why bother to struggle? She'd soon be dead—the doctors gave her only a month at most, probably much less than that . . . There had been no answer to the ad. Alan had probably been right.

Resignedly, she took the glass of water he held out to her, the pills he put in her hollow hand. After she'd swallowed them she leaned back against the pillows, queasy and aching, not knowing anymore whether that was the result of the cancer or the chemotherapy or the medications she'd been under, it seemed, for years . . .

Alan had probably been right . . .

She frowned. "I wonder why Alan hasn't called," she said, and Dutton gave her a smile and a shrug.

"Well . . . you know Alan," he said, with affectionate dismissal.

"That's just it," said Margaret, feeling her voice, like her thoughts, starting to blur. "I *do* know Alan . . ."

But the weight of the phenobarbital was dragging her down; she sank against the pillows, confused and tired and unable to think. Her last thoughts were of how the grass would look, wet and bright with the morning's rain, and the hope that when she woke, Alan would have phoned to tell her that Jacob had contacted him, that Jacob was back . . .

She whispered, "I'm cold," and Dutton pulled the covers higher over her as she slipped into cloudy sleep.

Eleven

CATHERINE left Margaret Chase's apartment feeling slightly uneasy, as she did when she was interviewing a witness whom she knew was lying. Maybe her own words to Dutton had had more truth in them than she'd known—maybe this suspicion of altruistic motives *was* an occupational hazard of working in the DA's office. Nevertheless, when she reached the City and County Courts Building and rode up to her floor, she sought out Edie's little cubicle in Data and put in a request for information about one Henry Dutton, allegedly connected with charities.

"Got any kind of a record?" asked Edie, jotting down the spelling of the name. Beside her the printer chattered, spilling out a long list of Hispanic males in whose names green Chevy pickups had been registered in the last five years with New York State license plates which may or may not have had the number 8 in them—the witness wasn't sure.

Catherine shook her head. "I don't know."

"Well, if he don't, it means he won't be in our system."

"Oh . . ."

"Not," added Edie, her liquid brown eyes glinting with mischief, "that I won't be able to get you what you want about him . . . but it means a little breaking-and-entering on the lines, if you know what I mean."

"I don't," said Catherine, straightening up and ostentatiously putting her hands over her ears, "and I don't want to."

Edie's grin broadened. "I'll let you know when I got it, girlfren', one way or the other."

Catherine stopped at the coffee machine on her way to her desk, the fatigue of the sleepless night catching up with her. Larry McKie, the office mother hen, must have made this batch, since it was remotely drinkable, but it only served to remind her of the savor of the Hawaiian Royal Kona which Dutton had served her. Her eyeballs felt like Shake'n'-Bake; she stretched a little to get the cricks out of her shoulders, then pulled from the desk drawer the standard list of hospitals, emergency trauma centers, and the morgue, and started her round of calls again. At this hour of the morning she should be able to get better information, she thought, if there were any to get.

Nearly an hour's calling—with two-thirds of the list to go—seemed to prove to her that there wasn't.

"No," she said, for perhaps the dozenth time. "No, he definitely has a beard . . . Okay. Thank you. Damn," she added, as she put down the phone and crossed yet another name off the list. Leaning forward on her elbows, she rubbed her eyes, massaged her forehead—the headache that had started over the microfilm readers had never quite gone away, except for those few brief minutes in which she'd walked in the rain-fresh air from the bus stop to the doors of the building. Why couldn't she have a job like Jenny's, and spend her days taking authors to lunch?

"Headache at nine a.m.," said Joe Maxwell's voice reprovingly. "Not a good sign." And against the

151

throb of her headache the crackle of the plastic bag in his hand sounded like machine-gun fire.

Catherine peeked up at Joe over her fingers. In his early thirties, boyishly good-looking with curly black hair and dark eyes, Joe was nominally Catherine's supervisor. Though it was fairly early in the day he'd already discarded his jacket—the tie would stay, but get looser as the day wore on, as if it were losing its will to remain knotted from sheer exhaustion. The crackling sound came from a brightly-colored bag of *something* he held in one hand, from which he dipped a handful and munched.

"If you keep eating those things, my headache's going to move into my stomach," groaned Catherine. "What *is* that?"

"Chocolate-cheese nuggets," murfed Joe, chewing happily. "Yummm . . ."

"For *breakfast?*"

"Want some?"

Catherine shuddered. "No, thanks."

He craned his head to look down over her shoulder at the printed list of hospitals. "So what are you working on?"

Casually she placed a file-folder over the list, and said, "Nothing."

"That's good," he approved, taking another chocolate-cheese nugget from the bag and popping it into his mouth. "Because you're fifteen minutes late for the Bartoli deposition."

Catherine said an extremely unladylike word she'd picked up from Edie and shoved the list into her desk, scrambled to her feet and, catching up her briefcase, headed for the door. "Have a nice day," said Joe, and went to get himself a cup of coffee to round out his breakfast and start his day off right.

Getting used to the city's holding jail had been

one of the hardest things Catherine had done in coming to work for the District Attorney. In a way it was an expression of the whole dichotomy between the leisured pace and gracious surroundings of her years as a junior corporate lawyer in her father's firm, with its atmosphere of leather armchairs, large expense accounts, and unemotional legal entities; and what she was doing now. It was humanity in the cells she passed, some of it innocent, some of it guiltier than anyone would ever know, but humanity at its filthy and foul-mouthed worst. The men whistled at her and called out obscene suggestions in several different languages as she walked between her flanking guards—they would have done so, she knew, at any woman, pretty or not, and she had ceased to take it personally or feel threatened. Some of the men blustered at her, or called her names—others sat quietly in their cells, too deadened to even care about who might be passing by.

And such a one, she thought at first, was a grayhaired man sitting on the end of his cot in a cell about halfway down the line, a few doors up from the cell where Peter Bartoli was being held. But he did look up as she passed, more from curiosity than anything else, and for one instant, Catherine found herself looking into the eyes of Father.

Then he turned his face away quickly, bringing up his hand so that she would not see. She did not pause, only made a mental note of the cell number, and, shaken and weary with her sleepless night, tried to get enough of a grip over herself to take down the deposition she had come to take. Another thing she had learned in the DA's office was, First Things First. And she owed it to Peter Bartoli—and to the DA—to give her full attention to the matter at hand.

But uppermost in her mind was the illogical thought, *I should phone Vincent* . . . and then, *dammit, he doesn't have a phone.*

She took Bartoli's statement in the interview room, a dreary cement chamber painted institutional apple-green and smelling of stale tobacco and anti-septic, the table that ran down its center divided by a screen of wire mesh. It was to this room, after Bartoli had been returned to his cell and Catherine had rounded out her notes for her report, that a uniformed bailiff brought Father. He took his seat quietly, laying across the table before him the cane they'd let him keep.

"Please leave us alone," said Catherine, and the bailiff departed, closing the soundproofed door behind him. Through the wired-glass judas on the door she could see a corner of the man's cap—he was just outside.

Then she looked across the table, into the haggard face of the man opposite her, the man she had seen half a dozen times in the shadows of the tunnels—the man Vincent called Father.

The man who had, nearly a year ago, saved her life.

"Are you all right?" she asked.

He nodded. He looked exhausted, as if he had gotten no more sleep than she and had spent a far more dreadful night. Without his rust-brown robes, without the thick vest of fur and leather that so many of the tunnel people wore, he seemed smaller, more vulnerable—just a stout, aging, gray-bearded man in the blue prison denims, one more man from the cells outside. Only his eyes were different, with their wisdom and tolerance and sorrow, but like the men outside, he watched her warily.

She was, she understood now, a rich man's

daughter, as Margaret Chase had been. She knew now what he had feared for Vincent.

"Can I get you anything?"

"No." He leaned forward a little in his chair, looking through the grilled wire at her earnestly. "Please," he said, "stay out of it. Anything you do to draw attention to me will . . ."

"You're being charged with murder," she broke in gently. A detective named Gutierrez had handed her his file, with a headshake and the comment, "I hope you have better luck with this one than I did." "You must tell me what happened."

He hesitated, his eyes upon the backs of his hands where they rested on the cane before him, then silently shook his head.

"Don't you know by now you can trust me?"

"It's not you," said Father, raising his blue-gray gaze to hers. "I may be a stranger to your world, but I'm no stranger to the betrayals of your justice system."

Knowing what she knew had happened to him, there was no retort she could give to that. Instead she said, "I'm the only one who can help you."

"If you want to help me," said Father, "please . . . go away."

"I can't do that . . . Jacob."

He had looked away from her—she saw him flinch, shaken badly by the mere sound of a name he had not heard in thirty-five years—shaken, too, by the fact that it was she who had uttered it.

"I know who you were," she whispered, "and what happened."

There was no fear in his eyes, or dread—just a kind of stripped look, as if a shield behind which he had hidden had been taken away, leaving him to face a foe unarmed.

"Vincent?" There was sadness in his tone.

"He knows, too."

Father sighed, his broad shoulders slumping a little. "I didn't want to keep things hidden from him," he said softly. "I only wanted to forget. Does he understand that?"

"Yes." Then, "You have nothing to be ashamed of."

He looked a little surprised that this would have been a concern for her. "I'm not ashamed."

There was a moment's silence, and she understood that he had truly put that part of the incident behind him.

"Was it Margaret who sent for you?"

There was a kindling of life in his eyes. "Margaret? You've seen her?"

"I tried," she said. "She was too ill to have visitors."

The grizzled brows pulled together with concern. "She's in the hospital?"

"No. She's at home."

Father was silent a moment more, digesting that, trying to imagine her in that setting . . . a setting, Catherine realized, he would know. He had been in that apartment, all those years ago, when that grim-faced old man in the portrait was still a living presence there. It was, she thought, the first news that he had had of his wife since the letter from Paris thirty-five years ago.

"She sent me a message," he said at last.

" 'The wreck of my memories'," she quoted softly, and his eyes met hers again, realizing that that was what must have led her to Margaret . . . that Vincent must have found the letter. After another moment's silence, "Do you know if the message meant that she was in some kind of trouble?"

He shook his head. "I don't know. I took it to mean she wanted to see me again."

Her hand moved a little to the file on the table before her, the scant file of the circumstances which had brought him here. "Who was Alan Taft?"

'A friend," he said sadly. "He defended me during the witch hunts, put his own career on the line—he could have been blacklisted as well, you know. They did things like that."

"Was he Margaret's lawyer, too?"

"He was the family lawyer."

And he had been murdered, thought Catherine. Murdered by someone who had ransacked his office. Murdered—since the crime took place very shortly after five o'clock, when there was still a chance there would be people in the building—in all probability by someone he knew well enough that it did not occur to him to shout for help.

Abruptly she asked, "Do you know a man named Henry Dutton?"

Father paused, fishing back in his memory for names, images, people out of that time—then he shook his head. "Why?"

"I'm not sure," said Catherine. "But what else can you tell me about Margaret? Maybe it'll help me piece this together."

"I don't know," he said slowly. "She was so young when I knew her . . . and so beautiful. She has had . . . a lifetime since then."

Catherine felt again the hot swelling of pity in her chest, and wanted more than anything to reach across the table and take the old man's hand. It was impossible, of course—even had the mesh wall not been between them, they were undoubtedly being filmed on a silent closed-circuit camera. So she only said, "I'll do what I can. I'll tell Vincent I've found you, that you're all right." She touched the button on the table at her side to summon the bailiff, and rose, gathering up her papers.

Before the door behind Father opened to admit the servants of authority once more, she added, "She never remarried, you know."

And Father's eyes thanked her as the bailiff led him away.

Vincent took the little plastic jar from the boy Dustin, unscrewed its lid. The message Pascal had tapped out for him on the pipes only said, URGENT MESSAGE PICKUP IN WALL ST. FR-PR TUBE—only "WALL ST. FR-PR TUBE," the site of the disused tracks of a private subway spur which had once served the now-demolished mansion of a man named Franklin, was all one word in Pascal's single-tap code. But he knew the message had to be from Catherine.

And it was. The jar held a sheet from a yellow legal pad; on it was written, *Father located. All right but in trouble with the police—working to clear. Meet me tonight.*

And it was as if he had cast off the weight of a lead-lined cloak from his shoulders, or had been trapped in a narrow tunnel and had finally worked himself free. His breath blew out in a sigh. "She found him, Dustin. He's all right."

The boy looked up, his face alight in the dim flicker of a rusty wall-lantern—then they both broke into a shaky laugh of relief and delight.

They were of course, thought Catherine, scarcely out of the woods yet. With deliberate concentration she closed Father out of her mind until she'd written up Peter Bartoli's statement about why he'd stabbed his partner six times with a broken wine-bottle (not beer, as it had been in the original statement—Bartoli had been particularly indignant at the implication that beer and not wine would have been served

158

in his *ristorante*). Mrs. Bartoli hadn't impressed her, in her earlier interview, as being worth that sort of activity no matter *what* she'd done with the partner, but, as Catherine was well aware, passion can be totally incalculable. But later in the afternoon, crossing the bustling cacophony of the bullpen after dropping off the deposition with DA Moreno, her thoughts returned to Father and to the file Gutierrez had handed her in the jail that morning.

And quite frankly, as a lawyer who was getting more and more experience in the thought processes of public prosecutors, she had to admit the case against him looked bad. Not only did the circumstances of the Taft murder point just as well to Father as to anyone else, but his refusal to give his name or any details about himself were doubly incriminating.

In time, she supposed, his prints would get back to the FBI . . . Or had security clearance files from the late Forties ever been computerized? But that would only further complicate matters. There was a thirty-five–year gap in his past, and that, Catherine knew only too well, was enough to get any policeman in the world thinking, *Hit man*.

No. Something had to be done about Father's identity—and something had to be done about finding the murderer of Alan Taft.

"Hey, Cathy . . ."

She glanced up, pulled from her puzzling as Edie fell into step with her. The programmer handed her a doubled-over sheet of tractor-paper, shrugged with her brows as well as her fashionably padded shoulders. "I gotta tell you, girlfren', if Dutton's a player he's playin' by the rules."

Catherine's mouth twitched in a wry expression. "How far back did you go?"

"All the way." They reached Edie's station—she

stuck the tip of one manicured finger into the coffee in her red stoneware mug to test its temperature, and grimaced as she looked over at Catherine. She amplified, "Poor kid from Queens, to four years in Cambodia with the Peace Corps, to his latest project."

"Which is . . . ?"

"A ten-million-dollar shelter for the homeless."

Catherine flipped the printout over in her hands, studying the credentials—law, business, social work . . . Why had the man impressed her as someone with something to hide? Why had the fact that she was from the District Attorney's office bothered him? Why had he been that evasive about Margaret Chase? According to what Kim had told her, Margaret wasn't *that* debilitated by her treatments, was able to be up and around . . .

Thoughtfully, she asked, "Where does he lay his hands on that kind of money?"

"Got his own foundation. Private fundraising, donations, grants . . ."

"And no history of misappropriation? No complaints filed?"

"Nothing."

Her voice was flat. "Impressive."

Edie folded her arms, looked at her in exasperation. "But you're not impressed."

Catherine sighed again, uneasy and not sure why. "I don't know," she murmured, turning the paper over in her hands. Something about that apartment had struck her as odd—something about the setup . . . The way the nurse had gestured, the way Dutton had herded her quickly out of the room . . . "It's just . . . I didn't think he'd come out so damn . . . spotless."

Edie shook her head. "I'm telling you, the man's Nobel Prize material. There's just no pleasing some people." And she flashed Catherine a grin as Catherine turned away to get back to her desk.

Maybe, thought Catherine, settling into her chair once more and studying the printouts before her. But she'd *met* Nobel Prize material before—humanitarians, good people, kind people—and somehow the furtiveness behind Henry Dutton's easy charm hadn't struck her as being in keeping with that kind of intention. Digging an interrupted lunch out of its wrappings—the remaining half of a now-cold take-out burger she'd bought off the roach coach in City Hall Park on the way back from the jail—she remembered her brief encounters on office business with the nuns of St. Regina's, the nuns to whom Vincent had given Mouse's pirate treasure.

Maybe she just had her own ax to grind, she thought, and wanted Dutton to be guilty because she knew Father was not, and she knew he would be found guilty if brought to trial. But something about the set-up that morning had bothered her, and bothered her deeply . . .

She took a bite of sandwich, and a sip of coffee, and wrinkled her nose—the stuff in the cup was not only stone cold now, but tasted like it had been brewed out of old gym socks. She was so tired now she was willing to drink almost anything, but comparing it with the coffee Dutton had given her . . .

And then she remembered. The man who'd brought the coffee in, who hadn't any idea of how to handle a tray . . . who didn't have the air of any servant she'd ever seen. Brought up in what was termed Society, Catherine knew jolly well that a woman like Margaret Chase wouldn't have a man like that serving coffee to her guests. And now that she thought about it, she realized what else had bothered her.

The neglected air of the apartment. The sense of emptiness.

The fact that, apart from the nurse, there were no servants. The place hadn't been noticeably untidy, as no one had lived there for a week or so—according to Dutton, Margaret Chase had just returned from the hospital the previous day—but the tables had all been dusty, the flower arrangements hadn't been tended to—something even the slackest servants would have done. Judging by the dust, there hadn't been any servants for probably a week.

She glanced across the bullpen at the clock, wondering if she'd be able to finish her backed-up work in time to go over to Homicide and talk one of her friends there into lending her the keys to Alan Taft's office.

The police were done with the place. The only signs that they had been there were the marks of tape by the doors, and, in places, a remainder of fingerprint-powder on the edge of a desk or an oak file cabinet; but even that, like the taped white outline that had surrounded Alan Taft's body, had been dealt with by the building's janitorial staff. The office was just an office, dark except for the dim glow of a security light when Catherine let herself in.

Taft's receptionist, she thought, closing the door behind her, had evidently cleaned up after the police, replacing papers in their files, files in their cabinets, and had gone, too; the office had a deserted air. The day's mail still heaped the floor in front of the door.

She gathered it up, and crossed to the glass wall which divided the outer office from the inner. Leaving the mail on Taft's desk she went straight to the file cabinets. The file marked DUTTON was empty, but though fairly new, was bent and worn in such a way as to tell her that it had contained something. *Dammit*, she thought, looking around her for some further inspiration, *now is that because Dutton—if it was Dutton—took something away, or because it just got spilled in the search and the receptionist put it back in the wrong folder? Am I really going to have to go through all those files . . . ?* She went back to Taft's desk, and stood for a moment, her hand resting on the massive soapstone panther that stood there, wondering where the key to the desk drawers would be . . .

But as she did so the mail heaped on the desk before her caught her eye. And among the legal journals, statements, and bills, there was one packet in particular—a 9 × 12 envelope marked CONFIDENTIAL—whose brightly-colored stamps drew her attention, stamps such as she'd seen only last week, on postcards her father had sent her from the Cayman Islands, that haven of tax-free corporations and intricately-interlocking phantom foundations.

Catherine opened it. Inside was a report, labeled:

DUTTON FOUNDATION AUDIT—CONFIDENTIAL—
REVISED MARCH 21.

To a layman the columns of figures inside wouldn't have meant much. To a tax accountant, or to a corporation lawyer such as Catherine had been for two years, they were damning.

There are evidently other ways of making $30,000—or $3,000,000—thought Catherine, sliding the audit into her handbag, *than winning the Nobel Prize.*

The building's lobby was empty as she crossed it, the security guard off making his rounds of the building—she had met him just outside Taft's office, nearly scaring her out of her skin. Her low heels clicked sharply on the black marble floor and the echo of it whispered like water dripping in the vaults of the ceiling, emphasizing the vast darkness of the place. Catherine shivered, hugging the red velvet of her jacket closer about her, made nervous by the eerie half-dark. Exhaustion made her feel even more chilled, and it seemed to her that she'd been awake for days, researching, worrying, puzzling over details of a larger and more complicated story.

And yet it had all gone quite easily, she thought. She had expected trouble tonight, expected . . . she hadn't known quite what. *Tiredness making me paranoid*, she thought. All afternoon, since deciding to come here tonight, she had been prey to a sensation of unease, as if she'd half-expected to see Dutton and his men lurking around every corner, waiting for her. She tucked her handbag more firmly under her arm, thinking, *Well, Isaac always says to get a backup if you can. Still, I didn't need to ask poor Vincent to . . .*

She pushed through the revolving door, and stepped into the hash glare of the streetlamps on Lexington Avenue.

And they were waiting for her, Connor and another of Dutton's henchmen, just outside the door.

Twelve

"Y OU'RE embezzling her estate, aren't you? Keeping her here against her will." Catherine looked from Henry Dutton's craggy, handsome face to the doorway of the hall, at the end of which was the room in which Margaret Chase would be sleeping her drugged sleep—sleeping away the last few weeks of her life. Through the long windows of one side of the living-room the constellations of New York's light glittered against velvet sky. The dying flower arrangements still hadn't been thrown away. Close behind her, Dutton's two stooges watched the scene with eyes more lifeless than those of Anson Chase, trapped forever in the portrait on the wall.

"You never had any intention of building that shelter."

It seemed to sting Dutton; he turned his head a little towards her, irritated. "In the beginning, maybe," he said.

"And instead you've funnelled everything into your private account."

The fund-raiser regarded her coolly, tapping the thick envelope that contained the audit up and down in one palm. His lips hardened, turned wry—all his charm had been put aside. "Do you have any idea what it's like to spend your life so close to so much wealth, and never see a dime?" He looked around him at the beautiful room, at the gracious air of money, perhaps badly earned but very well spent indeed. "I just got tired of doing unto others."

"Even though you had to kill for it?"

His eyes hardened. "Especially because I had to kill for it." And for no reason, Catherine remembered what Vincent had told her of the happenings earlier in the spring, the unhappy, tangled tale of gold and greed and what they did to even those who had renounced this world.

"You see," Dutton went on, "I've learned that under the right circumstances, a man is capable of anything."

She said softly, scornfully, "You think that's news? And now what?"

He sighed regretfully, and slipped the audit into his jacket pocket, sticking out like a newspaper under his elbow. "I wish I had a choice, Miss Chandler. I really do."

They left one of the stooges in the apartment, Dutton and the man Connor leading Catherine out into the marble-floored elevator lobby again. Catherine knew already from the lack of any outside noise in Margaret's apartment that the walls were sound-proofed—one didn't pay millions of dollars for a penthouse apartment to hear one's neighbor singing in the shower—and that screaming would do her no good at all. There was in any case only one other door onto this lobby—it was that kind of building. The elevator doors slid open. Dutton's hand was like iron on her elbow, urging her inside.

The quarters were cramped in the elevator. There wasn't much she could do, she thought, gauging the room she had, the possibilities, damning herself for not having brought her gun. Not that it would have done much good—they'd only have taken it from her when they surprised her outside Taft's office building. On the street it would be difficult, for they'd brought her in by the alley door and left the car there waiting; they'd undoubtedly take her out the same way. Vincent . . .

And then overhead came the grating jar of machinery misfunctioning, a smell of burning wiring, and the whole car lurched sickeningly, throwing all three of its riders off-balance.

Catherine, tense and ready, recovered first. Her heel ground down onto Connor's instep at the same moment her elbow jammed backwards into his solar plexus; taken off-guard by the lurch of the car he doubled up, retching, falling into Dutton who was already grabbing again for Catherine's arm. The light in the car was flickering already, throwing everything into a confusion of shadow, and overhead she heard the metallic scrape of the emergency access-hatch in the ceiling being forced open from the other side.

Vincent.

Dutton whirled at the noise, looking up at the sudden hole of shadow overhead; Catherine drove a knee into his groin and slammed the heel of her hand as hard as she could up under the septum of his nose. He gasped shrilly and his knees gave, and Catherine looked up in time to see a powerful arm, a huge, clawed hand, reaching down to her from the hatch. She grabbed the audit from Dutton's pocket, shoved it into the top of her handbag, and sprang up, grabbing at the corded wrist.

The men in the car below her were yelling as Vincent hauled her up through the hatch and slammed it behind them. A bullet crashed through the ceiling beneath their feet, whined angrily against the cement wall of the elevator shaft, and by the dim glow of a distant safety light Catherine saw Vincent's face, set and grim. It had perhaps been an exercise in paranoia, she thought, to have had him follow her tonight; but tired as they both were, they had agreed it was the only safe way. She had known he couldn't protect her outside the building on Lexington Avenue, but had only been hoping he'd find a way of stopping the car, not expecting him to have entered this building itself.

"Hold on, Catherine," he said, as she flung her arms around his neck and he began to climb the cables, his massive arms making nothing of either of their weight on the long haul to the top.

After phoning the police to get them to Margaret Chase's apartment before Dutton could make his getaway, and spending several hours giving evidence of embezzlement, fraud, conspiracy, murder, and attempted murder, Catherine would have liked to sleep until at least noon the following day, but she forced herself to get up early. There were an appalling number of things that had yet to be done.

Late that afternoon she entered the computer data center, rather baggy-eyed but triumphant, and greeted Edie with a sparkling smile. "It worked," she said delightedly. "Released on his own recon, no questions asked."

Edie shrugged, like a debutante in a thousand dollars' worth of Thai silk saying *Oh, this old rag* . . . "And why shouldn't it work? As far as the IRS, the DMV, and AT&T are concerned . . ." —she punched up a file on her keyboard— ". . . Benjamin Darrow is a tax-paying, phone-using, motor vehicle operator."

She hit the "Enter" key and Father's mug shot digitalized itself onto the screen, captioned by the name *Benjamin Darrow*, and accompanied by a great deal of convincing and totally spurious data concerning his birthdate, address, and Social Security number. Catherine shook her head. She'd known Edie could do incredible things with modems and other peoples' mainframes, but this was truly a tour-de-force.

"Edie, you are amazing . . ."

Edie twisted the end of one corn-row around a finger and mugged: "So tell me something I don't know." Then her smile faded, and she said more seriously, "So like, who is this guy, anyway? For all I know he could be working for the KGB."

Catherine sighed, thinking of the accusations made a decade before Edie had been born—thinking how little things had changed. "If it makes you feel any better, I can promise you he's not KGB."

"Then why all the intrigue?" Her fine-drawn brows pulled together a little at Catherine's silence; her eyes grew worried as she looked up at her friend. "I mean, I can keep a secret as well as the next person."

"I know," said Catherine. "Believe me, Edie, I wish I could tell you . . ."

"But you're not gonna." There was only a kind of comic resignation in her voice.

Catherine smiled ruefully. "Just trust me on this one, okay?"

"Yeah, yeah, famous last words," sighed Edie. "Go on, you get out of here and get some sleep. You look like you need it."

She shook her head, and put on the persimmon-colored jacket she'd held draped over her arm. "Can't just yet," she said softly. "Have to walk a friend home."

As yesterday had been, today was a day of spring brightness and showers, and as Catherine and Father walked along lower Broadway in the beginning eddies of rush-hour traffic, the passing of cloud-shadows high overhead made the wet pavement sparkle, the windshields of the jammed traffic flash as if mirrored. Woman in bright spring dresses hustled past them, clutching their coats about them; men in business suits kept one hand on their umbrellas and nervously watched the sky. Taxis wove and scooted like bumblebees among the heavier wash of traffic. A newspaper rolled along the gutter like an urban tumbleweed, propelled by a bus's backwash. Catherine glimpsed a headline: GOV'T AGREES TO PAY IN NUCLEAR WASTE SUIT . . .

And her eyes went, a little shyly, to the elderly man who limped along at her side.

He still wore his double-breasted tweed suit, looking oddly formal in his gray fedora—an unlikely Eurydice who, having followed the song of Orpheus, has decided to return to the darkness after all.

They paused where the steps led down to the Canal Street Station, the first step on the road down into the Underworld. "Goodbye," she said, wondering what else there was to say, and Father stood for a moment on the steps, his hands turning awkwardly on the handle of his cane.

"Catherine," he said at last, and looking up, met her eyes. "You've been more than a good friend to me. I know what you've risked, and for that, I am grateful."

The words must have come hard for him. She knew him to be a proud man in his way, as the leaders of men, no matter how good their rule and how small the groups they lead, are proud . . . And she knew that he had disapproved, not of her, but of Vincent's love for her, the love which put Vincent at risk every time he climbed the hidden ways of her building, to spend those nights with her on the terrace, talking, reading, listening to music—watching the turning of the New York nights. That, she understood; and he saw the understanding in her face, and smiled, thanking her for it silently.

"Goodbye," he said, and turned away, to return to his realm of darkness.

Catherine hesitated, then said, "Father . . ."

He stopped, and turned back. Men and women crowded past them in a torrent, faces set and abstract, business suits and Anne Klein dresses like smooth, expensive armor disguising whether they loved, and what they feared, and whose voices they heard in their dreams.

"I just wanted you to know," she said. "I would never hurt him. I love him." It was the first time she had said so to another person—the first time, she realized, there had been another person who knew Vincent, to whom she could speak.

Father smiled a little. "I know," he said, and in his voice she heard that there had never been any question in his mind. "I also know it can only bring him unhappiness."

All the nights shared on the terrace, with Vincent's arm warm around her—the nights they walked hand-in-hand in the cool glades of the park . . . Vincent's voice reading to her, or the sleepy gleam of his eyes as she read to him . . .

"Why do you say that?" she asked.

And with sad knowledge he replied, "Because part of him is a man."

Looking at the old man, Catherine found herself wondering how he had found his way down for the first time; what gate had opened for him there, when all the world had turned against him and all gates Above were closed. After the betrayal, the hearing, unemployment and life on the streets, the letter from Margaret must have been the final straw. No wonder he had wanted to forget.

But the song of Orpheus was the song of the

world of light. It was the song that drew Vincent to her, and Father knew too well the hurt that could lie at the core of that aching beauty. But he knew, too—and in his sorrow she saw that he knew it— that the heart of the song was love, and not to be denied.

Slowly he turned, and descended in that crowd of jostling backs into the darkness that led to his world, leaving Catherine to the sunlight of hers.

The pipes chimed softly, message and counter-message, the curious music of Below. Other than that it was silent here, save for the almost-inaudible hissing of a kerosene lamp on the octagonal table, and the leaf-fall rustling as Vincent turned a page of the book he read.

Vincent.

Margaret Chase studied him in the saffron haze of the lamplight, the odd, flattened profile that was more animal than human, the way the candlelight caught on ginger-colored eyelashes and in the rough, silky torrent of his hair.

Jacob's adopted son.

The girl Catherine had told her about him, care-fully, preparing her, as if she feared the sight of him might upset her—and, Margaret supposed, looking at him detachedly, it might, if one were taken unawares. But after coming out of her drugged slumber to find the police all over her apartment, Henry under arrest . . .

She winced a little. That had hurt. He had been so good to her in the beginning, the things he had done for her had been so kind . . . But of course, she thought, he knew how hungry she was for kind-ness, and how frightened. That warmth and humor, that kindness . . . He had known just how to win her trust. That had hurt, too. Catherine had been as gentle as she could about it, telling her that Henry's intentions had been good at the start, but in her heart Margaret wondered whether he hadn't picked on her as an easy victim all along. Alan had certainly never trusted him, and Alan was—had been—a good judge of people.

It was almost impossible to realize that he was dead.

She looked around her at that quiet room. It was so silent here, so peaceful; the stone walls lined with books, the tables cluttered with curiosities, maps, bits of broken astronomical equipment and antique medical implements in the rosy glow of the candles . . . Of course it was Jacob's room. It had been thirty-five years since she'd lived with him, and then he'd been so often on the move between New York and New Mexico—their apartment had always been tidy and well-kept . . . But it was as if she'd always known that, left to his own devices, Jacob would live in a place that looked just like this.

She had told Catherine about Taft's last visit to her, the morning of the day he was killed—about his protests to her about her new will, giving everything she owned to the Dutton Foundation, and the fact that he was having them looked into a little more closely. Ironic, she thought, smiling again, that now that Henry was going to spend a long time in jail for Alan's murder, the foundation which bore his name would proceed to really do that which it had been set up to do, before he'd started dipping money out of it . . . it really would build the Chase Shelter for the Homeless out in Brooklyn. That would amuse Alan, she thought, with a grim little inner laugh . . . In a way, it amused her. But distantly. By the time the shelter was built—in fact by the time Henry went to trial . . .

She shook her head, pushing the thought away,

and pulled the thick chinchilla of her coat-collar more closely around her. It was cold down here. But then, these days, she was always cold.

And then Catherine had introduced her to Vincent, and had told her that Vincent would guide her to where Jacob now lived.

Vincent looked up, as if his quicker ears had caught the distant echo of a familiar, dragging step. He set aside the heavy volume he was reading—Balzac . . . Jacob had evidently passed on to him his fondness for novels of intricate human relationships—and rose to his feet, the dulled metal hardware of his vest and belt glinting in the candlelight.

Jacob was standing in the doorway. From her seat in the shadows of the gallery Margaret watched them embrace, truly father and son . . . It was good to know Jacob had not spent all those years alone. Jacob still wore his best tweed suit, incongruous against the worn leather and quilting of Vincent's clothes, but infinitely dignified.

"Father," said Vincent in that soft, remarkable voice. "I'm glad you're safe."

He said simply, "It's good to be home."

His voice was as she had heard it for three decades of dreams. Then he turned his head, and his eyes met hers.

With her cropped hair, her ravaged cheeks and a face tracked-over with sorrow and experience and pain, all that he saw was the joyful maiden that shone forth from her eyes. With a gesture slow and completely subconscious, but ingrained in him to the marrow of his bones, he took off his hat, and the formality of it was so like him, so familiar, that she knew this could not be a dream. She rose from the carved chair where she'd been sitting and almost ran down the gallery steps, and all the years between them turned to smoke, and breathed away upon the wind.

"Jacob . . ." she whispered, as his strong arms gathered her in.

They walked a long way that day, through the galleries and tunnels of his mysterious world. Though it was not really, Margaret thought, so mysterious at all—just . . . another kind of world. A different world, a world of shadows and candles and quiet, a world protected. She asked about the messages along the pipes, and he took her to the Pipe Chamber and introduced her to Pascal, like a cheerful little spider in his mind-boggling webs of copper and steel and clay; asked about the Chasm with its three bridges, over which she and Vincent had passed, and Jacob stood with her on one of those railless stone spans, his arm around her protectively, and speculated upon who had built them, and when and why. He showed her where an underground river flowed through a channel cut long ago for a subway that was never built; showed her a four-block length of six-lane highway, dug deeper than some of the subway tunnels for some long-forgotten urban transit project and later forgotten; showed her a vault lined with mirrors which Mouse had found, for which nobody had ever come up with an explanation; and the tops of what had been an ancient forest, its trees buried forever in the city's subsoil— according to him they'd even recently found a pirate ship buried down near the old waterfront, complete with a treasure of accursed gold. Margaret had always enjoyed walking and had kept up several miles a day even in her illness. After the long, debilitating days dreamed away under drugs, it was good to walk again.

And as they had walked, arm in arm or with his

arm around her waist, they had talked, renewing an acquaintance which felt, at times, to have only been interrupted a few days ago. She told him about the new blocks of *immeubles* she'd seen going up near Orly Field on her last visit to Paris, the city where they'd spent their honeymoon—he groaned half-jokingly and shook his fist, for all the world as he'd used to when he'd groused about progress destroying the beautiful and the good . . . for all the world as if he'd been there with her and seen it for himself. She met Mouse, the little inventor, and Winslow the blacksmith, and the little ragged squad of the tunnel children, like Doyle's Baker Street Irregulars with their bright eyes and impish faces; saw Cullen's workshop where to his delight he'd finally gotten a piece of marble—the cornerstone of a wrecked building which Jamie and Mouse had nearly broken their backs hauling down for him as a surprise—and the wax-smelling workshop where Sara made candles and soap and lamps.

It was good beyond anything to feel the solidity of his shoulder, of his arm around her waist; good only to know that finally, he was there.

It was only when they returned to Father's room that exhaustion overtook her, and pain—the pain she'd fought daily, hourly, for so many months.

It caught her like the bite of some shark which had been lying in wait, making her gasp and falter—he steadied her, his face suddenly tense with concern. "Margaret . . ."

"I'm all right, Jacob," she said, easing herself down onto the carved chair again. "Really . . ." And she smiled quickly to prove it.

"We've done too much . . ."

"No . . ." She shook her head. "No, I just need to rest a bit."

To her, there was no such thing as 'too much'

anymore, and in his expression she saw that, for those few magic hours, he had entirely forgotten what Catherine must have told him, that she was ill. He said nothing about it, however, only perched on the corner of a table at her side, and took her hand. He had used to be more probing, trying to fix whatever was wrong—he had learned, she thought, that there are ills which can never be fixed.

After a time, she said, "You've built a remarkable world here, Jacob. I've never felt so at peace."

He smiled. "And all these years, I've dreamed of showing you."

"If I hadn't been such a fool . . ."

He shook his head. "No, don't, Margaret, please."

"No." Her hand sought his—he had changed back into the rust-brown robe of his patriarchate here, the sweaters and vest and arm-warmers that kept him from the Tunnels' perpetual chill. "No, I have to say this," she said. "I've been wanting to all along . . ." She paused, uncertain. "And now suddenly I don't know where to begin."

There was silence between them, like the silence between young people, when all the words have been said, and it is time for something else. Rising from her chair, she turned from him and walked a few paces away, staring into the liquid golden shadows.

"I'm dying, Jacob," she said softly. "And sometimes I think it's so damned unfair. That there's something in my own body turned against me . . . And then I remember what happened to you, and what I did, and I get that same feeling all over again . . . like somehow I'm being punished." It was something she had never said to anyone, not even Alan, but it was the first thing which had come to her mind, sitting in her internist's office at Bethesda, when he'd first spoken that awful word, "malig-

177

nancy." (Odd, she thought, they never said "cancer" anymore . . .) And it had returned to her mind nearly every day since.

He came to her side then, his face twisted with concern, appalled that she had lived with that thought for so long. "Margaret . . ."

She shook her head. "I know its absurd, but I just can't stop thinking it."

"Margaret," he said, "it's forgiven. I let go of the anger years ago." He paused, holding her hands in his strong, roughened fingers—fingers that had been so smooth, so unworked, when she had known him first—looking into her face and trying to find words that could erase that guilt, erase even its memory.

At length he said, "Yes, there was a time when I gorged myself on bitterness and self-pity. But then I came to know someone who had every reason to curse fate, to feel punished—and yet he accepted all that life had to offer, with gratitude and love."

"Vincent," said Margaret, remembering the strange inhuman face, and the way the world would treat a man who looked like that.

Jacob nodded. "Vincent," he said softly.

She whispered, "We must do that, too."

For a moment they embraced, desperately, hopelessly, as if he could hold her physically to him; as if, Orpheus-like, he could with the songs of memory keep her truly out of the grave. Then he sighed, and let the thought go. Time goes on, and one can either curse the river and die, or take what it brings. "I will miss you, Margaret."

She smiled, and drew her hands from his. "Come on, Jacob. Let's walk some more."

A week later the moon shone full, edging the clouds that parted around it with a rim of unearthly silver and spangling the new leaves of the park as if strange, bright coins, and not rain, had fallen earlier in the night. The rain-smell, the spring-smell, was a living whisper in the air, and the light from within Catherine's apartment made pale squares on the asphalt of the terrace and shimmered like the moonlight on the silk of her robe. Vincent's voice in the darkness was quiet, no more than part of the beauty of the night.

"Margaret said that the last seven days were the happiest of her life."

Catherine sighed, leaning against the frame of the French door, thinking about that photograph, about that beautiful girl and the worn face of the woman she had seen, and all the years wasted in between.

"How is Father?" she asked, remembering the gray old man who had parted from her on the subway steps, the sad wisdom in his eyes.

"Healing," said Vincent softly. "Alone. Grateful."

She shook her head, feeling again what she had felt ever since the night in the library when she had learned the story, the sense of sorrow for that old tragedy, the sense of things that had been taken away which could never be replaced. "It's so sad," she said. "To have had a beginning, and an end . . . and all the time in the middle, empty. Time is all we have, Vincent . . ."

"They had seven days," he said, and there was a wistfulness in his voice.

She stepped forward, into the sheltering circle of his arm, understanding what he meant. Seven days, she thought, her head pressed to the strength of his chest, was not so bad . . . This collection of stolen hours, strung like shining pearls in her memory, was not so bad, considering how easily she could have missed it—considering how little so many people had. It was what they would always have, no matter what befell; hours that would always be theirs. You cannot change the past, she thought. That was its curse, and that was its eternal joy.

Thirteen

MARCH gave place to April. Spring came to New York. *The time for lovers* . . . Margaret had written, all those springs ago.

Catherine thought of her often, those crystalline days, the nights when some quality of the air, some sense of everything being balanced on the point of some new and unthought-of wonder, made sleep impossible . . .

And she would remember that faded, beautiful woman whom she had met so briefly in that opulent penthouse apartment, and wonder how Father was doing, and what was taking place in the world Below.

She attended her father's fund raiser for the Chamber Music Society, and thought of Vincent as she leaned against one of the ornamental pillars which demarcated the formal dining-room of her father's townhouse flat from the living-room, listening to the string quartet execute a flirty Mozart aria . . . wishing he could be there to hear. Later she learned that Elliot Burch, in spite of not having been invited, had sent her father a very large check for the society, and was illogically furious.

"Maybe the man just likes Mozart," pointed out Edie a few days later, extracting a french fry from the heap on the plate between them and daubing it in the ketchup. Catherine, who'd ordered one of Tummy Time's notorious salads and was regretting it, said nothing, but her lips tightened . . . from across the room at the counter, a woman's voice floated over to them: *If I'm not losing money and nobody's died I figure I'm ahead of the game* . . .

Edie shrugged at her friend's silence, went on, "I mean, the man's always making the newspapers for passing out money to some worthy cause."

"That's just it," sighed Catherine. "He always *did* come across as an idealist, a crusader. A man who . . ." She paused, and shook her head, brushing back her hair from her forehead with one hand. "I don't know. I just felt . . . betrayed."

Edie studied her for a moment, her great brown eyes with their smoky whites filled with concern. "Well, honey," she said after a time, "the world's full of men handing out what they think women want . . . and full of women who let 'em get away with it. And they all pretty generally get what they deserve." She turned the french fry over thoughtfully in her fingers. "On the other hand," she added, deadpan, "you could have passed that lobster on to some of the rest of us poor peons instead of just sending the guy away . . ."

And Catherine laughed and threw a packet of salt at her, and the conversation turned to other things.

In those spring days Catherine was hard put to find time to visit Isaac Stubbs' Academy of Self-Defense, but the tough, broken-nosed street-fighter seemed always glad to see her, always willing to teach, whether she showed up with her sweats in her briefcase at five-thirty in the wet, freezing mornings or at nine at night under the glare of the steel overhead lamps. "The point is that you do it," he said, wiping the sweat from his ugly, shining black face. "You come in when you can, whenever you can . . . these people who take two lessons in Egg Foo Yung and think they can defend themselves are in for a hell of a surprise."

After which he proceeded to beat the hell out of her, driving her back into a corner of the big cement loft and attacking her, attacking her, not letting her out until she came after him with everything she had, with cold and calculating and ferocious rage.

"Damn those schoolmarms who told you never to raise your voice," he snarled at her, dodging, faking, striking while she strove and sweated to defend herself. "Make some noise, God damn it . . . I'm tryin' to kill you! Yell at me!"

And she yelled, roaring as she had heard Vincent roar when he had fought to defend her, an animal sound that broke the strangling restraints of twenty-seven years of polite upbringing as she lunged at him, smothering his attacks in an attack of her own, caring for nothing except his defeat.

"Not bad," he said later, when they were sitting, getting their breath back, in the little corner of his loft that he'd fixed up as a sitting-room, with a couple of old gray couches and his iaido swords on the wall, and the single graceful bronze of a woman that was one of his prized possessions. "You keep at it, Cat, and you'll get the technique—you got the spirit, and that's the thing that can't be taught. You ever watched an animal fight?"

And Catherine hesitated, then nodded slowly. As as child she had always been frightened of violence, avoiding it by making herself the sweetest and most compliant of girls—avoiding confrontation of any kind by making herself as perfect, as beautiful, as nice as she could.

Isaac took a pull at the beer he'd opened for himself, and went on, "I don't mean that circling and waiting animals do—I mean when they finally get

183

down to real fighting. They don't worry about timing or strategy or what-the-hell-comes next. They go in fast and they don't think about nothing but getting the job done. That's what's scary about a police dog, or even an alleycat: they don't care who you are or how big you are; they got nothin' in 'em that thinks about what happens if they lose. They're gonna do it or die trying."

Catherine nodded again, not speaking, thinking of Vincent—of the times he had fought to defend her. It was the side of him that was not human, the beast side of him, powerful and innocent as a hunting lion; the side of him that would do anything, unthinkingly and to the limit of his life, to keep her from coming to harm.

It was a side of him that she understood, after a fashion—but it was not until that month that she came to learn, terrifyingly, how much of that single-minded instinct lay within her as well.

Father's recovery from Margaret's death was slow. The joy that had purged away the last of the old sorrow had been followed, Vincent thought, too swiftly by the sorrow of her loss, and for weeks the old man kept to his chamber, reading or meditating, playing endless, nearly wordless, games of chess with Vincent or working on his maps far into the lamp-lit nights. Vincent knew that this mourning was in itself healing, and kept a judicious distance, saying little, sometimes only sitting with him for hours in silence.

By the time that Mouse's latest transgression forced the summoning of a council-meeting of the entire community Father was recovered enough to preside over it, but standing quietly under the spiral of the twisted iron stair, Vincent thought that Father looked older than he had, grayer and tireder and more stooped.

His voice, however, had its old crisp note as he said, looking over the tops of his reading glasses at the culprit before him, "You've broken our rules, not once but time and time again."

Mary, standing to Father's right in her homespun gray gown, looked unhappy; Winslow, to Father's left, folded his massive arms and looked grim. The other members of the community were silent, gathered along the gallery above, sitting on the dais of the vestibule or its short flight of steps, standing grouped around the walls. Even the chiming of the pipes had stilled, for Pascal sat hunched like a bony cricket in his reddish mantle at the top of the gallery steps, his stethoscope hanging like a bizarre medallion around his neck. Below him the curve of the iron staircase was thick with children, sitting between and among the piles of Father's books heaped there: Kipper, his too-big cap jammed down on his black curls; Dustin; Eric and Ellie, silent and a little awed at this, their first meeting as members of the community; even Alex and Jeannie, the youngest of the Tunnel children but already old hands at sitting quiet and following as much of the discussion as they could. They knew, at least, that it concerned Mouse, who made toys for them . . . and that Mouse was in serious trouble.

"Your repeated forays Above put all of us at risk," Father went on sternly. "You've been warned again and again and yet you've persisted in this wilful course of action."

There was a murmur from those who grouped around the walls and along the book-cluttered gallery. Since Jonathan Thorpe's invasion of the tunnels with his gun, many of them had become uneasy about contact of any kind with the world Above.

They had been reminded of how fragile their secret world was, and in many ways it had drawn them closer together. But many were troubled about how easily the way they lived could be taken away from them by a careless act.

"Do you have anything to say in your own defense?"

Mouse, standing in front of Father's octagonal conference table, looked around the circle with a puzzled expression in his guileless blue eyes. "Why's everyone getting so upset?" he wanted to know. Vincent sighed inwardly and shook his head.

"Mouse," said Father, "you've been *stealing*."

"Not stealing," argued Mouse logically. "Taking." He shrugged. "Just stuff. Needed it, found it, took it . . ."

"From a warehouse!" pointed out Winslow.

"That's where the stuff was," agreed Mouse, surprised that he'd need to tell him so, and Winslow rolled his eyes heavenward in a mute plea for strength. "Lots there," he added. "Won't even miss it. Left plenty, too," he concluded, proud of his own restraint.

Father's voice was taut. "That's not the issue."

"You set off a burglar alarm!" added Winslow.

Mouse nodded, brow furrowing with the unpleasant memory. "Very noisy," he agreed. "New kind. Tricked me. Won't happen again."

Mary was looking worried. Vincent guessed she was thinking about Mouse spending the night—or a weekend—or two-to-five—locked up in some cement blockhouse Above with the worst scum of a world he barely comprehended. Winslow, his dark face turning even darker, was clearly thinking about the kind of information Mouse was likely to blither about the Tunnels to all and sundry on his way there.

To Father, the big blacksmith said in disgust, "He hasn't heard a thing we've said."

"Heard everything," protested Mouse indignantly. "Lot of silly noise. Everyone takes stuff from Up Top. That's what Up Top is there for."

"Mouse," pointed out Father patiently, though Vincent suspected by his tone he knew it was hopeless, "there's a difference between foraging and stealing. We take those things the world above has cast off. We accept what is given to us freely by our Helpers above. But we *do not steal*."

"Not *stealing*," insisted Mouse. "*Taking*. Using. Couldn't wait. Needed elevator cable, hydraulics . . . big project."

"What big project?" demanded Winslow. "No one was told anything about a big project."

"Winslow's mad," grinned Mouse at this display of temper. "No one got his permission . . ."

"Mouse . . ." Father removed his square-lensed reading glasses and turned them over in one shabbily-gloved hand. "We live down here, too. It would have been nice to consult us, don't you think?"

Mouse scuffed with one toe of his furry boot. "Would have ruined the surprise." Vincent was ruefully amused to see that he *did* understand that—the keeping of a secret from those who had a right to know it clearly loomed larger in his mind than his attempted theft as an infraction of the rules.

"It's my fault, Father." Jamie stepped forward from where she'd been sitting on the steps leading down from the vestibule, her hands in the pockets of her quilted vest, her fair hair dyed honey-gold by the soft flutter of the candlelight. "You know that old iron ladder down by the Pipe Chamber? It's all rusted out, and that's a hell of a climb when you're carrying something. I asked Mouse if there wasn't some way he could fix something, to make the climb easier . . ."

"Moving ladder," said Mouse eagerly, his hands sweeping the air, gesturing the schematic of the thing in his mind. "You'll see! Run it off water power, all hydraulic. Just hop on, ride it down . . . hop on, ride it up . . ."

"But it still does not excuse stealing!"

"Not *stealing!*" Mouse looked baffled by this display of deliberate obtuseness. "*Taking!*"

Father sighed in genuine distress. He'd had this discussion with Mouse a dozen times in private, and knew Mouse didn't understand and wouldn't understand—perhaps couldn't understand. But that fact changed nothing of the seriousness of last night's excursion. If they didn't want to have a squad of New York's Finest poking around in the steam-tunnels something would have to be done, and done quickly.

Still, the punishment for repeatedly breaking the rules was something he wouldn't wish upon anyone. He looked uneasily around at the circle of faces in the lamplight—young and old, black and brown and yellow and white, the soft, washed-out colors of their makeshift clothing all tinted by the perpetual hazy amber of firelight which had never, he thought, quite replaced the brightness of the sunlit upper world . . .

And for an instant the memory of Margaret came back to him, Margaret in the bright Parisian morning, a mingling of exquisite joy and pain. Mouse had made an automatic water-pitcher-pourer for her, that last week, after she'd taken to her bed for what was to be the final time. It had never misfired in the same fashion twice and watching each fresh mechanical catastrophe had been a source of never-ending, appalled delight for them both.

"I suppose it's time, then," he said. "Mouse has admitted the charge . . ." Mouse opened his mouth to protest, but Father's voice rode inexorably over his. "Those who favor imposing the punishment, please so indicate."

There was a hesitation, a stirring in the crowd. Those who had been sitting rose slowly, like Father, remembering all Mouse's kindness, all his help . . . but like Father all too aware of where his continued forays into warehouses and construction-shacks would eventually lead. His face resolute, Winslow turned his broad back on Mouse. Slowly, after long deliberation, others followed suit. Some did so with glances of apology, others, not able to meet his eyes. Mary remained facing him, her lined face filled with compassion and the desire to believe that this time he'd keep one of his promises. Jamie, and Vincent, and a small handful of others did so too. A little to Vincent's surprise, Cullen was one of those voting for the punishment. But then, Cullen had been burned the worst in the incident of the pirate treasure—it had left him gun-shy about anything to do with the world Above.

And after a long moment, Father, too, turned away.

Mouse stood alone in the center of the big candle-lit chamber, arms folded and shoulders hunched, drawn in on himself like a wounded animal, hurt and uncomprehending. A subway rumbled by overhead and the silence in its wake lay heavy as lead.

In time, Father turned back. "Mouse, I'm sorry," he said. "But since you refuse to listen, perhaps our silence will teach you the lesson our words could not. For one month, no man, woman, or child among us will speak to you. The sentence will begin . . ." He paused, knowing that once he had spoken it would be a violation of his own authority to go back upon it, ". . . now."

There was a long moment of absolute stillness, while Mouse looked swiftly, hopefully around the circle of faces, puzzled and scared and not wanting to believe his friends would really do such a thing to him. As the crowd began to disperse, making their way slowly through the little vestibule and out into the tunnel of the Long Gallery and so to their own chambers, their voices were a soft murmur among themselves, but none of them looked at him, or spoke to him, or acknowledged his existence even when he called out their names.

"Joke, right?" he pleaded. "Okay good, okay fine . . . Pascal . . . !"

But Pascal averted his eyes and moved through the stone archway, anxious to return to the simplicities of the Pipe Chamber he loved. Mouse caught at others as they passed, the hope in his face turning to fear. "Cullen . . . say something . . . Kipper . . . Jamie!" He seized her arm, holding her back. "Big joke, huh? *You* were on my side . . ."

The slender girl looked helplessly across at him—for they were of a height, like brother and sister in their blonde fairness—with her great eyes full of tears. Then in silence she pulled her arm free and turned away. Desperate, Mouse reached to stop her, but Vincent stepped between them, and Jamie, head bowed, hugging herself in her quilted vest, slipped away through the door.

"Vincent!" Mouse pleaded, frantic. "Vincent breaks their stupid rules, too . . ." He looked up into his friend's face, begging him to acknowledge. "Vincent's my friend. Found me, caught me, brought me here . . . read to me, talked to me . . . Talk to me now, Vincent . . ."

But the rules could not be broken—the more so

because they were all that the community Below had. Hurting for his friend's sense of abandonment and confusion, Vincent looked at him for a long moment, trying to tell him with his eyes that he was still his friend . . . and then turned away.

"Vincent, too . . ." whispered Mouse, as if Vincent had struck him. Then, hurt and furious, he whirled and dove for the doorway, shoving those still in the passage outside as he dashed through, and away into the dark.

"You wanted to see me?" Catherine asked, cautiously opening the door to Joe Maxwell's office—cautiously, because the dartboard was about three feet from the door and his aim wasn't nearly as good as he liked to think it was. As she'd suspected, he was sitting, jacket off, feet on desk, tie at half-mast, lobbing darts at the board—which for once didn't have anyone's picture on it. He stood as she entered, his boyish face grave and a little sour.

"Yeah," he said awkwardly, and Catherine thought, *Oh, great, he's going to hand me something nobody else wants to touch* . . . She knew the look. "Come on in."

"What is it?" She stood before his desk, neat and slender in her teal-blue silk shirt and trousers. Morning sunlight slanted through the Venetian blinds of the office window and splashed across the desk's surface, which as usual gave the impression of a government records-office recently sacked by terrorists.

Joe sighed glumly. "The Avery case."

Inwardly Catherine groaned, *Oh, God, not another witness backing out* . . . But she shouldn't recall that at this point they even *had* a witness.

Joe got to his feet and started pacing, summarizing from habit what they both already knew. "Max Avery's as dirty as they come," he said, with a gesture reminiscent of the city courtroom. "I know it, you know it, the guy that sells hotdogs across the street knows it, only nobody can prove it. We've already talked to Waldrop, Snodgrass and Mertens, and a dozen others that we know damn well have paid off to keep their buildings going. Want to know what we got?"

And he perched on a corner of his desk and made a big "zip" sign with thumb and forefinger. Catherine nodded, remembering her own frustrations in just collecting data for the case and feeling, for a moment, before things clicked together in her mind, only the impersonal anger at Avery, at a world where such a man could exist . . .

And then she thought, *Why is he trying to convince me?* Suspicion flooded her, suspicion that exploded into certainty as Joe's dark eyes slipped aside from hers. "Moreno thinks you . . . Well, there's one major developer who hasn't given us a flat-out 'no' . . ."

Anger hit her, hot rage so intense that it crinkled the muscles of her scalp. "No," she said quietly. "Don't ask me, Joe, don't even think it."

He gestured helplessly. "Gimme a break, Radcliffe. You think I want to do this? I just work here." His voice took on a false-jolly note, as if to say, *Hey, it's no big deal* . . . "Just have a little talk with Elliot Burch . . ."

Catherine's voice turned icy cold. "My relationship with Elliot Burch was personal," she said, surprised at how level it sounded. "Not to mention painful. And it's in the past tense."

"Take it easy," urged Joe, knowing he was doing a dirty and illogically wishing that she'd make it easier on him by not taking it so hard. "We're asking you to interview the guy, not have his children. If Burch talks, we can put Avery away."

"Well, then subpoena him."

"He's got an army of lawyers, he can stonewall and tie us up for years . . ."

Catherine's lips tightened in fury. She had encountered Burch's army of lawyers before.

"But he'll talk to you."

"And what makes you think that?"

Joe sighed, knowing the murder had to come out sometime. "Because he told us so." And, seeing the hard white look around her mouth as she bit back remarks better left unsaid, he added, "Personally, I think it stinks, but there it is."

Easy for you to say, she thought bitterly as she left his office to storm in frozen silence back to her own cubicle. *You're not the one who made a fool of herself falling in love with the man.*

If it had been love, she thought later, staring at the outside of the folder Joe had had sent over to her desk, the folder marked AVERY and containing all those reports of on-the-job injuries of those who tried to buck the kickbacks, all those informants who changed their minds after receiving things in the mail like the severed ear of the family dog and a note, *We know where your daughter goes to school* . . .

She owed it to herself, she knew—she owed it to them—to do whatever would get Avery behind bars.

Even letting Elliot Burch get the chance he'd been angling for all these months, the chance to justify himself—the chance to see her again.

Had it been love?

Catherine wasn't sure.

Ending it had hurt like hell. Going to his office and coldly informing him that she knew he was the man angling to buy that old rent-controlled building in Chelsea, that it was his money paying the goons who beat up the old people for refusing to move out . . . that she was going to institute a full investigation. She'd walked calmly out through the gaggle of reporters in the outer office and had calmly taken the elevator down to the street. It was only when she'd walked away, holding her coat about her in the sharp February wind, that she'd started to cry.

Did the pain she'd felt then, the agony of betrayal and hurt she'd experienced when she'd first learned who was paying Mundy Security, mean love?

She didn't know. She had always been of two minds about Elliot Burch.

That he had loved her—still loved her—she had no doubt. They'd met at a gallery-opening at the Met, to celebrate his donation of a collection of abstract paintings, including two of Picasso's vivid, fragmented figure-studies, and in the short weeks that followed he had made a determined, but oddly boyish, effort to sweep her off her feet.

And a part of her had wanted to be swept.

It had been a time of doubt for her, a time of wondering just where her love for Vincent could possibly go. She was not a part of his world—could not be even without Father's disapproval, if she wished to carry on the work with the DA to which she felt more and more committed each day—and he could never be a part of hers. When she was with him, when they shared those quiet evenings on the terrace, she felt utterly right, utterly at peace. But in the daylight hours, doubt would creep in. *Let's be practical about this, Cath . . .*

But was it practicality or fear of a situation which she could not control? The intensity of her feelings for Vincent frightened her—the practical side of her, the lawyer side, fought the deep need for him as surely as the debutante still lurking within her fought the idea of roaring like a beast and tearing into Isaac with teeth and nails.

And then Elliot had come along. Undeniably

handsome, with his light-green eyes and smooth brown hair, the wide lips that promised sensuality at odds with his controlled neatness, the straight nose and cleft chin and slim, muscular swimmer's body. Humorous and cheerful, appreciative of the classical music she loved though his own tastes ran to show tunes and certain types of jazz, taking a delight equal to hers in the ever-changing silly wonder of the New York streets . . . Rich, and generous—though he'd never, she thought now with an involuntary smile, given her anything quite so spectacular as a seventeenth-century necklace out of a pirate's hoard . . .

Her father had been discreetly thrilled. He tried not to show it, remembering her fury during her debutante days when he'd try to hint her toward "suitable" marriages, but she could tell. And indeed, she thought, why shouldn't he be? "He got a darker brother?" Edie had asked, with frank unrancorous envy.

How could she explain to them—how could she explain to him—that she loved someone else? Someone with whom there was no hope of a future—someone whom they would never see? She still had trouble dealing with that one herself.

Vincent had said simply, "Follow your heart," accepting that her heart might very well lead her away from him forever. He had known, too, that the sensible thing for her to do would be to leave him, to marry a man of her own world, a man who would cherish her, whose company she enjoyed, a man she could live with . . .

It would help, she had thought, exhausted, if she knew in which direction her heart wanted to go. But she hadn't.

The hurt of their breakup still rankled, made worse by his telephone messages, his maneuverings to get her back, to force her to see him again. He was an ambitious man and would stop at nothing, let nothing stand in the way of getting what he wanted.

What made her angrier still was that he'd known just how to get to her, after all, as he'd known just who to call when he wanted a group of people on fixed incomes to leave their homes and friends and drastically lower their standard of living for his convenience. In letting him get as close to her as she had, she had handed that power to him, had as much as told him that she was dedicated enough to her work to do almost anything to get an extortionist like Max Avery behind bars.

Even, she thought, getting wearily to her feet and collecting briefcase, scarf, and her long blue coat for the brief bus ride to his offices, *see him again.*

Fourteen

"Am I disturbing you?" asked Vincent softly.

Father looked up from the kaleidoscope into which he had been looking. The brass tube, with its complex of inner prisms and mirrors, bound around with iron and copper wire and bands of various kinds of metals, was mounted on a smooth oak stand so that it faced a small lamp, whose light gave life and brilliance to the changing flower-patterns of the colored glass within.

"No," he sighed, and put the beautiful little implement from him. "No, I was just . . . just . . ."

Vincent touched the brass tube with fingers surprisingly light and gentle for their fearsome appearance. "I remember when Mouse made this for you," he said, tilting his head a little, his mane a long tangle of saffron over the shoulders of his short leather vest. He was glad to see that Father looked much more his old self, as if the exercise of his responsibility for the community at large had gone far toward healing that terrible wound in his heart. "His tube of colors . . . all the colors we lacked. The colors of the world above."

Father nodded, smiling at the recollection. In all the years he had been Below—in all the years Vincent had known him—he had spoken seldom of his longing for the world he had left. But Mouse could be surprisingly sensitive to nuances of inflection and tone, and must have heard it in his voice, when he had described the places he had been—must have realized, as Father had not, that he invariably described them in terms of color and light, colors so different from the soft hues of candleflame and lamplight with which they lived. And he had given him this.

"I was afraid he'd stolen it," Father remembered, his hand, in its fingerless brown glove, stroking the careful workmanship of the kalidoscope's carved base, the delicate soldering along the seam. "He promised me solemnly that he'd made it himself. He was ten years old at the time . . ."

Ten years old, remembered Vincent. Still feral, wild, almost never speaking. After Vincent had caught him in the tunnels and begun patiently, gently to tame him, it had been nearly a year before he had spoken at all. Then for weeks he would only parrot all that Vincent said.

"I was very touched," added Father, with a rueful smile. "And then I found out that he'd stolen the parts." And he laughed, remembering, too, that scruffy little boy, blue eyes bright as an animal's under the wild shock of his sandy hair, ready to flinch and run if one only extended a hand . . .

The first thing he'd said on his own, if Father remembered correctly, was when he'd reached out to pat Vincent's sleeve, and had muttered, "Vincent—friend." His smile faded.

"You were silent in the circle today."

"I had nothing to say," replied Vincent slowly, settling himself in the great chair of leather strapwork which stood beside the table. On the carved sideboard behind him a band of candles burned, their fluttering light picking sharp glints in the buckles of his vest and belt and boots, leaving his deep-set blue eyes in shadow. "The problem is a grave one . . ."

"You disagree with what we did?" Father had not missed it when Mouse had turned hopelessly to Vincent, had cried, *You break their stupid rules, too . . .* There was, in fact, no rule against going Above— people did it all the time on foraging expeditions— but Mouse knew perfectly well how deep Father's objections were to Vincent's friendship with someone who was a part of the world Above. And, Vincent knew, with every good reason in the world. His visits were fairly regular, and growing more frequent as their friendship, their love, deepened. Each visit increased the chances of being seen, of drawing attention to the world Below.

At length Vincent sighed, and shook his head. "It troubles me," he said. "The Silence can be terrible."

And more terrible, thought Father, for Mouse. He remembered how the young man's shock and hurt when Cullen had stabbed him over the gold had had nothing to do with the wound itself—it was the fact that Cullen would hurt him which had left the scar.

"Not half so terrible as what he'd suffer if he were ever caught Up Top," he said, thinking of his own two nights in the New York City jail. Horrible as they had been, as an older man, a man who had lived in the world Above, he had had enough experience to keep quiet and stay out of everybody's way. For a boy like Mouse . . .

"No," he said, turning aside from the thought. "We did the right thing. But that does not make it any easier to live with."

Vincent nodded, though it still troubled him. For all his brashness, Mouse had a curious streak of sensitivity, almost more animal than human. Silence, to him, meant other things . . . the years of darkness and fear from which Vincent had rescued him, the years of lonliness.

"Father . . . !" At the sound of the girl Ellie's voice from the tunnel Vincent swung around, hearing in it, and in the swift tread of her running feet, barely controlled panic. She burst into the chamber, the curly ends of her brown braids slapping her shoulders, her freckled face tight. There was mud on her dress of worn white sacking, the thin bluish mud characteristic of the deeper levels near the quicksand-filled South Pockets. She nearly fell against Father, clutching at his arm.

"Come quick! It's Eric . . . he fell . . ."

"Where?" Father came around from behind the table, his eyes sharp with fear—there were places in the Tunnels where a fall could be a terrible thing.

She hesitated, not wanting to admit it, but knowing she must get help. "The Maze," she said.

Father was appalled. "You *know* the Maze is dangerous! That whole area is saturated by ground water, the walls are unstable . . . there are warnings posted and I *know* that Mary has told you to stay away from there a thousand times."

Ellie looked unhappy as Father turned swiftly to gather up his stick and his old black medical bag. "We were playing hide-and-seek," she blurted unhappily, and Vincent felt a pang of sympathy for her. Father had told *all* the children a thousand times not to play there, and had done so for thirty years, and Vincent wondered if he were aware of just how seldom he was ever heeded when he did so. The Maze was such a wonderful place to play, with its vast, echoing caverns, its myriads of tiny passageways and hidey-holes seemingly designed for games. He remembered a time when he and Devin had sneaked there to play, and a minor rockslip had trapped his legs—Devin had spent six and a half hours patiently digging him out of the debris, his hands frozen and bleeding, and then had had to drag and carry him back to his rooms. Since he had been an adult Vincent had joined his voice to Father's unceasing chorus of warnings, but knew full well that he wasn't obeyed, either.

Ellie's voice was shaky with unshed tears. "Kipper *told* him not to climb up there, he told him . . ."

Vincent knelt at her side. "It's all right, Ellie," he said gently. "Can you take us to him?"

"Yes, quickly," said Father, kindling a lantern from one of the candles on the table and handing it to Vincent. "That area's dangerous—we've no time to lose."

The Maze itself lay far outside the purlieu of those who had gone to dwell in the Tunnels, outside even the perimeter of most patrols. The little community of the Tunnels tended to cluster fairly close to one another among the twisting corridors of the old steam-pipes, subway tunnels, and water-mains, within the ring of the gates and bars set up over the years against incursion from without. Within those boundaries, the young adults of the community, men and women, took their turns at walking patrol, checking the gates and renewing the torches and lanterns which burned where the tunnels crossed— even outside the ring the main lines of communication to the ways Down used by the Helpers were frequently kept lit.

But the tunnels that connected to the Maze led downward. They dropped below the level of the subway lines, even the deep-dug Broadway Local, down through faults and fissures in the Manhattan bedrock, where there were few of the curving concrete walls of human construction, and where the clanging of the pipes faded to a distant mutter in the dark. Even in these deeper labyrinths occasional torches flickered in makeshift sconces, for Vincent knew full well that Father and his people were not the only dwellers Below and liked to keep some kind of illumination in even the most deserted places. But as Ellie led them deeper, for the most part the bobbing glow of his lantern was the only relief in the utter darkness, gleaming softly on the unshaped rock of the walls.

The way to the Maze led through old water-tunnels, decaying canyons of gray granite which narrowed and widened erratically, sometimes lowering above their heads so that Vincent had to duck his great height to pass beneath, sometimes vanishing into an eerie slot of whispering shadow above. Now and then they passed through caverns alive with the muffled gurgle of underground streams, or smelling of black, silent ponds or bogs where the niter glowed blue and eerie upon the dripping walls, a reminder that the water which had shaped these places still moved there. More clearly than the distant rattle of the deeper subway lines, they heard the groaning of the strange winds of the underworld, hair-raisingly human, like the cries of souls who had somehow lost their way on the road to Hell.

At length they came to the warnings Father had posted, old signs painted on the rock of the walls and renewed a number of times as the trickle of ground water had decayed them: KEEP OUT. DANGER. A torch burned over each sign—Vincent, in his endless patrols of the deeper tunnels, saw to it that they were always renewed. A little beyond that, the Maze itself began.

"It's this way," whispered Ellie, ducking through a narrow side-tunnel whose entrance was marked in the chalk that all the children carried. Father grumbled a little, turning sideways to squeeze his bulk through the constricted place. The long walk had tired his bad leg, and he moved more slowly and stiffly than usual. Vincent, holding his lantern high, brought up the rear, edging carefully along the descending seam. He had feared the children had taken this way into the Maze—there were half a dozen entrances into various parts that most of the children knew about, and two or three more besides, but to this portion of the Maze he knew only this one.

That was, alas, one of the things which made it so much fun.

As Vincent remembered it had, the narrow way dead-ended in a blank wall, pierced by a low-set hole where some long-ago stream had carved a crawlspace, perhaps a yard high, through the wall of harder rock that enclosed the maze's windings. "Through here," said Ellie, ducking down and vanishing like a rabbit into its burrow.

Father rolled his eyes, as if he should have known it would come to this, and Ellie's head appeared a moment later, clay daubing her braids. "It's only a little crawl," she pointed out, with childish impatience, and vanished again.

"Only a little crawl . . ." muttered Father, handing Vincent his bag and his stick and getting to his knees with difficulty. As Vincent helped Father down he glanced over his shoulder back up the seam behind him. The place had always made him uneasy, his instincts telling him, even when he'd come here as a child to play, that there was danger here. The rock, he knew now from studying geological surveys of the island, was decayed and friable. There had been a bad flood the previous winter when a water-main broke that had further weakened portions of these walls. Still, when Father vanished through the hole he tucked the bag under his arm and followed.

As Vincent had suspected, the children had been playing in the big chamber they called the Dungeon, whose high walls were honeycombed with a network of tiny tunnels, like capillaries, winding around and providing a very satisfactory succession of hiding-places. He and Devin and the other children of their age—Mitch, Alys, Candy, and others—had, after overdosing on Kipling's *Jungle Books*, played stalking games here, climbing the ledges on the towering walls and dropping onto each other in the character of Bagheera the Black Panther slaughtering deer (or defending the Jungle against the evil hunters of the Raj); or sometimes they were Lord John Roxton evading hordes of ape-men in the volcanic holes beneath the Lost World of Maple White Land, or John Carter battling Tharks and Warhoons for his very life.

It was easy to guess what Eric and the others had been doing. A pale shear-scar showed where a rock ledge had given way, twenty feet up the wall—pieces of rock lay around the shallow, uneven funnel of the chamber's floor. Among them, close by the giant rock column whose shadow had always provided such a wonderful cover for ambushing whomever tried to leave by the little crawl-hole, Kipper knelt, with Eric's head in his lap. Kipper was shivering, for he'd taken off his heavy vest to wrap it around Eric's legs. Eric, fair and skinny and small for eight, looked even weedier with his thin, bespectacled face drawn in an effort not to show pain. His patched green sweater was damp on one sleeve and shoulder, for when he'd fallen he'd rolled into one of the pools of stagnant water which dotted the dungeon's floor. There were more of them than Vincent remembered—the center of the chamber had been dry when he'd played there as a child, and now a sheet of water about eight feet across lay there, gleaming in the lantern-light like polished lead. The dim rushings and drippings of water behind the walls came to his sensitive hearing in a disquieting murmur. The stalagmites rising like wavery columns and stalactites hanging like the white teeth of a shark high overhead gleamed wetly, and were patched here and there with niter and whitish lichens; the air smelled of damp. Kipper, remembering Father's cautions about first aid, had taken off his jacket to keep Eric warm.

"It's all right, Eric," said Father gently, kneeling beside the two boys in the wavering lantern-light. Vincent held the lamp down low over them as Father removed the boy's shoe and gently began to manipulate his ankle. "What happened here?"

"The rock broke," whispered Eric, his voice shaky with pain and fear.

"These stones are not as strong as they look, Eric," said Vincent softly, the echoes of his voice muttering away in the vaulted chamber's ceiling overhead. "See how damp the walls are? The same water that carved the Maze eats away at those rocks . . ."

"Which is *precisely* why none of you were supposed to be down here in the first place," added Father, with acerbity. Looking down over his shoulder, Vincent could see how swollen Eric's foot was, though not particularly discolored. A break, he knew, would turn blue, if only in a small spot sometimes, almost at once.

"You're a lucky boy, Eric," added Father, a little more kindly, seeing how white Eric's face looked in the lantern-light, how it gleamed with perspiration in spite of the cold. "It's a bad sprain, but I don't think anything is broken. Vincent . . ."

Vincent handed him his bag. The old man opened it, pulled out a roll of thick, knitted bandage and, as Vincent held the lantern over his hands to illuminate what he did, bound it in a neat, competent X-dressing to support the ankle. As Father worked Vincent heard from somewhere beyond the walls a kind of wet clatter, as of stones falling—truly, he thought uneasily, the place was unsafe, far less safe than it had been even fifteen years ago . . . not that it had been any Rock of Gibraltar even then . . .

"There," said Father, affixing a final safety pin. "Kipper, Ellie, help him—gently, try not to put any weight on it, that's right . . ."

And suddenly, beneath them, the floor moved. In the swaying lantern-light Vincent saw the walls lurch, as a torrent of dust and debris poured down on them from above—with a second jolt he seemed to hear, in the darkness around them, the terrible, sliding grind of huge masses of rock shifting.

"I want this place sealed up!" cried Father, scrambling awkwardly to his feet, his stick slipping on the rock. "It's too dangerous . . ."

Another lurch loosened bigger chunks of rock from the blackness above, and Vincent realized this was no minor slippage, but the prelude to a major fall. Father shouted "Go! Hurry up, kids, now!" to the three children who still huddled, white-faced with shock and terror, in the shadow of the huge pillar—the whole cavern shuddered convulsively as Kipper, galvanized into sudden action, thrust the other two ahead of him towards the crawlspace. At the same instant, through air suddenly thick with powdery dust, Vincent saw to his horror the giant column which he had always thought of as supporting the ceiling jerk downwards. With a hideous, grating pop the brittle limestone of its tapered base faulted under its own weight and broke, a rain of chunks and dirt pelting from above as its vast top began to rip free of the ceiling which had supported it.

With a gasp Vincent dropped the lantern and lunged forward, catching the column as it began to shift and roll free. Father sprang after him, letting stick and medical bag fall unheeded, adding his strength to Vincent's great power to hold the weight from the children cowering beneath. Vincent yelled "Get away!" as he felt the weight of it lean past its point of balance, start to slide, and, when Kipper hesitated, panic-stricken but unwilling to leave him, he roared at them, baring his fangs in a fury of terror that they would not get through the entry before the column covered it, before the entire ceiling came down.

Terrified into movement once more, the children fled, dragging Eric into the narrow mousehole of a tunnel. "Go, Father . . ." gasped Vincent, fighting desperately as the weight of the column heeled over onto him, more rock raining down around him, the whole chamber shaking as fresh cascades of rock and dust broke free, clogging their lungs, smothering the flames of the broken lantern, promising worse to come.

Whether Father heard him or not Vincent didn't know. He felt the column slide in his grip, heard a dreadful rending, crashing boom in the darkness behind him, the vault of the chamber picking up the echoes in skull-breaking thunder and knew the decayed rock of the Maze was falling in on itself. He cried "Father . . . !" as the great rock toppled, releasing more debris, huge stones from above, then something struck him on the head, and darkness enclosed the chamber like the slamming of the door of a tomb.

Fifteen

CATHERINE entered Elliot Burch's office in a state of icy calm, determined to give him nothing. Elliot, she knew, was a self-made man, an ambitious man who would go to nearly any length to get what he wanted, be it ordering catered lobster lunches brought into the office of a woman who had said she was too busy to go to lunch with him, or having his lawyer hire thugs to beat up the people who wouldn't vacate a building he wanted to tear down. When she would not return his calls—when he could not bribe her father to invite him to the same fundraiser—he had used her sense of decency, her dedication to her job, to get her in here—fine. He'd have his interview, since he was paying for it. And that's all he'd have.

His office was as she remembered it, a beautifully-appointed suite in a building he'd designed himself. After the slick modernism of so many architects' and developers' offices, the room had an Edwardian solidness to it, the graciousness of carved wood paneling and leaded glass windows. The blue-and-brown Picasso on one wall, the long table bearing a model of the high-rise condo complex that was his latest project, were counterpoints rather than anomalies—they had the integral harmony of objects chosen by a man supremely sure of himself.

Like Catherine's former fiancée Tom Gunther, Elliot Burch was a developer who had started as an architect, and he still retained a close hand upon—and a deep, fierce pride in—his buildings. Photographs of them, or framed elevations he had executed himself, dotted the walls. Tom, Catherine had known, had wanted his buildings to be the best because they'd sell the best, because that was a way of becoming known, of being in demand. Elliot wanted them to be the best for their own sake, because they were *his:* his art, his life, and not just the source of his fortune.

She wondered bitterly what he'd done with the model that had been here when first she'd known him three months ago, the vast apartment complex near Madison Square Garden which her investigations had halted stillborn.

"Catherine . . ." He rose from his immense, immaculate oak desk as she entered the office, the doors closing soundlessly behind her. "It's so good to see you again." There was a warm delight in his voice—*As if he's sure all he has to do is smile at me*, she thought angrily, *and say, I'm sorry, honey, these things happen in big business . . .*

He started to come around the corner of the desk to reach for her hands, but she stepped back a little, her eyes forbidding him to take another step towards her, and he stopped. Even the smell of his aftershave brought a stab of feeling to her that was easiest to read as rage.

"Let's skip the amenities, shall we?" she said quietly. "I'm here to talk about Max Avery."

Elliot stood for a long moment, seeing how the land lay. "You're angry," he said at length, his voice steady and his handsome face grave. The impetuousness, the almost adolescent bounciness of his old dealings with her, was absent. "I understand that,

Catherine. You may not believe it, but this is as difficult for me as it is for you."

"Then maybe you should talk to someone less difficult," she replied. "That can be arranged." And she saw that she'd hurt him—or that he wanted her to think so. *No,* she thought. Tom used to play games like that, used that hurt-little-boy look to get her to regret putting him at a distance. *Follow your heart,* Vincent had said, and her heart told her— though she wasn't sure now that she could believe it—that Elliot played cleaner than that . . . at least with people who weren't in his way.

He asked her, "What did I ever do to make you hate me so much?"

"I think we both know the answer to that." Their gazes held for a long moment. Then he stepped back a pace, and gestured her politely to one of his brass-trimmed cordovan chairs. She took it, opening her briefcase and extracting a notebook with a small, steady hand, coolly signifying that if that was the question he'd put the pressure on John Moreno to get her here to ask, he'd asked it and she'd answered it and that was that. "Can we get on with it?"

Whatever else could be said about Elliot Burch— arrogant, single-mindedly selfish about what he wanted to attain—he wasn't stupid. Nor, Catherine had to admit, was he insensitive. He knew when to retreat. He retreated now, to his own comfortable chair opposite her, the great, polished plain of the desk lying like a deserted battlefield between them, unsullied and unoccupied save for a single thick file aligned with compulsive neatness in its exact center. Reaching out, he picked it up, as if he, too, recognized that the part of the interview he'd paid for was over. "It's all here," he said. "Every threat, every bribe, every kickback. Dates, times, amounts. The names of the go-betweens. Enough to put Max

Avery away for twenty years." He placed it on the desk and Catherine reached for it, but he kept his hand there, and his eyes met hers again. "Not yet . . ."

Catherine stood half-risen, as wary as she had been yesterday in combat at Isaac's loft, waiting for his next demand.

"I have something I want to say first."

She settled back into her chair, but her green eyes remained upon him, and her silence was the defensive silence of one who has heard all the arguments before. In their former dealings she knew he was a man who would push, and not stop pushing, and though she was better these days at confrontations than she used to be, she dreaded the clash to come.

But instead of asking why, instead of speaking of what had gone before, Elliot got to his feet and paced to the sideboard, where the brown-and-blue Picasso hung in disquietingly logical splendor—a Cubist exercise in showing several perspectives of the same object at once.

"I've dealt with a dozen Max Averys since I began," he said, like a man recounting the simple facts of his career, without self-justification or apology, simply as facts. "Not because I wanted to. Maybe in your life the choices have all been black and white, but mine have been . . . gray."

Catherine nodded, knowing that what he said was true. Working for the DA's office, she had been made uncomfortably aware of how much her upbringing had sheltered her from the choices people made simply to remain alive, of how easy things were if you had money . . . For no reason, she remembered Vincent telling her about Cullen, who had spent his life waiting for his ship to come in . . . Vincent himself, whose choices were so harshly curtailed by whatever bizarre accident had closed that strange, wise soul in a form automatically feared and despised.

"I wanted to build," went on Elliot, the sudden fervor of an artist in his voice. "And it was easier . . . and cheaper . . . to play ball with Avery than to fight him."

He sighed, and waited a moment for her to speak, but she did not. Whatever she had expected, it had not been this—and she knew from every interview she'd had for the past three months that what he said was true. It was the source of Max Avery's power.

"Maybe you were right to walk away from me when you did," he went on, his light voice deepening with emotion at the memory of that time. "Employees were breaking the law in my name. Things were done that were inexcusable, and ultimately, I'm responsible for that. But Cathy, I didn't know. Maybe I didn't want to know."

She was silent, understanding once again that he was telling the truth.

"My life has been full of regrets." He returned to his desk, standing beside his chair, green eyes carefully matter-of-fact as they looked into hers. "Losing you is one of them. Max Avery is another. All I can say in my own defense is that I've made this city a better place to live."

For people who can afford to pay for it, thought Catherine.

But again she said nothing. It would be an injustice to blame him for it if he had in fact not known. And in fact, she knew from her days of dating him that his projects *had* frequently improved the city . . . anything that improved the housing situation would.

He seated himself again, picked up the file, which she had not touched. "My attorney advised me to shred this." He did not smile at her, but his eyes changed somehow, a kind of hardening of resolution mingled, somehow, with that old impulsiveness, that boundless energy she'd known of old. "I have a new attorney." And he slid the file to her across the desk.

Catherine took it, uncertain. She had expected . . . she wasn't sure what. Maybe a bottle of Dom Perignon and two glasses, a gold bracelet, 'something I thought you'd like . . .' Something, she realized, she could have had contempt for. If this was a bribe, an attempt to buy her affection or even her respect, it was going to come *awfully* expensive for him. And difficult as it was for her to give anything to this man, she knew it was time for her, too, to do justice.

"It may take us months, even years, to put Avery away," she warned him, telling him, she knew, what he already guessed—like the Surgeon General's Warning on a packet of cigarettes. "Until we do, you'll have crews walking out on you, shipments disappearing, every kind of nightmare you ever imagined. Max Avery plays hardball."

"Avery is in a position to cripple four of my current projects," returned Elliot calmly. "He'll cost me millions of dollars. But when it's over, the city will be rid of him. And so will I." He smiled, and the smile did not bode well for Max Avery. "I can play hardball, too."

Catherine put the file into her briefcase, slowly snapped shut the clasps, and sat for a moment, looking at him and thinking that if Elliot were the kind of man he seemed now to be, he'd probably been close to the edge of going up against Avery for some time. The man she had known, the man who'd given so generously to charities, the idealist who wanted to see the world a better place, would have hated paying off an ambulatory snail-track like that for the sake of convenience . . .

But the cost to him, she was aware, was going to be staggering. Compared to it the donation of a gallery full of paintings, Picassos or not, was straight out of petty cash.

And though she had been determined not to give him any opening to her, she could not help asking, "Why, Elliot?"

He replied, very calmly, "Because I'm not one of the bad guys, Cathy—no matter what you think."

Catherine took a cab back down Lafayette Street to the City Building in a troubled frame of mind. Her very real sense of triumph at finally making substantial headway on the Avery case—a sense of having done something to make the world a better place such as she'd *never* had from arguing a really good corporate tort—was underlain by an odd sense of shame at having done an injustice to Elliot Burch.

Thinking about it, she sensed that he truly had not given her the file which weighed so heavy in her briefcase to win her back. He was, she understood now, a crusader at heart, a man whose instinct was to sweep all before him, whether his goal was a woman he loved, or a crook he despised—or a housing project which would open up better living space for hundreds of people. It was entirely possible that he had not known—that his lawyer, a softspoken little man whom Catherine had always disliked, had deliberately kept him in the dark, playing expertly upon an ambitious and idealistic man's desire not to know that a project he treasures is harming others.

Sitting in the back of the cab, she felt embarassed, as if she had thrown a tantrum at a debutante's ball.

And there was something else, she thought—

something . . . She wasn't sure what. A gnawing feeling of something wrong, of disaster . . .

She glanced behind her, and across the street, as she got out and paid off the driver, uneasily aware that the file in her briefcase was damning to a very powerful man who had few scruples about what he did to people who got in his way. Her training in the martial arts had made her sensitive to her instincts.

Yet it didn't feel like immediate danger . . . She didn't know what it felt like.

Joe Maxwell was waiting for her at her cubicle in the bullpen, perched on a corner of her desk with a broad grin on his face amid the chattering chaos of daily business. She'd phoned him from the black marble lobby of Burch's building to tell him she'd gotten the file, and it was he who'd suggested the cab . . . which she'd already decided to use her own money to take, if the department wouldn't pony up.

"If Burch will corroborate on this, I'd say Max Avery is out of the construction business," he said, thumbing through the thick sheaf of vouchers and photocopied ledger pages.

"It's going to cost him," Catherine pointed out, remembering that, like it or not, she owed Elliot. And indeed, her anger at him, her sense of betrayal, had gone, leaving only that strange, gnawing uncertainty that made it difficult for her to think about Elliot at all. "I don't think immunity for Burch would be out of line."

Joe raised an eyebrow. "Am I wrong, or are you whistling a different tune than when you left?"

"Elliot is doing the right thing, Joe," said Catherine, determinedly ignoring his tone as she'd ignored his good-natured teasing about Elliot during the period of Elliot's determined pursuit. Odd, she thought—it had all been so important to her only

215

that morning . . . "That's got to count for something."

He grimaced in agreement, seeing by her tired
eyes and taut mouth that now wasn't the time for
big-brotherly ragging. "I'll talk to Moreno," he said.
"Immunity for Burch and his people is a small price
to pay for Avery."

Catherine nodded, relieved by the sense of a debt
honorably discharged, and Joe rose to go, pleased,
as the saying went, as a dog with two tails. Catherine circled around toward her desk, then paused,
looked back at him, and said, "Tell Moreno he owes
me one. And tell him that if he ever tries to trade
on my private life again, my resignation will be on
his desk by morning."

Joe smiled slowly, and gave her a discreet thumbs-
up as he jostled off through the bullpen, heading
for Moreno's office with the folder in hand.

Catherine returned to her desk slowly. The interview with Elliot and the emotional upheaval which
had preceded it had left her feeling drained. She
wondered if after this morning's coup, Moreno
would let her take the afternoon off . . . Probably,
she guessed. Then she thought, *No*, recalling the
wrap on the Bartoli case, the write-up of the Pitts
affadavit, the dozen other matters needing her attention . . .

But she wondered why her thoughts kept whispering to her with images of silence, and darkness,
and pain.

"My god, look at it," whispered Jamie, as the
shaky yellow beam of her makeshift miner's hat—a
flashlight firmly duct-taped to a motorcycle helmet—
moved over the dripping rockface with the turning
of her head. "It's worse than Kipper said."

And behind her there was a kind of awed muttering from those crowded in the tunnel behind. Mary, with her own small kit of the medicines and bandages she used for midwifery slung over one shoulder, put a thin, strong hand to her mouth and gazed in shock; Winslow, setting down his pick and crowbars against the rock of the tunnel wall, swore softly and vehemently. Cullen lowered his lantern to better illuminate the huge chunk of rock which had collapsed inward, blocking the low crawl-tunnel completely, the fragments and pebbles and mud oozing thickly around its sides.

"Can we clear that tunnel?" asked Winslow, looking at Jamie.

She shook her head doubtfully. "Even if we clear the hole, that crawlspace is twenty feet long. Once you're in, there's no room to turn around or swing a pick . . ."

"There must be something we can do." Panic edged Mary's soft voice as she looked around at the narrow tunnel behind them, now filled with torch- and lantern-light as people crowded its entrance to mutter and stare. "We could pass the stones out, hand to hand . . ."

Feeling their eyes on him Winslow felt the cold touch of panic, and, as usual, hid his fear and uncertainty under a hot flash of temper.

"One rock at a time?" he demanded. "They'll be dead for sure before we reach 'em that way."

"Don't say that!" Mary's voice shook. "They're not dead, they're not going to die . . ."

Winslow looked around him, remembering his own days of defying adult authority to play in the Maze, trying to stay calm, knowing full well that the greatest enemy to those trapped in the cave-in would be time. If they panicked here outside, Father and Vincent would be lost. "There's got to be some other way in," he said. "All these little twisty tunnels, they all feed into each other . . ."

Running feet echoed in the tunnels behind them, splashing in the seep-water and punctuating a child's panting breath. There was a jostling in the passage and Kipper was let through, clutching a dozen scrolls of Father's maps. Winslow snatched them out of his hands.

"About time," he muttered, and unrolled one, Cullen holding high his lantern and the others pressing in close. "Dammit," he swore, and threw the stiff brown roll aside, unfurling another, clumsy in the confined space, cursing again as the heavy paper tried to roll itself back up again. "There's got to be another way in . . ."

"There isn't . . ." whispered Kipper, really scared.

"Quiet," snapped Winslow furiously, refusing to accept defeat, and threw the map aside with a hand that shook. Sweat stood out on his broad brow. "Dammit, this isn't right either. There has to be another map. The level below this one, maybe . . ." He swung back upon the boy. Mary had washed the mud and grit from the cuts Kipper had sustained dragging Eric out of the path of the avalanche, but mud still soaked the boy's curly black hair, and, beneath it, his face was very pale in the torchlight.

"Run back to Father's chamber, get me the rest of the maps. You must have missed something."

"I did not!" insisted Kipper.

"Don't you take that tone with me, boy!" he yelled. "You weren't supposed to be down in the Maze in the first place! None of this would have happened if you'd done as you were told!"

Kipper turned away, biting his lip, knowing he had been at fault. As senior of the three children he should never have suggested the game . . . and now he'd gotten Vincent and Father killed . . .

"Stop it, Winslow." Mary caught the boy by the shoulders before he could run away to hide his grief and guilt. "Kipper feels bad enough."

Winslow's strong lips tightened with shame. "Kipper, I'm sorry," he said, and drew a deep breath, fighting for control over his temper, fighting against the fear that made him lash out at anyone near. "I didn't mean . . ."

Standing beside Mary, Kipper met his eye, and nodded.

"We're all to blame," Winslow went on grimly. "We should have sealed up these tunnels years ago." And he looked down again at the low entranceway in the rock wall, stopped solid with one massive boulder like a cork in a bottle and who knew how many behind that. And behind him, around him, he could feel them looking at him—Mary, Pascal, Sara, Benjamin, Jamie, Cullen, all the others, waiting for him to take charge. Wanting *someone* to take charge, to tell them what to do, to direct them—to show them how to save their friends. The men they would have turned to for leadership in an emergency were both buried behind twenty feet of bedrock, perhaps badly injured—perhaps dead. Winslow's strength, his loud voice and blustering temper, had always made him something of a leader . . . how ill-equipped, he only saw now, when sole leadership was being thrust into his big hands. It was terrifying—but not as terrifying, he thought, recalling the fights over the disposal of the treasure, as the chaos that would result if two or three of the others started different plans. Their only hope was in speed, and in a single effort.

Right, thought Winslow grimly. *Well, if I'm elected, let's get to it . . .*

And he turned back to face the rock of the wall, willing his fear into anger, his anger into strength.

"There's no way through, is there?" said Mary, her voice close to tears. "No way to get them . . ."

"There's only one way I know to get through twenty feet of bedrock." Winslow reached behind him, lifted his pick and hefted it, the weight of it reassuring in his hands. With a grunt of fury he swung it high over his head and sent its steel point crashing against the rock that blocked the crawl-hole, splinters and sparks flying back and the echo of the blow reverberating in the narrow space like an explosion.

"And that," he went on grimly, "is one foot at a time."

His anger, his strength, settled into a rhythm, the smashing of steel against granite deafening in the tunnel but the action itself a relief to him, the crack and swing of his muscles untwisting the fear in his soul. There was just room in the widening of the tunnel for Benjamin and Nicholas to gather up picks and join him, three points of steel crashing against the rockface in clanging rhythm, loosening chunks of stone that others could creep in and haul free. The ringing clamor of the picks seemed to shiver deep into the bones of the rocks, a desperate, word-less pounding in darkness.

And at her desk, Catherine Chandler winced, the dull ache in her head, the sense of fear and the strange thoughts of darkness which had grown stronger upon her, not less, as the afternoon went on, coalescing suddenly into a kind of rhythm, a throbbing clang, like something heard very far away.

She leaned forward, cradling her head on her hands, wondering what the hell was the matter with her. She'd never felt like this before, never had this sense of . . . of peril, not to herself, but . . .

At the same time the queer pain in the muscles of her back and arms eased and vanished, and the uneasy, recurring half-image of darkness in her mind became at once clearer and more detached from her. She realized with abrupt certainty that the thought was not hers at all, but Vincent's.

And as if the words had been spoken in her ear she knew—as Vincent had frequently described his own feelings when she was in danger—that Vincent was somewhere in peril of his life.

Sixteen

VINCENT'S eyes opened to blackness. The smell of rock dust hung thick and choking in the air, along with the smell of mud and damp; he coughed, and pain stabbed him in the ribs, leaving him breathless and sick. He tried to move, and couldn't. The pain jabbed him again. A massive weight lay across his chest and hips, crushing him into the muddy rock.

The column, he thought. It had slipped from his grip, come down on him ... .

Then darkness.

He closed his eyes again. He had dreamed of Catherine. As he frequently did in dreams he had seen her, in teal blue with a rosette of amethysts at her throat, her face grim as she stepped through a great oak door which swung soundlessly to behind her. Felt her worry, her upset, her hurt . . . her fear of being hurt again. And then, like sunshafts falling through a steam-vent when he'd turned a corner out of shadows, triumph had come through . . . a blazing sense of strength, of some dreaded obstacle cleared, of something good well-done. He'd been dreaming of sunshafts falling on her face, of seeing her eyes smiling in daylight, when the pain had wakened him to the darkness.

Father, he thought, his mind clearing with a jolt. He remembered Father behind him, remembered desperately holding the column up as the ceiling had fallen in over them both.

He tried to turn his head to look, but saw nothing. There was the thinnest thread of gray light from somewhere—phosphorescent lichen, maybe, such of it as had survived—but he lay, he guessed from scent and feel as much as sight, in a depression in the Dungeon's uneven floor, the rock fragment beside him the only thing which had kept him from being crushed to jelly under the column when it fell. The dip of the floor in which he lay blocked his view of anything else.

Slowly he moved his right hand, agony flashing along the muscles of his arm as he groped at the sides of the column. It did not lie directly over him, but obliquely—his left arm, wedged next to a chunk of broken stalactite, was mobile enough to shift it around under the column's bulk. His hands felt at the stone, seeking a grip, then thrust.

It was like trying to move the earth.

He flexed his hands, panting. The cold wet of seep-water soaked his hair and the back of his shirt and leather vest. Through the choke of the dust he smelled the fumes of kerosene, burned out, smothered by the fall of rock and earth from above. How much, he wondered, of the Dungeon remained?

Father, he thought again. His last sight had been Father being struck by the falling stones.

He twisted, shoving at the weight that imprisoned him, sprained muscles screaming under the shock of it, and felt the stone shift a little above him. The silence around him was terrible, only the far-off noise of dripping water to tell him that he lived, that he was still in the real world at all . . .

Unless, he thought with grim humor, *it is the River Styx*. Even the soughing of the underworld winds was stilled; he could feel no movement on the coarse fur of his hands. The walls, the little wind-trap tunnels around this place, must all have collapsed. The children . . . ?

Gathering his strength together, he let out a roar, a bellow of rage and frustration and fear, as he shoved at the stone, all his will, all his strength channeling into the sound and the thrust, heedless of the wrenching agony of muscle and bone. He felt the stone move, and twisted, sliding his body from beneath it, and then lay for a time on the rough stone of the floor, gasping for breath, glad only to have his ribcage free of the pressure, to be able to draw unfettered breath.

Then slowly, he got to his feet, swaying for balance, dizzy and ill with shock. "Father?" he called out, and the echoes told him instantly that most of the room had collapsed inward on itself. He looked around him desperately in the darkness, eyes vainly trying to adjust. "Father . . ."

Somewhere he heard a cough. "Vincent?" The voice was very weak—then another cough, broken off short, as if in an effort to suppress pain.

Dropping carefully to his knees, Vincent searched the floor with his hands, his eyes slowly changing to match the near-total blackness of the little pocket that was all that was left of the cavern they had entered. His hand touched Father's arm, feeling the texture of the coarse wool now clogged with grit; his fingers sought along it, downward, to touch the old man's hand. It seemed to him now that he could make out shapes in the darkness by the pallid gleam, less than that of a single firefly, of the few remaining patches of lichen. He saw the glint of Father's open eyes, and felt a surge of relief when he saw them blink.

"Father, I'm here."

He groped further in the blackness, feeling Father's

face—cold as the stone on which he lay, save where a hot streak of blood tracked down it and matted into the side of his beard. A broken-off stalactite, perhaps twelve feet long and thick at the top, lay across Father's body; another chunk of rock pinned his legs. "I'll get you out . . ."

Father groaned as the weight shifted, then whispered, "The children?" His head moved blindly, and his hand clutched at Vincent's sleeve.

"They were well up the tunnel," Vincent said, hoping that what he remembered—or thought he remembered—was true, and not some desperate wish or dream. "Let's just pray they're safe."

"Vincent . . ." Father coughed again, the sound of it bad, thick with an agony that he tried hard to stifle. "Can you see anything?"

"Dimly," said Vincent, working as he spoke, heaving the stone aside which had fallen on the old man, clearing away the wreckage of the chamber around them. "Shapes and shadows—shades of gray . . ." Somewhere in the darkness he heard the grinding slither of rock falling, smelled new dust thicken the air. The chamber was still unstable, he thought. Another heavy tremor and they could be enclosed like two seeds, crushed in the fist of the earth.

Gently, he cradled Father in his arms. Waking in the darkness, it had been his first and deepest dread that he would find nothing but this man's body . . . or perhaps, buried under tons of rock and earth, nothing at all. He wondered if there were a place to drag him where the floor was not so damp—wondered if he dared try to move him at all.

In the blackness Father reached up and touched Vincent's thick mane. "Your eyes are astonishing," he whispered. "In this darkness I'm as good as blind." He tried to move, the effort wringing another cry of pain from him—then he lay still, his breath like the drag of a rusty saw.

"How do you feel?" asked Vincent softly, and Father coughed again.

"I've been better," he managed to say. But it was clear to Vincent that Father was very badly hurt.

Looking around him, it was difficult to judge distances in the blackness, but Vincent estimated that fully three-quarters of the Dungeon had collapsed, isolating them in a tiny chamber under what had been the funneled apex of its ceiling. A huge slab of rock walled off most of what had been the cavern, and around it, in the thin, blue glow Vincent could make out other rocks, broken pebbles, fallen screes of gravel and earth. In addition to the utter lightlessness of underground, the air was still filled with dust, and the filtered phosphor-gleam caught in it, giving everything a curious gray cast unlike either sunlight or the moonlight of outdoors in the park . . . an eerie, leaden quality that hurt the eye with a lying facsimile of sight.

After a time Vincent laid Father gently down again, and groped his way back to the column, feeling among the heaps of shattered rock for Father's medical bag. After nearly fifteen minutes of patient work he located what was left of it, squashed and broken, and extracted from it a knitted bandage which he soaked in a pool of seep-water, to wash the blood and some of the dirt from the old man's face. He could feel by Father's hands that he had not gone into deep shock, and for that he was thankful—even if his head injury wasn't as bad as Vincent feared, even if there were no serious internal hurts, shock alone could kill a man. Straining to look down into Father's face, he saw that he had drifted into unconsciousness, and gently shook him, whispering to him until his eyes opened again.

"Father . . ."

His breath had almost sunk away—now his chest heaved again, with a deep sigh, and he whispered, "Vincent?"

"Listen . . ."

The old man moved his head, his brows pulling together. "What?"

"Pounding . . ." Vincent reached out and touched the wall behind them. Through it he could feel— and perhaps feeling and not hearing, through the stone, was what he had done before—came the deep vibration, like the clang of a metal heart.

"Someone hammering against the rock."

Father's voice was barely audible, even in the thick silence of the buried chamber. "I can't hear a thing."

"It's coming from the far side of the tunnel," murmured Vincent, leaning down to speak to him. "The children must have made it out . . ."

"Yes," whispered Father. His hand groped feebly at Vincent's arm and chest. "Thank God . . ."

"They're digging us out."

Father's lips pursed a little, his breath slipping through them with a sibilant little hiss of pain. "It's a long way." His voice drifted, and Vincent shook him again, as hard as he dared.

"Father, you must stay awake," he said urgently. "You have a head injury. You may have a concussion."

"I feel . . . very sleepy," agreed Father, detached and faint, as if speaking of someone else.

"Let's keep talking," urged Vincent, frightened by that detachment, that dreamy note in his voice of no longer really caring whether he slipped away into darkness or not.

Father nodded, and his breath caught sharply at some pain the movement brought. "Of course," he added after a moment, "if the head injury was that severe, I wouldn't be lucid . . . and I *am* lucid, am I not?"

"So far."

"So far?" That seemed to rouse him a little; some animation came back into his voice. "Why, in that case I shall recite from Vigil by the hour to make sure . . ."

Vincent smiled a little. "Then *I'll* be asleep."

Father made a little sound that might have been a laugh, but which ended in a gasp of pain; his hand tightened convulsively again on Vincent's wrist. Somewhere deep in the earth Vincent heard the rumble of shifting rocks, and with a splintering crash another fragment of stone plunged down from the ceiling, bursting like a cannon-ball on the floor a few feet away. Father flinched as Vincent moved instinctively to protect him with his body, and for a moment there was silence, each wondering if the vibration caused by the distant diggers was what had shaken free the new shower of stone, and if, as they drew nearer, the next avalanche would be worse.

But, thought Vincent, looking around him at the dark confines of their tomb, they did not seem to have much choice.

It was perhaps fortunate for Winslow and the other diggers that they did not have Vincent's sharpness of hearing, his awareness of the noises of what passed deep underground, and did not hear the distant, grinding rumble of the new rockfall. In the narrow confines of the outer Maze the clanging of the picks drowned out all other sounds, even the hoarse, dragging breath of the men, exhausted by the unaccustomed manual task.

Benjamin and Nicholas had yielded their picks to

others and were leaning back against the tunnel wall, resting on their feet and drinking the water Mary had brought for them in a tin cup. Winslow, driven by desperation and concern, pounded on. The air in the tunnel felt close and stifling now, heated by the crowding bodies there and the torches which flickered in every crack in the walls. Other men were working with picks and crowbars, trying to widen the narrow tunnel around them a little to permit more men to work on the hard granite blocking the crawlspace itself while the stronger-backed of the teenagers and women were shoveling dirt out of their way or carrying rocks back as they were dislodged. There was little of this yet. The granite was hard.

"Winslow . . . Winslow, this won't work!" said Jamie desperately, coming up behind the big blacksmith to tug at his sleeve. She could see—they all could see—how little headway the picks had made on that first boulder, how difficult it was for even two men to work in the confined space. "There's got to be a better way."

Winslow swung around, lowering his pick. He'd taken off his jacket and vest; his homespun white shirt was sodden with his sweat and his face glittered with it in the torchlight. "I don't hear you coming up with no brainstorms."

"We could . . ." Jamie hesitated, knowing what the big man's temper was like at the best of times and sensing that in his fear he was likely to lash out at anyone. "We could tell Mouse," she blurted out hastily. "Break the Silence."

Winslow heaved an impatient sigh, flexed his aching hands. "Jamie, if I thought it'd do any good, I'd sing him a hymn. Mouse will just get in the way, slow us all down with all his talk, get everyone arguing again." He'd seen his friend in action before, and his instincts told him that his own leadership was precarious at best, especially as men grew tired, and the tunnel crept forward so slowly. Give everyone something to do, and they'd do it. Give them a choice between alternatives—and Mouse's outlook on life consisted of a toyshop of alternative plans—and they'd do nothing, or devolve into the dozen small arguments over what was to be done, as they had in the matter of the pirate gold.

"Winslow, he knows the tunnels better than anyone, even Father. Maybe he knows another way in."

"There *is* no other way in. How many times did I go over those damned maps?"

She gestured desperately, acknowledging that he was right but driven by the fear that the present course of action wasn't working either. "Maybe he could build something, some kind of machine."

"I've seen his damned machines," retorted Winslow, his temper rising. "Half of them don't work . . ."

". . . and half of them *do!*"

Winslow sighed heavily, his own frustration, his own exhaustion, making him want to shout at this slender, blonde-haired girl, tell her to shut up and get working . . . do something instead of nothing . . . Beside him Randolph and 'Nardo, the relief team, had set down their picks, listening . . . *Dammit, in another minute we're going to have them going off looking for another way to do this . . .*

He pointed to the rock wall. "Vincent and Father are in there, maybe hurt, maybe dying," he said. "You want to get to them? Talk don't break no rock, girl. Sweat does. You get my meaning?" He turned back—after a moment, the other two did as well. Winslow attacked the wall as if his strength, his anger, could move the bones of the earth—could move the dark fate that he saw rising before him, the dread of Father dead, Vincent dead, and all that could come after that.

For a moment Jamie watched them, huge, clumsy shadows flung on the gray rock of the walls by the lanterns set nearby, the steely flash of pick-heads and the firefly sparks on stone. Then, unable to stand it, she whirled and ran off down the tunnels.

In the mildew-smelling dampness of the service-closet, Catherine listened for a time to the silence of the basement laundry room outside. No sound, except the steady whirring of somebody's clothes in a dryer, and the deeper, heavier heartbeat of the building's heating plant . . . no voices, no footfalls, not even the dim, tinny chatter of the super's TV set which would have told her he was somewhere near. *Good*, she thought. It was the slow time, late afternoon, rush hour outside . . . rush hour in the laundry room would be in another couple of hours. Now the whole building's basement was virtually deserted.

Cautiously, she tucked her big flashlight under her arm, zipped up the brown leather bomber jacket she wore, and, bending down, lifted free the grate on the floor. She transferred the light to one hand, shined its beam briefly down into the pit to satisfy herself that it was free of some of New York's less appetizing fauna, then climbed quickly down, replacing the grate over her head. The cluster of steam-pipes ran down next to the ladder, varying in diameter from the size of her calf to that of her waist, reddish paint peeling off them to show the rough iron underneath. She flashed the light once more around the sub-basement, with its mouldering boxes, its unnameable junk dating from some Lovecraftian epoch in the building's past, and turned back to the pipes.

With the butt-end of the flashlight, she banged on the pipes the simple code Vincent had taught her—a location code, and the syllables of his name. And waited.

All the way back home—while she had stuffed her papers hastily in her briefcase, while she had made her rapid excuses to Joe—the feeling that Vincent was in trouble had been growing. By the time she reached her apartment it had taken hold of her like a fever, driving her as she'd changed rapidly into jeans and a workshirt and boots; it gnawed at her now. But other than the one brief flash of darkness, of pain, it was far less conscious than it had been. She knew only that something was desperately wrong.

When, after ten minutes, Vincent neither came nor signaled back—as he frequently signaled if he was a long distance away, to give her a time estimate of when he would arrive, seldom more than fifteen minutes—she rapped on the pipe again. She wondered if the others heard their signals, those unseen others who made up Vincent's world: Pascal in his cavernous Pipe Chamber, Father, who had had his seven days of happiness . . .

She hoped, suddenly, that Father was all right.

Still he did not reply.

She turned her flashlight beam back towards the rear wall of the chamber, hidden behind immemorial junk. After a moment she walked back towards it, fingering in her jacket pocket for the chalk Vincent had given her, her heart beating fast. Vincent was in trouble . . . she knew it, as surely as he knew when some peril threatened her. He could neither come, nor signal, and it came to her suddenly that she might very well be the only one who knew of his danger. The only one who could save him.

That decided her.

Taking a deep breath, she stepped through the low arch, and moved into the darkness of the Tunnels alone.

She had a vague idea of the direction in which the dwellings of the subterranean Tunnelfolk lay. Following the route by which Vincent had taken her to the library, she located the winding iron stair that led downward to levels below the old main in which she walked. Another tunnel at the bottom of it, its wide, tiled sides and rusted iron rails marking an ancient private subway line; an access ladder in a dropshaft going still further down. Her boots splashed softly in puddles of water, or scuffed through the thin mud there; now and then she heard, far off, the dim clanging of the pipes. If the Tunnel children marked their way in chalk, she thought, moving hesitantly along another, narrower tube, too low to stand in upright and bearing upon its walls half a dozen smaller pipes, she'd find their markings sooner or later . . . wouldn't she? Maybe even meet those she'd helped find their way to the world Below, the orphans Eric and Ellie . . .

And she smiled, thinking about that thin, matter-of-fact little boy, his tougher, gutsier sister, as she move down deeper into the dark. She found herself wishing she had brought a compass, or a ball of string . . . A *big* ball, she added, chalking yet another arrow on the wall in the hopes of guiding herself back. Another ladder, iron staples vanishing in the blackness of an ancient riser-vent . . . How many levels down was she? Estimates put the subway tunnels down as deep as two hundred feet, water-tunnels incredibly deeper than that . . . How on earth did Vincent know his way around this place? It was worse than trying to locate a restaurant in Greenwich Village . . .

He was in trouble, in danger, in pain. The awareness was like a constant whispering in her bones, stronger and stronger, a growing nightmare in her brain. She had to find him . . .

She was deep down now, in the scabland bedrock of granite seams and blind canyons below the level of the subways, where water dripped incessantly down the uneven walls, and niter gleamed palely on stone. The damp breath of the deeper earth rose in clammy wind from an ancient well in the middle of the tunnel; as she passed it, the heel of her boot knocked a stone from its rim, and it was a long time before she heard a splash. The rumbling of the subway was dim and far off; she had come the wrong direction, she thought. But she wasn't sure what the right direction would be.

And then, as she turned a corner her flashlight-beam glanced across the ornate shape of a wrought-iron gate set firmly in the tunnel rock. Hurrying forward, she grasped the thick iron bars. Vincent had spoken of such gates, sometimes barred, sometimes solid sheets of metal or wood, which protected the inner levels of the Tunnels . . . She pushed against it, and felt the solid clang of a bolt. Beyond it, the flashlight showed her the gray and dripping length of a tunnel, curving away into darkness.

"Hello!" she called out, and the echoes traded the word, *Hello . . . hello . . . hellohello-oh-oh-oh . . .* away into nothingness. "Vincent! Is anyone there? Kipper? Ellie . . ." *(ellie-ellie-ellielliellie . . .)*

She tried the bars again, but the grate was firmly locked. Vincent had spoken of trip-levers and releases . . . She flashed the beam of the light around the sides of the gate, seeking for such a device, anything to let her past, to let her in . . .

In the upper corner, set in the rock above the gate, she saw the chunky shape of a little stone lion-face snarling down at her. The carved face was canted slightly, turned a little to one side—the whole thing, she thought, reaching for it, probably turned. She grasped it with one hand, twisted . . . it was heavy, and stuck fast. She tucked the light under her arm, reached up with both hands as well as she could, twisted again, and this time felt it give.

Her flash of triumph lasted only an instant. Then the floor under her feet dropped away, the hidden trapdoor upon which she had been standing pitching her down into darkness like a stone.

Seventeen

CATHERINE hit what felt like an enormous pile of cushions and spun, rising to her knees—with a certain amount of difficulty on the bouncy surface—ready to fight. She was, after the split-second that it took her to determine that she wasn't hurt—for she had fallen through the trapdoor into what felt like a long, polished chute, and from that through another trap into this place—more angry than scared, as if someone had dumped her unceremoniously into some kind of silly funhouse. And looking around her, she had for a disoriented moment the impression that this was precisely what had happened.

In the lamplit gloom around her she made out all sorts of things—mannequins built out of old auto parts with glowing lightbulb eyes, an espresso maker half-dismantled and hooked up to power a sewing machine, a pachinko machine the size of Elliot Burch's desk, and stalagmites pieced painstakingly together from broken glass and airplane glue. A lamp in the shape of the Empire State Building rose in a softly-glowing blue spike above it all—a lighted barber-pole whirled mindlessly nearby. Unimaginable machines crouched in the dark corners of the room, their mechanical guts strewn over half the floor and every horizontal workspace. She had fallen, she saw now, through a trapdoor in the ceiling and into an immense Victorian four-poster bed covered with cushions, old comforters, and quilts.

Noise and movement—she whirled to face it, still not sure where she was or why she'd been whisked there. But it was only a black-faced raccoon, perched high on top of an elaborate sand-castle, peeking at her cautiously from between its towers.

Yet she knew the room wasn't deserted.

She slid to the edge of the bed, wanting more than anything to get traction on a more solid surface. "Hello?" she called out, pointing the flashlight's beam at the shadows. Movement again, in another corner, and she turned to face it, ready for anything now. "Is someone there?"

And from the shadows a young man stepped hesitantly into view. He was, she guessed, sixteen or seventeen, stocky, fair-haired, and clothed as Vincent and Father were generally clothed, in a patched mish-mash of leather and cast-off rags reassembled, a pair of thick wooly socks cut into fingerless gloves for his hands, and thick leather moccasin-style boots on his feet. Someone had sewn what looked like a collection of ornamental belt buckles on the brown leather of his vest, and they gleamed oddly where the light struck them, like the medals of some cock-eyed military campaign. He eyed her warily, and she had the impression that, like the half-feral cat that haunted the little garden of her father's place in Gramercy Square, he'd bolt at a sudden move.

And she relaxed a little. He didn't look particularly dangerous, though of course that was no guarantee—if he wasn't armed she could probably take him at a pinch . . .

"Me," he replied to her question. "Who?"

"My name is Catherine," she said, realizing he

needed reassurance as much as she did. "I was looking for Vincent . . ."

"Catherine . . ." Awe filled his round, open face. "Vincent's Catherine." He nodded toward the trapdoor over the bed, and grinned a little. "Express route," he said, very pleased with himself for creating something that clever. "To the deepest chamber of all. Mouse's hole . . . no place for a Topsider."

"You're Mouse?" Catherine smiled, holding out her hand. "You gave me a necklace . . . I've always wanted to thank you . . ."

He grinned shyly, shook his head. "Pretty," he explained, and gestured with a sweep of his arms. "But didn't work. Anyway . . . Vincent's friend."

Catherine nodded, touched by his tone, as if that explained it all. Then her brow clouded. "Mouse, I think Vincent may be in trouble."

"Vincent takes care of himself." From the sandcastle the raccoon scrambled confidently onto his arm, then up to his shoulder—Mouse caressed it, frowning at her, as if remembering Father's precepts. "Shouldn't have come."

She shook her head stubbornly, and, gripping her flashlight more firmly in hand, strode toward the door which she now made out in the shadows beyond. "I've got to find him . . ."

Mouse caught up with her, blocking her way. "Hundreds of tunnels, chambers," he insisted. "Wander forever, never . . ."

"Then take me there! Vincent may be in danger!" And, when he still frowned, uncertain, "I need your help, Mouse. Please."

Mouse hesitated, chewing his lower lip, fighting his own instinct to keep outsiders away from the tunnels which were his home. For a frightened moment Catherine wondered what she'd do if he actively tried to stop her from going further—then he looked at her again, seeing the desperation in her eyes, and came to a decision. "Okay," he said slowly, and then, more quickly, "Okay good, okay fine." With a quick, darting movement he shooed his pet aside, and grabbed a big sodium-bulb flash-light from his workbench—Catherine had to almost run to catch up with him as he darted through yet another tunnel out of the room.

"Grew up down here," Mouse confided in her, as he led the way with swift, unerring steps along the silent dark of the tunnels beyond. The beam of his flashlight, hard and white, slashed deep into the darkness before them, and his voice echoed queerly in the low concrete vaults of the tunnel roof. "Know these tunnels better than anyone." With a hint of pride in his voice he added, "Vincent's my best friend. We hang out."

And Catherine smiled, remembering all Vincent had told her about the little engineer. Like two ghosts in the blackness they climbed a long spiral of metal stairs, ducked through a rudely-cut opening into the low brick vaults of what seemed to be a pre-Civil-War water-main, hurried along, their feet splashing softly in the puddles on the floor and their shadows bobbing and looming darkly at their heels. Far off in the darkness Catherine heard the echoes of running feet, and at the same moment Mouse stopped, head up, listening . . .

"Something's wrong, something's broken, needs fixing," he said softly. "They come to Mouse. Even in the Silence."

The crossed beams of the two flashlights caught a slim, hurrying form as it emerged from a cross-tun-nel and came swiftly towards them. A girl, Cather-ine saw, about Mouse's age, her blonde hair pulled back in a ponytail, clothed like Mouse in the charac-teristic garb of the Tunnel dwellers: jeans, thermal sweater, gray vest quilted out of what appeared to be moving-pads. Coming toward the light she did not see Catherine until she was within a few feet of her and Mouse—then she stopped, frozen, uncertain and ready to bolt.

"It's okay," said Catherine quickly, trying to reassure her. "I'm a friend of Vincent's."

The girl nodded, though her eyes were cautious, almost frightened—but she clearly had other things to think about than an intruder in the Tunnels. Turning to Mouse she said urgently, "Mouse, you've got to come . . ."

"Thought you broke the Silence because you missed me, Jamie," returned Mouse sarcastically.

"Listen to me!" cried Jamie. "There's been a cave-in. Father and Vincent are trapped!"

Mouse gulped, all the sarcasm shocked out of him. Catherine thought, *Darkness. Pain . . .* understanding now what she had felt.

"My God . . ."

"Where?"

"The Maze . . ."

Mouse darted forward almost at a run, Jamie and Catherine hurrying at his heels. "Bad," he muttered, holding the flashlight low and taking the turnings, the stairs, the rusted metal ladders from memory, hardly glancing at the walls around to check his bearings, knowing exactly where he was, and where he must go. "Very bad, worse than bad, worse than worse . . ."

And Catherine, hastening in the darkness at his side, thought, *I knew it. Dear God, don't let him be dead . . .* But there was cold terror in her heart.

Winslow looked up when he heard the murmur of voices behind him from the other workers in the tunnel. After hours of work they'd broken the boulder plugging the neck of the crawlspace, only to find, as they chipped and dug the pieces painfully out by hand, that another boulder—or maybe a section of the crawlspace wall itself—had fallen in behind it. In the limited space work was more difficult, with less room to maneuver the picks. His muscles ached, but the fear still drove him, the fear they'd be too late, and he sensed this fear, heard it peripherally in the quiet talk of those hacking beside him in the tight confines of the tunnel, or hauling back the broken fragments of rock.

He heard also the silence that fell on them, and caught a quiet voice speaking Mouse's name.

And turning back, he saw Mouse standing in the dark gap of the tunnel, flashlight in hand. Jamie was beside him, and at his other side, illuminated in the hot blaze of the torchlight, was a woman Winslow had never seen before, slender, blonde, green-eyed and extraordinarily beautiful, wearing the jeans and leather jacket—whole and store-bought—of a denizen of the upper world.

Shocked, he demanded, "What the hell is this?"

"She was with Mouse," Jamie said helplessly.

"I'm a friend of Vincent," said Catherine, stepping forward through the crowd. The big black man, with his angry eyes and sweat gleaming in his short beard, had to be Winslow . . . the others must also be people Vincent had spoken of, his friends, the people who made the warp and weft of his days . . .

"Are they alive?" she asked, sick with dread.

"We don't know," said Winslow grudgingly. *I'm gonna kill that boy one of these days*, he thought in exasperation, but now was not the time to take issue with Mouse for violating yet another of the community rules. Behind him, Mouse was poking at the shattered rock and the partly-cleared crawlspace, picking up rock fragments, looking at the fallen boulders yet to go, the torchlight flashing on the ornaments of his vest as he muttered to himself.

"Can you help, Mouse?" asked Nicholas eagerly, putting down his pick, speaking, Winslow thought dourly, as if Father had never pronounced the Silence—though he knew in his heart this wasn't the time to enforce it.

"Maybe with one of your machines . . ."

"We don't need no damn machine!" retorted Winslow furiously.

"Yes you do," returned Mouse, straightening up and looking into Winslow's dark, angry face. "Never get through this way, one rock at a time."

"It's the only way in!" insisted Winslow. "We can do it . . ."

"Not in time," Mouse argued, his wide-set eyes intent, the almost childish face suddenly grave, the face of a man recognizing an almost hopeless situation. "Run out of air in there before you get through."

"There must be another way," said Catherine, her eyes luminous with fear, and Mouse nodded.

"From the other side."

"That's crazy!" Winslow rounded upon them both. "It's solid rock!"

"No," insisted Mouse. "Another tunnel. I remember."

"Then you remember wrong!" Turning, Winslow seized the maps which had been thrown into a corner, brought the one of the area nearest the Maze over to Mouse and shoved it under his nose. "There's no other tunnel. See for yourself."

"Maps are wrong," Mouse yelled back, snatching it from Winslow and slashing it aside. "I know what I know . . . and I *know*."

Men were looking at each other, muttering agreement, muttering doubts, speculating on which course to take. Appalled, Winslow calculated how long it would take to clear the blocked crawlspace—twenty feet, Jamie had said, maybe more if that part of the Dungeon had caved in . . . *Dammit, why couldn't those kids have played someplace else!*—with half the workforce he now had at his command. He'd seen cave-ins before in these tunnels, knew how what had originally been a sizable chamber could be reduced in seconds to a hatful of airspace.

Angrily, he shouted, "I'm not risking their lives because you say you know."

Catherine turned to him, her own anxiety striking sparks in those green eyes. "What if Mouse is right . . . ?"

"Got a new machine," Mouse was saying eagerly to the other diggers, to Mary and Benjamin and Cullen. "Best one yet. Dig in from the other side . . ."

"Winslow," pleaded Catherine, "if there's even the slightest chance . . ."

"Leave it alone!" he yelled. "We've wasted enough time."

Mouse retorted, "Do it your way! Waste more time!" his arms slashing in a windmill gesture of disgust. He turned to the others. "Any of you coming with me?"

Dammit . . . thought Winslow furiously, as, after a long moment, Jamie stepped over to stand beside Mouse and Catherine. There was silence, men and women looking from the towering blacksmith to the cocky youth in his battered leather vest . . . "I'll come," said Cullen, and set down his bucket of rocks. A moment later Nicholas downed his pick and followed.

With a contemptuous snort Winslow turned away from them, and hefted his pick once more. The first shattering blows of iron against rock shook the narrow tunnel as Mouse and his little party hurried out, heading back for his room at a run.

"Catherine is with them." Vincent raised his head.

'Catherine?' Father, who had seemed to drift off when Vincent had left him to listen at the wall, seemed for a moment not to remember that name. Then his brows pulled together—crouching only a foot or so away, Vincent could see his face now, saw how black the grizzled beard and eyebrows were against skin chalky with exhaustion and strain under the mask of grime. "How could she know?"

"She knew." Part of him felt a kind of wonderment, but, when he thought about it, very little surprise. Of course Catherine would have known . . . would have come. "She must have known. Our bond is stronger and deeper than either of us can begin to imagine . . ."

"As if both your destinies," said Father gently, "were inextricably linked."

Vincent nodded, hesitant, wondering that Father would speak of her now, wondering that he would understand.

"As if," father went on softly, as Vincent picked his way back over the fallen stone to where he lay, "your hearts in their search for union could transcend time and space, circumvent the laws of physics and probability . . ."

"Yes," said Vincent, settling down again at his side, knowing in his heart that it was true. That it was more than simply love he had always known. They were yang and yin, linked at some unknowably deep level of the soul. Even had she wed the man Burch, as he knew she had been thinking of doing earlier in the year, even then, they would have continued to be a part of one another, to their mutual sorrow. Though he would no longer have seen her, no longer have even attempted to do so, he knew there would never have been a night that her voice would not have haunted his dreams.

He wondered suddenly whether she had known this, too.

Very quietly, Father went on, as if speaking to himself. "One June afternoon nearly forty years ago, I was walking on 57th Street, and as I approached Fifth Avenue I saw the loveliest woman I've ever in my life seen. She was walking toward me in a summer dress, a soft breeze was blowing . . . she was . . . a vision."

His hand, which Vincent had taken, tightened slightly, and Vincent knew that his father saw, through the darkness that now surrounded them, that waking vision again; as if by speaking of it, reliving it, he could reach into the time-stream and pluck forth that moment, dripping diamonds, to taste its joy again. "She wasn't merely beautiful," he continued softly. "Her eyes were beaming with intelligence and humor, full of life. Her gaze met mine for a moment, and left me utterly speechless. I knew then that this was the woman I'd searched all my life for."

Yes, thought Vincent. When he had seen Catherine's face, not beautiful, not serene . . . streaked with blood, mutilated, soaked by the wet grasses of the park as he'd turned her over . . . How could he explain that for him, it had been the same? When he had heard her voice, touched her hand . . . They had become friends without sight, for with her eyes bandaged, her face covered, she had not seen his ugliness, nor he her beauty, until later.

And yet it had been the same.

Father's voice flexed, oddly ironic at the vision of that younger man, the man, thought Vincent, in that double-breasted tweed suit and fedora hat, leaning on his smooth London-made cane . . . doctor, professional researcher, respected employee of the Chittenden Institute . . . that young and long-vanished Dr. Jacob Wells. "Before I could even think of doing anything, she climbed into a cab and was . . . gone."

As Catherine had stepped into the downfalling column of light, when they had parted first in the subcellar of her building—when she had returned to the world above, and he had known that he must never see her again. How did a man of the world Above, he wondered, deal with something like that, even if the choice was his to make? In Father's whispered voice he heard the finality of that shutting cab door, the shock of being left alone on a crowded street in the bright sunshine of a world suddenly, utterly, and irrevocably changed . . .

"What did you do?" he asked.

Father shrugged a little, a gesture more of his eyebrows, his face, than of his broken body. "Tried to find her," he said simply. "I went back to that corner the next day . . . and the next. A day didn't go by when I didn't think of her . . . and wonder."

Vincent was silent. For eight months, he too had thought . . . and wondered. And he knew to the marrow of his bones that he would have wondered for the remainder of his life.

At last he said, "I hope that's not the end."

Father smiled a little at the memory. "Well, a year passed by. One day, I was walking along 57th, when a cab drew into the curb, and . . . out she stepped. At almost the same spot. A year later we were married."

"Margaret," said Vincent softly, and Father nodded.

"Yes," he breathed. "Margaret. So you see, Vincent, I too know of miracles."

246

Vincent was silent for a time, thinking about the woman he had spoken to first in the basement of that big, luxurious apartment building; thinking about that wasted, beautiful, charming woman he had known for only the seven days that she had lived in the tunnels. The woman who, dying, had touched his hand and whispered to him, *Take care of him . . .*

"That's a wonderful story," he murmured.

"I wanted you to hear it." Father's voice trailed off, and Vincent felt the hand in his tighten again, as the old man fought against pain, against the unconsciousness dragging at him, against the weary darkness . . . Who knew? thought Vincent. Perhaps against the thought of Margaret's death itself, and the sadness it had left.

"Vincent," said Father softly, "I understand more than you think about Catherine, about your bond."

Deep in the bones of the earth Vincent could sense the ringing crash of the picks, striving at the rock which blocked the crawlspace. It was impossible to tell how near they were, how much time had passed . . . He felt infinitely weary, and heard in the timbre of Father's voice that he was weakening steadily. They had played chess, as they had used to when Father first taught him, without a chessboard or pieces, each remembering where the men were set, and he had tried vainly with his voice, with his mind, to hold Father to him, to keep him from slipping away.

"Are you in much pain?" he asked now, quietly, and had to lean close to hear the old man's reply.

"Enough."

Somewhere in the dark above them he heard the grinding shudder of slipping rocks, and drew Father close against him, bowing his head over him, shielding him with his body as more rocks fell, in a cloud of choking dust, from the dark overhead. They fell close, clattering harshly among the rubble of the cavern floor, and the dust made the scant air harder yet to breathe.

"It looks bad, doesn't it?" whispered Father hoarsely, when Vincent tentatively sat up again. The hand that groped for his felt weaker than before, and cold . . .

(*"His nose was sharp as any pen,"* Mistress Quickly had said of Falstaff's death in *Henry V*, *"and 'a babbled of green fields . . ."*)

Vincent tried to force the lines from his mind, but they returned, a tragic whisper on the death of a man who had lived hugely . . . *"So 'a bade me lay more clothes upon his feet: I put my hand into the bed and felt them, and they were cold as any stone; then I felt to his knees, and all was as cold as any stone . . ."*

As cold now as Father's hands felt when he touched them, as Father's face . . . *cold as any stone . . .*

"So many things I have to tell you." Father's voice was barely audible now, and Vincent pressed his hand, willing his warmth into the failing flesh.

"We'll walk out of here together, I promise you."

But Father did not reply.

Catherine's confidence in Mouse's ability to rescue Father and Vincent suffered an abrupt check when the little group returned to the Mousehole. "This is a machine?" she demanded, aghast, as Mouse proudly pulled back a tarp from a shadowy agglomeration of junk heaped in one corner. Some of it she recognized—part of a jackhammer, what looked looked like three-quarters of a four-stroke car engine—while the rest of it, belts, gear-wheels, mysterious camshafts and housings, seemed to have been cannibalized from alien spacecraft or Captain Nemo's *Nautilus*.

"Will be," he promised cheerfully. "Not here. There." He gestured towards the empty crates and boxes stacked in every corner of the room. "Come on, everybody help."

In boxes, then, they loaded up the pieces of Mouse's machine and carried it back along the twisting tunnels, with Mouse hurrying in the lead, half a dozen nail-scarred two-by-fours balanced on his shoulder with the lantern swinging like a bindlestiff on their ends. Neither Cullen, Nicholas, nor Jamie seemed to question that Mouse knew what he was doing; Catherine, her arms aching under the awkward weight of the load, brought up the rear, trying to convince herself that this would work—that Vincent and Father would still be alive when they got to them.

"Mouse is a genius," Vincent had told her, one of those nights sitting on the terrace, sharing the warmth of his cloak. "He can fix anything, analyze how anything works . . . put any two machines together to make a third . . ."

She had said, "What a shame he hasn't had the chance for an education—he sounds like he could make a fortune as a research engineer."

"Possibly," Vincent had agreed, "if he made it through college and didn't blow up the laboratory of any educational institution unfortunate enough to house him. But I believe research engineers limit themselves to things of practical value—I suspect Mouse would be likelier, in your world, to languish in semi-starvation as a toymaker. His inventions are erratic at best." And his blue-green eyes had smiled with deep affection at the thought of his friend.

Looking at the junk in the box she carried—looking ahead of her at Mouse's broad back, glimpsed now and then through the jagged shadows of those who walked between them—Catherine had to admit she saw Vincent's point.

"He knows the tunnels better than any of us, better than I," Vincent had said on another occasion, a night of sluicing rain, she recalled, one of the few occasions on which he'd actually entered her apartment, and even then he'd kept one cautious ear cocked for the slightest threat of intrusion . . . "They are my home, the territory I patrol and explore, but for him, they were not only that, but his sole defense, his only refuge. How long he'd been prowling them, living in them, stealing food from Mary's cookpots and the communal stores, I don't know—and he certainly has no idea, any more than he remembers where he comes from or how he got down there. Years, certainly."

Jogging down the tunnels, following the others deeper and deeper into the bones of the earth, Catherine could hear Vincent's voice as if he were beside her, textured like the stone but soft as a silken scarf—hear it, along with the rattle of the rain against the French doors that night. The lights had been out, she recalled—a further measure of protection in case of interruption—and Vincent had been no more than a warm shadow at her side, a voice in the dark, as he had been when first she knew him . . .

"Half the time he doesn't need a light, doesn't even need to feel the walls or count the turnings as the others do—he knows instinctively where he is, as I do, by the smell of the earth, by sound of the subways, by feel of the wind below the ground."

And as they traveled deeper, leaving once more the realms of concrete pipes and brick water-mains and entering the bare rock-seams that ran deep beneath the city's bones, this seemed to be the case. They passed warning signs, illuminated by fluttering torches, passed makeshift gates and, in one place, a barricade of half-rotted timbers, and the passages grew narrower and far more dank, where greenish water trickled down the walls and the floors were twisted and uneven, and strange winds blew down fissures and chimneys in the walls.

"The Maze," whispered Jamie to Catherine, as they followed Mouse down a sudden steep tunnel that wound around like a corkscrew in the dark. "We always got in trouble for coming here—I haven't been here in years. I got lost here once. Mouse and Vincent found me. They know this place . . ."

"Here." Mouse's voice was decisive. They had emerged into a small chamber, hardly more than a widening of a very dank little tunnel where a second tunnel ran into it—low-roofed, damp, glistening with niter and blotched with strange fungi and smelling strongly of water somewhere near. He walked to the right-hand wall and ran his hand along it—Catherine could see it was the same hard, blackish granite that Winslow had been hammering on the other side. "Okay good, okay fine," he said, and nodded. "Here."

And unceremoniously dumping down his burden of lumber, he took his battered red toolbox from the top of Cullen's load and flipped it open, and started to work.

Curiously, his drilling machine fitted together with startling precision and speed. Watching his face, watching his eyes as she handed him parts or helped Cullen and Jamie fit together the drill's cradle from two-by-fours and pieces of pipe, watching his deft, sure hands in their fingerless gloves, Catherine could see what Vincent meant when he said Mouse was a genius. There was nothing in him now of the good-natured, slightly scatterbrained air he had formerly had. Fitting hoses, clamps, joints together, rigging a whole series of jerrybuilt gears to increase the small power of the little four-stroke engine, Mouse worked with the skill and speed of a trained mechanic.

"Got gas," he explained, concentrating on adjusting a balance-wheel by the light of Catherine's flashlight but motioning with one elbow back at a can that Nicholas had carried down. "Siphon out of old cars, junkers in the yards—got a tap into a station tank, too. Too far down to tap the city power. Besides, Father says that's dangerous."

"I expect Father's right," agreed Catherine, thinking with a shiver what the results would be if ConEd started investigating power-leaks. In the silence while Mouse worked she had strained her ears, listening for the strident clatter of picks, but though Winslow and the digging party could not be more than a hundred feet away, the twisting tunnels baffled all noise, the thick granite of the walls muffling even the echoes. She wondered if Vincent and Father could hear.

"There," said Mouse, straightening up and giving the compressor that ran the drill a proprietary slap. "Should work good—better than good . . ."

"It damn better," said Cullen softly, wiping his bony hands on the tail of his rusty leather vest. "Because god only knows how much air they got left."

When fired up the compressor made a hideous din in the confined space of the tunnel, the air filling with blue exhaust smoke, the echoes headsplitting when the drill-bit contacted stone. Her eyes burning, Catherine backed away as Mouse threw his weight against the drill-cradle, driving it forward on its makeshift tracks . . .

Any doubts she had had about the efficacy of the

machine itself were put to rest. Amazingly, the drill worked . . .

It was the bits that broke.

"No good no good NO GOOD!" cried Mouse, after the heavy engine lugged a third time, and with a resounding crack the drill-bit splintered, the shock of it throwing Mouse to the floor. He scrambled to his feet, tearing off the motorcycle goggles he wore as an eyeshield, and kicked the drill furiously. It sputtered and died.

"NO GOOD! Three drill bits ruined for three inches of hole!"

"We've got to keep going," said Catherine, her voice quite steady but the panic of failure, of terror, building up in her chest. "We can't give up . . ."

"Could go Above," muttered Mouse, walking around his machine, picking up and throwing away the shattered fragments of steel that had been one of the earlier bits. "Find what's needed . . . construction shack, maybe . . . big building . . ." He shook his head furiously, looking back at the unyielding wall of rock. "No time!"

Catherine, for some while, had been aware that time was growing terribly short. "You need more tools?" she asked. "I might be able to get them. Tell me what you need."

"You?" Mouse regarded her with bitter scorn. "Tungsten carbide drill bits?"

"Maybe . . ." said Catherine, running swiftly over her mind how much those might cost, where they could be obtained . . . Thank God for credit cards . . .

"Explosives?"

She was silent, knowing that explosives were a virtual impossibility to someone not in the construction trade . . .

In the construction trade. Her hands and feet suddenly turned cold.

"Yes," she said softly, turning back to Mouse, her heart beating so hard it almost nauseated her as despair shot up suddenly into a wild fountain of hope. Her voice shook as she said, "I know a man who can help. Come on, Mouse! Guide me up. You can tell me exactly what you need on the way."

"No time to waste," he said doubtfully, picking up his leather vest, which he had discarded for the work, and pulling it on, all its strange ornaments flashing. "Better be sure."

"I'm sure," said Catherine grimly. "Let's go."

Fingers pressed to the wall to pick up the slightest vibration, ears straining to hear the sound of the drill, Vincent was aware when it stopped. It had stopped twice before—he listened now, but it did not resume. The intermittent metallic pounding of the picks continued, but they sounded no nearer than they had hours ago . . . how many hours ago?

Father's voice was very weak. "Are they . . . still drilling?"

Vincent hesitated, not wanting to answer. So many things could go wrong with machinery, particularly, he was well aware, machinery put together from salvaged parts, tinkered cast-offs, cannibalized substitutions. Many of Mouse's machines ran on gasoline, and it could simply be a matter of running out . . . He knew how long it took to salvage any substantial amount of that. Instead of replying directly, he said, "They'll break through to us soon. Then all this will be no more than a memory."

It took him several breaths to say it—he had been conscious for some time that the air was less and less easy to breathe.

Father coughed raggedly, whispered, "I can't seem to get my breath . . ."

"Help is coming." Vincent moved back to him,

able to see now quite well in the strange myriad of charcoals and pewters that made up all the world, and cradled him in his arms. He felt heavier than he should, terribly limp. "Father," he whispered, "stay with me . . ."

Father moved his head a little, started to speak, but did not.

"Father," he said desperately, "listen: *To see the world in a grain of sand . . .*"

Still no reply. He brushed back the thick, grizzled hair from the old man's face, shook him gently, trying to summon him back. *"To see the world in a grain of sand . . .* What's the next line?"

Don't be dead, he thought helplessly. *Don't die now. They will come . . . they must . . .*

After a long time, he heard the unvoiced whisper, *". . . and heaven in a wildflower."*

He cast Blake's line forth as if it were a rope, a lifeline to the soul he felt sliding farther and farther into the darkness. *"To hold infinity in the palm of your hand . . ." Stay with me . . . stay with me, please . . .*

Father's voice was barely to be heard as he echoed, *"And eternity in an hour . . ."*

Eighteen

Thank God Elliot Burch is a workaholic, thought Catherine as she watched the lighted readout above the elevator door flick through the numbers between 1 and 25. Though it was almost six-thirty and nearly full dark outside, Burch's receptionist had answered her phone call from the lobby with the news that yes, Mr. Burch was still in . . .

She hadn't sounded particularly thrilled about it, but to Catherine the news was like a stay of execution. For Father and Vincent, she was burningly aware, it could be a reprieve from death.

In the oak-paneled outer office she heard the receptionist send in her name. Through the woman's headset and through the slightly open door of Burch's office itself she heard him grouse, "I said no calls . . ." and then, in a changed tone, "Of course I'll see her."

And it occurred to Catherine that she had never doubted that he would. Even, she thought, with a flush of shame, after this morning's interview, in which she certainly hadn't taken any points for poise . . .

He rose from his desk to greet her, as he had this morning. Only now the broad walnut surface was spread with blueprints and elevations of a condominium project, a calculator, notepad, protractor, and a thick-bottomed glass of brandy-and-soda—the desk of a multimillionaire developer who was still a working architect. Elliot himself was in his shirt-sleeves, the blue pinstriped suit-jacket hung neatly away in some invisible closet—the office, Catherine was well aware, was only one room of a suite—and his pale blue shirtsleeves rolled up to show his forearms' golden tan. As she stood in the doorway looking at him Catherine felt again the sense of his enormous vitality, the singleminded drive and energy that had so drawn her to him, had made it so easy for her to believe that he was capable of doing any-thing to get his way. Yet at the same time, seeing him like this, she had a sense of his vulnerability, of seeing behind those highly-polished defenses to the man who really lived there . . .

The thought flashed across her mind in a moment and was gone, like candleflame in the rising wind of fear, the hideous conviction that time was short-ening by the moment for Father and Vincent. She tried to keep the panic out of her voice, out of her face, but she realized she must look a sight, with her dusty jeans and the tunnel mud splashed on her boots and jacket. And indeed, after one look at her pale, shaken expression and frightened eyes Elliot dropped his polite conventionalities and strode swiftly to her side.

"Catherine, what's happened to you? What's the matter?"

"I need a favor," she gasped.

He had never seen her like this, never seen her shaken out of the calm self-assurance which she had worn like armor that morning. "Are you all right?" he asked, moving quickly to guide her to a chair. "Here, sit down, you look a little shaky. Let me get you a brandy . . ."

"I don't want your brandy!" She stepped away

from him, the panic in her pounding like a fever in her veins, driving her with the knowledge that time was running out. Then, catching herself, fighting the panic, she went on more evenly, "What I need is your help."

"Tell me what you want."

Silently, she produced from her pocket the list she'd scrawled by flashlight as she and Mouse had hastened along the tunnel—Mouse, a world away from everything Elliot was and represented, sitting in his shabby gray sweater and fur-and-leather vest down in the basement of a deserted tenement three blocks away, where the nearest way Down was . . . waiting for her. Trusting her. Giving up time, that precious, terrible commodity, because he trusted her . . .

Elliot laughed uncertainly at the list. "A tungsten carbide drill bit? Plastic explosives? Detonators? Giving up law for hard rock mining, are you?"

"It's no joke," she lashed at him, his laughter grating like a rusty nail at her nerves and goading her to irrational rage. "The need is real and immediate and I don't have time to spar with you." And if he didn't help her, she thought desperately, she had no idea what she would do. If she didn't get the things Mouse had listed—if she didn't get them soon—Vincent would die.

And beyond that there was nothing. She could not think—literally could not imagine—life with the knowledge that she would never see him again.

Elliot studied her for a moment, matching, like pieces of a jigsaw puzzle, the terrible urgency in her face, the fear in her eyes, with the incomprehensible list she had given him. "And I don't get an explanation?"

Catherine took a deep breath. It crossed her mind briefly that she probably should have come up with a story of some kind, an explanation that would help her cause with this man—after all, simply giving explosives away was massively illegal, and for all he knew she could have been leading a double life as a terrorist. But aside from the fact that the panic that now consumed her like fever made that kind of creativity impossible, she simply respected him too much to pull something that cheap, "I can't," she said simply. "I'm sorry . . . I'm asking you to trust me."

"It's all I ever asked of you." He turned away from her to his desk, picked up the phone as he flicked through the rolodex beside it, the stream-lined muscles of his back flexing lightly beneath the fine cotton of his shirt.

"I must have called you fifty times," he went on quietly. "Are you always so certain you're right?"

Catherine was silent, having nothing to say—and indeed, abashed and feeling herself blush, there wasn't much she could have said, even had she been able to think about anything but Vincent . . . and time . . . It was just as well that whomever Elliot was calling picked up the phone just then.

"This is Elliot Burch," he said, his voice crisp. "Gimme Jack, quick . . . Jack? I'm sending a friend down there to see you. Give her what she needs." He hung up, pulled a clean piece of paper from a drawer and jotted a quick message on it. "Jack's the night man down at the building site," he informed her, without looking up. "He'll be expecting you."

He handed her the paper; she was barely conscious of the brush of her fingertips against his as she took it. The address was somewhere up on 108th Street and she made a rapid calculation of how quickly it would take by cab at this hour, how long she had, or might have . . . Dear God, how long?

She had a hideous sense of watching sand in an hourglass, gray sand trickling away . . .

She almost ran to the door, leaving him standing beside his desk. But then she stopped, and in spite of her panic, her dread, she looked back at him—efficient, single-minded, wealthy, ambitious—handsome and powerful and all her father had ever wanted for her . . . and yet, at this moment, curiously alone. He hadn't asked. Because he still loved her . . . She hoped some day he'd find the woman he deserved.

"The next time you call," she said, "I'll be in."

He hadn't expected that—in fact she had the impression he fully expected never to see her again. "Why?"

"Because you didn't put a price tag on this."

Never again a lover, she thought, as she rode down the elevator, her heart beating hard. If she hadn't been sure of it in the first burst of rage that had triggered the initial breakup, she was sure of it now, sure of it by the sheer sense of panic, of dread at the thought of what she would do with her days if Vincent were not a part of them. But she wondered if he could accept being a friend.

As she stepped out through the heavy plate-glass doors and scanned the teeming glitter of Lafayette Street for a free cab, she found herself hoping that he would.

The weight of the darkness had grown with the hours. Though the dust poured into it by the latest rockfall was gradually settling out, the air was no easier to breathe. Vincent's eyes, thoroughly accustomed now to the darkness, traced the prisoning walls of the rock, black and dripping and streaked with the faintly luminous threads of the niter, taking in how narrow was the space confining them, how little air had been trapped. He wondered how much longer they had.

The distant, clanging rhythm of the picks formed a thin loom of sound in the background, but it sounded not much nearer—certainly far too distant to be of much help to them before the end. Putting his head to the stone behind him, Vincent could hear no sound of the drill which had given him such hope.

Beside him, Father's voice was a thread of sound. "I'm thirsty . . ."

Water, at least, in that place, was easy to find. Vincent edged over to the nearest puddle and scooped up some in his hand, held it to the old man's lips. It frightened him, how Father's hand moved to touch his arm, but slipped down again; it frightened him to see in the darkness how sunken his features were, how gray.

"We haven't much air left," Father whispered after a time. "No use fooling ourselves . . ."

"We must not lose hope." Not, he thought, as badly hurt as the old man was. In this grayish darkness, this leaden cold that seemed to deepen as he grew more weary, it seemed a perilously easy thing to die.

Father shook his head weakly. "I haven't much time," he said, and faint though it was his voice sounded resignedly matter-of-fact.

"Father, please . . ."

"No," sighed Father, "listen to me." And, unspoken, Vincent knew the rest of the sentence was, *while I can still speak.* It cost him some effort now, his breath laboring in the spent air, his face tense with the pain in his ribs, in his body, of trying to breathe, trying to speak. "Our world must continue, Vincent. A lot of good and trusting people depend on this place . . . it's all they have."

"Our world *will* continue," insisted Vincent, his hand seeking out Father's, holding it as if the physical grip could somehow stay his weakening spirit. "And you'll live to see it for many years."

The grizzled eyebrows flinched, fighting . . . *What? A hope that is too heavy to carry anymore?* "If I don't," he breathed, "*your* voice will be needed . . ."

And Vincent realized that that was Father's chiefest concern—that the fragile world Below not sink back into a leaderless anarchy and despair. He remembered the bitter quarrels over the gold Cullen had found, the reminder that they were, for all their striving, no more than humans doing as well as they could. For thirty years Father had worked, to bring justice where there was no law to enforce it, to organize help and care for all who had taken refuge there, to make of it a world where they could all live peacefully, caring for one another . . . and he had seen, over and over again, how delicate that justice, that care, that peace, was. Their world was all they had.

Thinking of Cullen's pirate gold, he said, "Mine is not the only voice."

"But it's the truest, and the strongest." Father moved a little, as if trying to sit up, struggling to make him understand. "Please, promise me . . . you'll keep . . ."

"Shhh . . ." Vincent stroked his face, his hands, trying to quiet him, sensing that his mind was beginning to drift. His own body ached, the strained muscles stiffening with cold and damp, his own lungs laboring against dust and suffocation.

"Keep our dream alive . . ."

And all that Vincent could say was, "I promise."

Father relaxed, settling back again; his eyes slid closed. "It won't be without sacrifices," he murmured, his fingers loosening in Vincent's grasp.

"The colors . . ." And his brows twitched together again, wistful at recollections long since put aside. "I think I miss the colors most of all. They've even begun to fade in my mind's eye." And his mouth, beneath the gray dust coating his beard, turned down a little, sad, not for his own sake, but for that of his adopted son. "I wish you could have seen the blue of the Pacific under a summer sun . . . the green of the grass at Ebbetts Field . . . fall leaves blazing orange and yellow in Vermont . . ."

It was that, thought Vincent, marveling, that he remembered . . . not the gray of their jails, the brown of the courtroom walls, the grim monochrome of the city streets he had walked for such a brief time in his one quick visit to the world that he had left. This world Below had long since been his, with its concerns and hopes, its simple law, its deep and silent peace . . . but the song of Orpheus still wove its threnody in his heart.

"But I have seen them all, Father," whispered Vincent, remembering his own childhood yearning for colors other than the hazy gold of lamplight, the strange, eternally varied grays of Underground. Father's brows puckered, questioning, and Vincent said, "No child ever had a better guide. Your words painted pictures I will never forget. You took me around the world . . . Twain's Mississippi . . . Kipling's India . . . Jack London's Klondike . . . You made them come alive for me." His hand tightened over Father's again, willing him to believe, willing him to hope, as Vincent had never ceased to hope . . . willing him to trust. "There are many places left to go . . ."

But he was not sure the old man heard.

"You're good at finding and taking," said Mouse in delight, rolling a ball of plastic explosive between his hands in a way that made Catherine nervously remind herself that the stuff was absolutely safe without a detonator cap. Behind them, Jamie trotted, the bulky cardboard box of drill-bits under one arm and the flashlight in the other hand, its gritty yellow glow throwing sprawling shadows on the curved brick of the tunnel walls. From a basement near the building site Catherine had signaled Mouse of her success—Jamie had been waiting with him when she'd reappeared, clumsily manhandling the three awkward parcels of drill-bits, detonator equipment, and plastique down the chipped cement steps to the abandoned cellar where she had left Mouse to ascend to the world Above.

Jack—Elliot's night-man on the site—had read her note and handed over the three packages to her without a word, not even of caution . . . as a lawyer, she recognized with grim amusement that if by any chance things ever reached court Jack's silence could be construed as an argument that no, he hadn't known he was handing plastic explosives to someone who had no business with them. But he'd looked like he had his doubts.

Not, thought Catherine, casting a wary eye at Mouse, that she blamed him. The little engineer had exactly the expression of a kid with a new toy as he balanced the plastique in his hands, sniffed it, played with it like a gob of modeling-clay. "I love this stuff!" he grinned happily. "Tried to find some once—didn't have any bolt-cutters."

"You *have* used it before . . . ?" inquired Catherine anxiously.

Mouse made his blue eyes wide at her, his round face ingenuous. "Yeah sure you bet, yeah, lots of times," he said. "One little glob and POW!" His teeth flashed in a delighted grin at the prospect.

As she gripped the box of detonator-caps and the

radio triggering device under her arm and followed Mouse down into the blackness towards the first of the protective gates which guarded the world Below, Catherine reflected that she really would like to believe him.

"Catherine . . ."

At the sound of Vincent's voice, Father half-woke, drifting slowly up out of a depth of blackness worlds deep to the blackness that was all the waking world had become. He had been dreaming, dreaming of Margaret—not, as he had so often dreamed in the long years of their separation, of that beautiful fair girl in her yellow summer dress stepping out of the cab and turning to smile at him, but of the thin, strong, radiant woman he had known in that last week, holding his hand and talking of Paris and politics and of what she had seen in Russia, a country he had never visited and had always longed to, though of course in the Fifties such a thing had been out of the question . . .

Sadder and sweeter, as Heine had written, *like pain dipped in honey* . . .

And out of that he had waked to cold and airless dark, and the strong touch of his son's hand warm upon his own. "What . . . ?"

"Catherine's returned." He could hear the deep relief in Vincent's voice, the joy of his knowing that the woman he had so cherished was near. What it would have been, he thought, to have had that close a link with Margaret . . .

Though it could only have brought him misery, in those parted years, could he have felt her sorrow as well as his own. And he felt a stab of pity for Vincent, realizing that the grief that Catherine could bring Vincent, as well as the joy, was in some ways not within his control.

They were what they were—and in that, his son was deeply to be envied.

A moment later Vincent said, "They're drilling again," and Father closed his eyes and sighed. He'd mapped some of the tunnels around the Maze, though, he was sure, by no means all—people came here seldom (*Or at least*, he thought with a flash of his old irritation, *they were SUPPOSED to come here seldom* . . .) and it was more important to map the upper levels, where the likelihood of children and newcomers getting lost was greater. He knew how hard the granite substructure of the island was, how inadequate were the tools at their command.

Softly in the darkness he heard the rustle of Vincent's clothes and mane, knew he must be looking around him—wondered what it was that he saw. Perhaps it was just as well, thought Father, that he himself was blind in this darkness. If he were aware of how narrow the confines of their prison were, how scarce the oxygen was becoming, it would have been harder to listen to Vincent's words of hope.

"I must move you to safety," came Vincent's voice from the darkness again. "There isn't much—an overhang over there that looks solid. It may hurt . . ." And then the muted creak of belt-leather, the clink of the hardware on his boots, the warm strength of those powerful hands taking as gentle a grip as they could.

He bit down hard on a groan of pain he did not want Vincent to hear. Fearsome as Vincent looked—though Father had long since ceased to notice his appearance—Father knew he was tremendously soft-hearted, more so than most men Father knew. It would hurt him if he knew the agony even that careful movement caused. Through shut teeth and a wave of nausea Father managed to whisper, "It's

266

all right," and knew that Vincent was perfectly aware of the lie.

"We'll be out of here soon," promised Vincent softly, but Father had fainted.

Nineteen

"NOT working . . ." gasped Mouse, and Catherine, wincing at the hideous noise of the drill-bit on rock, ducked forward to put her shoulder to the drill-cradle and throw her weight along with Mouse's against the rock. The air in the narrow tunnel was almost unbreathable with the choking blue smoke thrown off by the laboring gasoline engine; in the enclosed space the noise was deafening. Squinting through the fumes she could see the drill-head itself whirling in the little pocket of rock cut by the previous attempts, and the juddering buck of the machine told her they were making no further headway against the denser rock.

"Can't bore through," yelled Mouse, sweat matting his fair hair, and behind the motorcycle goggles his eyes were filled with dread. "Not strong enough . . ."

"I'll go for Winslow!" she yelled back. When they had passed close to the tunnels where the blacksmith and his crew had started their efforts, Catherine had heard the patient, furious strike of the pick. The man must be made of iron . . .

"Won't come!" shouted Mouse over the whine of metal on rock, straining his weight once more into the buck of the drill. "Too stubborn . . ."

But Catherine had already gone.

She heard the strike of Winslow's pick long before

she—and Jamie, who guided her—came into sight of the lamps in the work-tunnel. It was striking alone now, hard, angry, despairing. How many hours had it been? *Vincent*, thought Catherine helplessly, *Vincent, hold on* . . . Everything she had ever read about cave-ins and mine disasters trickled back into her mind from behind the wall of her conscious refusal to remember . . . Cases in this very rock, when they were digging the subways, where rescuers had tunneled for two and three days, only to find the trapped victims dead of suffocation or starvation or injuries . . .

Then the bobbing glow of the torches smeared the tunnel walls in amber, and against that shine she saw first shadows, then moving forms—a fat man with a reddish beard leaning on a pick and rubbing his back, a faded, gentle woman with gray-blonde hair dragging aside a basket of rock-chips . . . and Winslow, like some terrifying subterranean John Henry, smashing his pick stubbornly into the rockface, all his dark muscles shining with sweat.

He turned his head as she and Jamie approached; there was fury in his dark eyes, incompletely hiding despair.

"Listen to me, Winslow!" cried Catherine, and, turning frantically to the others, added, "All of you! There *is* another tunnel, just like Mouse said. We've been drilling there, but we can't break through without your help."

Something hardened in Winslow's eyes—he turned back to the crawlspace, littered with debris and still blocked with a great boulder in which only a small tunnel had been chipped. "If you aren't gonna work, get outta the way."

"Please!" she sought his arm, desperate. "You'll never get through in time this way!" It might only have been her panic speaking, her despair, but there was a growing sense within her that there was more to it than that. She could feel through her link with Vincent no despair, no fear, but she could feel also his awareness that time was very short.

But it was not something she could explain, and looking up into the black man's hard face, she knew that even if she might have, under ordinary circumstances, he was too caught in his own fears to listen to hers.

"That fool and his damn machines . . ."

"It's our only chance!"

Winslow's eyes moved around to the others, standing uncertainly in the circle of the lamplight, weary and sweating and waiting for his word.

Pleading, Catherine went on, "Vincent always said that you looked out for one another . . ." But even as she spoke the words she understood that the situation cut both ways, and that it was only unity that could save them, on one path or the other.

Then with an angry gesture Winslow hurled his pick at the wall of the little tunnel he had worked so many hours to dig, and cursed, roundly and richly, at Mouse and all of Mouse's ancestors. "Come on," he growled, "where's he got that fool contraption set up?"

They streamed back down the tunnels, the light of the lanterns wavering and swaying like fireflies in the gloom. In the dank plexus of tunnels Mouse and Cullen were still stubbornly leaning their weight into the shuddering drill-cradle, while the bit sparked and whined against the rock; Winslow shoved his way forward and batted Mouse's hands away like a child's.

"Outta my way, fool . . ."

And Mouse stepped back, panting, a grin of joy and relief spreading over his grime-covered face.

With Winslow's strength, and the strength of the men who had accepted his command, behind it, the drill-bit inched into the harder strata of the rock, chewing five straight bores perhaps eighteen inches long apiece. Then while the men pulled the drill back and disassembled it, taking it back out of the way through the clearing fug of smoke, Mouse scurried up to the rockface and began to tear off and shape the chunks of plastic explosive in his hands.

"That seems like a lot," said Catherine worriedly, coming up to crouch, holding the flashlight, at his side.

Mouse thought about it, then tore off half his intended dosage and patted it back into the main glob still at his feet. "Maybe," he agreed.

"*Maybe?!?* You don't *know?*"

Mouse shrugged innocently, and Winslow, who had arrived behind Catherine in time to hear this last, growled, "You'll blow us all to kingdom come!"

Benjamin—the fat man with the red beard—and Cullen had finished dismantling the drill-rig by this time; they and the others had begun to back off down the tunnel, where a turning and a screen of stalagmites would protect them from the effects of a blast. Mouse hefted the wad of plastique in his hands, then pinched another half-handful from what he had discarded and shaped it back into what he held. "Pack the stuff in the holes, put the little gizmos in, set it off with the other gizmo," he recited cheerily, though Catherine could see now that sweat stood out on his face despite the tunnel's cold. "Read all about it."

"You've never used plastic explosive!"

"Yeah," admitted Mouse, now deftly packing the holes with the pale, grayish wads. "Might blow Vincent and Father up . . . might blow Mouse up. Might save their lives." He glanced back at her, and

271

for the first time she saw the fear in his eyes. "Hand me the little gizmos."

"You can't do this!" protested Catherine.

Quite simply, he said, "Then they die for sure."

He held out his hand for the detonating antennas that Catherine had tucked under her arm. She hesitated, desperately canvassing her mind for another solution. Elliot had taken her out once to where his men were blasting a deep foundation for a high-rise—ironically, one of the high-rises that would be put in jeopardy if Max Avery put on the pressure—and she'd seen the hideous strength of plastic explosive, even when handled by experts. Mouse met her gaze, and in his face she saw that he knew it, too. After a moment she pressed the small electronic firing-devices into his shabbily-gloved hand.

He rigged them neatly, whistling tunelessly as he set the wires and the explosive caps. Catherine, holding aloft the flashlight to illuminate his work, guessed that he'd either read about how to do it or, more probably, had watched the men on building-sites doing the same thing—to the best of her recollection it looked like the same arrangement Burch's men had made, though she couldn't be sure. Maybe, she thought, Mouse couldn't be sure, either . . . How close could he have gotten for a look?

She glanced sideways at him as he stripped the wires with his teeth, twisted them deftly together, his face intent. She had known him only a few hours, but he seemed to her already like a younger brother . . . He had given her a gold necklace, she remembered for no particular reason, because she was Vincent's friend. Because he was glad that Vincent had a friend . . .

He looked up at her, and then at Winslow, standing behind. His voice was steady, but stripped of its usual ebullience—he knew exactly what was coming. "Want to blow up with me? Go on . . ."

"I'll do it," said Winslow quietly. "You two get on outta here."

"My gizmos," he muttered, shaking his head. "Go."

"You can't detonate it from the tunnel?" Catherine nodded back to where the tunnel narrowed and turned, the rock walls sheltering the others who had already taken refuge further back.

"Signal won't go through solid rock," said Mouse quietly. "Go with Winslow."

Dammit, thought Catherine helplessly, *he's only a kid* . . . "Show me what to do," she said slowly, desperately frightened but not wanting this boy to be hurt—to be killed, crushed by the falling masses of rock. "I'll do it."

His eyes, as they met hers, were the eyes of a man who understands the risks he runs. "He's my friend, too, Catherine," he said softly, and then, with a shaky attempt at humor, "You die, Vincent will kill me anyway. Go now."

Winslow half knelt, put a hand on Mouse's shoulder. "You're crazy," he said softly. "You know that, don't you?".

Mouse nodded, and looked back up at his friend. "If I'm dead, you take care of Arthur."

"Best not get yourself killed, then," grumbled Winslow, taking refuge in his usual dourness. "I ain't gonna nursemaid no raccoon." And, patting him on the back, "Take care."

Then he followed Catherine down the tunnel to where the others crouched, waiting. "Move back," he ordered, with a quick glance over his shoulder at the glow of light still visible from Mouse's flashlight. "And I mean *way* back . . ."

* * *

Crouched in the suffocating darkness Vincent raised his head suddenly, feeling Catherine's fear. Not grief or despair, as if she had given up and thought him dead, but fear . . .

The drilling had stopped . . . Endless minutes of waiting . . .

Then blinding light and a crash like the splitting of the earth. Vincent flung himself over Father's body to shield him from the torrent of rocks and dust pelting down on them from above, and beneath him felt the sloping stone floor jerk, heard the booming reverberation of echoes rolling through the tangling passages of the maze . . .

And light flooded over them, shockingly bright after the Tartarean grayness of the last hours. Diffuse and hazy with a fog of dust, he could see the amber glow of it pouring through a crack in the opposite wall. Voices calling out . . . Catherine . . .

And then they were scrambling through the crack, blotting the inflowing lamplight. Bright saffron gleams caught on Catherine's fair hair as she scrambled down the pile of broken rock, threw herself into his arms . . .

"Vincent . . ."

He held her, fast and desperately, fighting the urge to crush her against him . . . Then he turned back, putting her aside even as she broke from him to look to where Father lay, half-covered with dust and debris. "He's badly hurt . . ." Vincent said, going to him, Catherine at his side and the others—Winslow, Mary, Sara, Cullen—crowding behind. Looking around him at the tiny chamber, he saw that it was even smaller than it had appeared in the darkness. He had no idea how they had lived so long in that sealed space.

"We can make a stretcher out of the PVC pipe from Mouse's drill-cradle," Winslow was saying, and sudden silence fell at the mention of Mouse's name.

Catherine whispered, "Mouse . . ." her face white; she turned from looking back at the ruin of the tunnel behind them to Vincent. "He stayed behind to set off the explosives . . ."

Through the crack Vincent could see that where the tunnel had been was only a fallen-in jumble of gray rock. Half its ceiling had caved in with the force of that massive detonation, filling the space outside with smoking rubble.

Then the rock moved. He saw that what he had taken for a curved boulder-fragment was in fact the shape of a hunched back and shoulders, half-buried in smaller stones and tinted a monochrome gray with fallen dust. Dust and pebbles trickled down as Mouse stirred, then sat up dazedly, coughing and shaking the dirt out of his hair.

He looked around him and coughed again, one hand held pressed against his bruised ribs, and managed to say, "Used a touch too much."

Winslow reached him in two strides, pulled him to his feet in a huge bear-hug of joy, then, with almost equal promptness, shoved him brusquely away, embarrassed by this show of affection. "Only mouse I ever saw with nine lives . . ."

The others laughed as Mouse and Winslow came back to them, Mouse leaning on Winslow's mighty shoulder for support—laughed with relief and joy. At the sound Father's eyelids creased, then flickered open; he lay for a moment looking up at the faces surrounding him. At Mouse's, gray with filth through which his teeth flashed in a grin of triumphant pleasure; at Winslow's, streaked with sweat and grime. At Vincent's, dusty and exhausted in the matted tangles of his long mane, and, beside Vincent, at Catherine's, no different from the other faces of his people—like theirs, smutched with mud and dirt, like theirs, smiling with happiness, with the triumph over despair and death.

Not a rich man's daughter, he thought; not a representative of a world rejected, a world by its very nature rife with danger and greed. A person, as they were people, from a world both good and bad, as theirs was . . . a person bound to them by experience and by love. And now one of them.

He smiled at her, and reaching out, took her hand.

"I've never been so frightened . . ."

Vincent put his arm around Catherine's shoulders, and gave her a reassuring hug. In spite of his own bruises and exhaustion, he had insisted on guiding her back to the sub-basement of her apartment building, though there were any number of the Tunnel dwellers, now, who would have been willing to do so—any of those who had shyly greeted her, hugged her welcome, shared with her that huge pot of tea Sara had made in Father's room while Vincent and Mary were closeted with Father, treating his injuries. Mouse, with his raccoon Arthur perched on his shoulder; Jamie, who already felt like an old friend, young and shy and coltish; gigantic Winslow and gangly Cullen, who'd given her an embarrassed grin and said, 'Vincent probably told you about me . . .' She had replied, 'What Vincent told me was that you're the best woodcarver in the Five Boroughs,' and he'd ducked his head with shy pleasure, not sure what to reply. And of course Mouse had blurted out tactlessly, 'Found the gold. Him and me and Winslow. There was this ship . . .' and Winslow had cuffed him lightly and said, 'Less said about that the better, fool,' and they'd all laughed, Cullen as well.

But Vincent had insisted, and had walked with her up the winding tunnels, along the old brick mains and through the disused subway tube that Catherine was beginning to recognize and feel familiar with, like the sidewalks between her building and the one over on 72nd where Jenny lived, or the route down to the corner store. As they had walked she had told him about getting the drill-bits and plastique from Elliot, and about her interview with him, that morning that already felt a week's distance away.

And Vincent had nodded, understanding both what that had cost her, and what she had gained out of it for herself. "It took courage to go back," he said quietly, turning his head a little to look sidelong at her through the still-damp curtain of his mane. "That courage saved our lives."

Catherine shook her head. "I don't even think I thought about it," she said softly, reaching out to take his hands—the hands of a beast, wrapped in the bandages Mary had put over the abrasions of the rocks, thick with reddish fur and bearing nails, claws, that could rip apart a brick wall. Their touch upon hers was delicate as a dancer's.

They stood now in the archway of broken bricks that led through to her building's sub-basement, the scene of so many quiet talks, so many gentle memories. On the way up she had given a good deal of thought to Elliot Burch, and she wondered now whether part of her quickness to jump to conclusions about him last February had been a desire to resolve her choice, to find a reason not to choose him over Vincent . . . a reason to follow her heart.

She had found that, thinking about him, with the disappearance of her anger at him had dawned, not love, but a profound respect. She had no need to hate Elliot anymore, for after today, there was no question in her heart of the depth of her love for Vincent, her need for him.

"I felt like I was losing the best part of myself," she said softly. "I would have done anything . . ." Done it without question, she thought, remembering the diamond-hard fire of resolution which had consumed her these past hours, the implacable ferocity which would not accept defeat. Even had she, those months ago, decided to marry Elliot Burch, she knew now, even had she been practical and chosen a life with him—which would, she had no doubt, have been a good life—she could have survived his loss and gone on.

She wasn't sure she could have survived Vincent's. She had fought for him as she would have fought for air if she were drowning. Like an animal fighting, as Isaac had said, without any thought of what comes next—with the same fury, the same singleminded strength, that filled him when he defended her. She understood that now, understood it in her gut and her heart and her bones.

They were more alike, she reflected, than either could have guessed. The seeds were in each of them, of both beauty and beast.

The light from the sub-basement's grating reflected in the blue-green of his eyes, the electric glow of the upper world, steady and bright. Her world. Except that now she would be a denizen of two worlds, her own and the secret, lamplit one Below. She had been accepted there, something she hadn't even thought of during the crisis . . . something she hadn't had time to think of.

Her only thought, now as then, was that he was alive; that they would not be parted; that she could count on the touch of his hand, the strength of his presence, the joy of knowing he'd be there.

"It wasn't courage, Vincent," she said softly, as his arm tightened around her again, drew her to him as somewhere in the darkness a subway rumbled by. "It was love."